SILENT HUSH

BREAKING THE SILENCE
BOOK ONE

SARAH JD

PA: Obsidian Author Services (Bibiane Lybaek)

Cover by Simply Defined Art

Formatting: DAZED Designs

Cover Model: Trista Duncan

Many thanks to my Beta Readers: Anoesjka, Kathy, Melissa, and Tamarra.

CONTENT WARNING

Silent Hush is the first book in the Breaking the Silence duet, which ends on a cliffhanger.

Please note: This is a dark contemporary MF romance that contains subjects that maybe triggering to some readers, including, but not limited to: Detailed violence, killing, bullying, harassment, dub-con, explicit sex scenes, blackmail, and issues relating to crimes against children.

DEE

With trained silence, I crawl through the cramped cavity of the air duct, mere feet from my target. This hit is a little more complicated than most, given the fact that my target is under police guard. But something like that isn't going to stop me. This man must die, simply because I feel it's what he deserves.

Underestimating me is the biggest mistake people make when they come across me. It's fine though. It works in my favour. My need to stick to the shadows and fade into the background is all that much easier when people underestimate me.

I've been using it to my advantage for years, happy to be given a wide berth as the *'weird chick'*. I have little interest in making friends, and those who do know me are more allies than anything more personal.

The only thing that fuels me is revenge. Mainly revenge for other people since I got mine years ago, and tonight's target is the scum of the earth who used his position and power to blackmail people and ran a black-market operation selling porn. Specifically, involving underage unwilling participants.

As I ease myself to hover over the air vent that sits above the small bathroom, I get myself into position to make my entrance. With gloved hands, I shimmy the vent loose and let it hang open on its hinges before I slowly lower myself down into the darkened bathroom. As soon as my feet touch the linoleum floor, I glance at the door and wait, making sure I haven't been made.

After a beat, I move with stealth to the door and slowly grip the handle. Using the skills I learnt a number of years ago, I ease the handle down, maintaining my cover, and cracking the door. My eyes adjust to the dull light filtering in from the hospital room beyond, and they catch on the lump of a body in the bed. *My mark.*

Honestly, I'm kinda pissed that I have to be so careful so I don't get sprung by the cops. It would have been really damn satisfying if my mark was well enough to try and run from me. The chase is fun, and I would have loved to chase this fucker and see the fear in his eyes as he begged for mercy.

He wouldn't find it in me. Not after what he's done.

Of course, he'd try to fight me. The men always do. They take one look at my small frame and five-foot height and assume I'm weak.

Idiots.

Skill overrides size, and more often than not, it's all over for them sooner than I'd prefer. Most of the sick bastards I hunt deserve a long, drawn out, torturous death, much like this twisted fucker does. The police guard just outside his door means traumatising my mark is out of the question. They are also the reason I couldn't just stroll into the hospital's burns unit. I don't mind the challenge of breaking in, though. My small height and level of fitness and flexibility makes this break and enter easier for me than most. And the beauty of it is that I'll be in and out before anyone realises what's happened.

Slowly, I ease the door open as I assess if there are any obstacles, like a police officer sitting inside the room I didn't know about, or a nurse checking on the patient. It would be unfortunate, for them, since I'd have to take them out too, and I really just want to end the existence of my target and get the hell out of here.

Relief washes over me as I confirm the room is all clear with the only people in here being me, and the soon to be dead man. I glance over his sleeping form and the monitors beside the bed. There's no heart monitor on him, which works in my favour since it means I can avoid the nurses being alerted when their patient stops breathing.

Again, I grin. This is just too easy.

I don't waste any more time, moving across the small space to the side of the bed. I'd researched what this guy looks like before I came here, even though I wasn't sure if he would be recognisable due to the extent of the burns covering his body, but this side of his face seems to have come out relatively unscathed, and lying before me sure as shit is the one and only, Terence Hill, from Fox Pines.

Slipping my extra sharp sidekick from my pocket, I lift her, my trusty knife who I call Thana, appropriately named since she is the deliverer of death, and ready myself to pounce. In one swift move, I leap onto the bed and straddle my mark. His eyes fly open, a gasp springing from his lips before his brows furrow and his body stiffens in pain.

My weight is obviously aggravating some of the burns covering his flesh.

Oh, I'm sorry.

Not!

Before he can make a noise, I hold my finger up to my lips in a shhhh motion. Confusion contorts his face as I pull out a piece of paper from my pocket and hold it up, and I smirk, my eyes flaring in anticipation as he reads the words.

I'M HERE ON BEHALF OF THE GIRL YOU CALL KITTEN TO DELIVER YOU TO HELL!

My note is short and sweet. He gets the gist. I know he does because he tries to move, but I'm too fast, my other hand whipping out in a flash, and a moment later, pretty crimson oozes and then spurts from Thana's slice across his throat, which has opened up his jugular vein.

I leap off him quickly, trying to avoid the spray, but I'm not fast enough. The crimson splatters across my face. It's an unfortunate part of this sort of work, and something I've had to get used to over the years.

I quickly re-pocket Thana, shifting closer to the bathroom door as I watch the life drain out of this monster. I don't watch for long, though. There's no coming back for him now, so I shut myself back inside the bathroom, peel my gloves and black hoodie off, revealing another pair of gloves and another hoodie underneath, and I quickly shove them and the note in my small backpack.

By the time I have lifted myself up into the air duct and re-sealed the vent, the room below still remains empty aside from the dead man, and with great satisfaction, I creep out the way I crept in.

It feels good to close this chapter for the poor girl in Fox Pines who was violently abused by my now dead mark. Rhys George, otherwise known as Kitten, can finally move on, which is a good thing I think, since she is soon to be my new foster sister.

2

JARED

My mates have turned into pussy whipped saps. Apparently, they are in love with the same fucking sex addicted chick. The problem is, as happy as I am for them, it means I'm third wheeling all the fucking time.

Wait, no. More like seventh wheeling, because four of my mates are screwing the same chick in some bizarre group relationship, which also involves some older dude as well. Which means Rhys George has brainwashed five guys with her pussy.

How the fuck does that even happen?

Fucked if I know, but I'm sick of having it shoved in my face. With them and Lexi—the girl I always thought I'd end up with—all finding love, I'm about ready to set this world on fire.

Ok, yeah, I guess burning the world has more to do with Lexi choosing Ayden Mitchell as her fella instead of me, but in general, anyone flaunting their happy fucking love life deserves to burn right now.

Shit, I've turned into a pissy motherfucker lately.

"We'll be five minutes, Crowley." Marcus, my best mate,

and now love-struck fool, lies straight to my fucking face as he follows the other guys into Rhys' bedroom. Like fuck, he'll be five minutes. More like thirty minutes or an hour.

I knew coming here to hang out was a bad idea. Why the fuck did I let Marcus talk me into this?

Oh yeah, because I have no one else to hang with.

I need to find some new fucking friends.

As the door closes to Rhys' bedroom, I glare at it for a moment before turning to take in the room I'm in. It's some sort of living area, but with kids' stuff everywhere. Rhys has younger twin brothers, so I'm guessing the drawings of dinosaurs stuck haphazardly on the walls are their works of art. Either that, or Rhys has a dinosaur fetish and can't draw for shit.

Movement out of the corner of my eye causes me to flinch in surprise, and I scan the space to see someone sitting in a round armchair in the corner. Big brown eyes glance up to lock onto mine, peering out from the confines of a black hood, while long mousy brown hair tumbles out the sides.

"Oh, shit." I frown. "Sorry. I didn't see you there."

The girl doesn't respond, and I try to hold back a scowl, not wanting to be a rude prick just because I'm in a pissy mood.

"You must be Dee. I'm Jared," I jab my thumb to my chest, "and I'm not part of that weird shit." I gesture my head to Rhys' bedroom door.

The guys told me that Rhys has a new foster sister, but for some reason, I thought she'd be younger. From what I can see of her shadowed features, she looks to be close in age to me.

I shift uncomfortably when noises I don't want to hear come from Rhys' room. I wait for the girl to say something, but she remains quiet, staring at me. Glancing to my left, I take in the widescreen TV and game console that I was told we were coming here to play before turning my attention back to the girl.

"You wanna play with me?" I point to the game console and take a step towards the girl, but I pull up short when I notice her flinch back. At first, I think she must be scared of me, but the look in her eyes doesn't show fear. Her eyes tell me really fucking clearly that she's ready to attack if I take a step closer.

Fuck. What's her problem?

"I'm friend, not foe." I raise my hands in surrender, hoping to get her to crack a smile, but she gives me nothing but her death glare, those big brown eyes turning darker.

Sighing, I drop my hands back to my sides. "Fucking whatever. I'm just trying to be nice."

I sound like a whiny bitch. Fuck, maybe I should check to see if my dick has turned inside out. It was there when Courtney Ellis wrapped her hand around it at the Fox Pines High party I crashed last night, but the fucking thing turned limp so fast that I'm starting to wonder if it might drop off soon.

The girl in front of me shifts, dragging me out of my pissy thoughts, and she slowly unravels her body from the chair, coming to stand mere feet from me. Fuck, she's little. Like really short. I mean, a lot of girls are short compared to my six three, but man, this one must only be five foot. Perhaps a little taller. The black hoodie she's wearing is huge, hanging off her like a fucking dress, doing a damn good job of hiding what's underneath.

I keep my gaze locked on her, curious as to what she's doing as she stares me down. Is she finally going to speak to me? Sit down on the couch and game with me so we can turn up the volume and drown out the slapping and moaning coming from Rhys' bedroom?

As she approaches, her glare remains in place, her big

brown eyes looking darker than they did before, staying locked with mine, like she is filled with sudden anger.

I keep still, waiting to see what she will do as we fall into a silent battle of wills, staring at each other. When she moves again suddenly, I flinch like a little bitch, and I don't miss the slight upward pull of the corner of her lips as she walks past me, before slamming her shoulder into my ribs as she passes by.

An *omph* flies from me as I cradle my ribs, anger spreading through me like a hot wave.

"What the fuck was that for?" I glare daggers at her retreating back, but she doesn't turn at my words. Doesn't even fucking acknowledge me. Just keeps walking before disappearing behind another door with a slam.

"Fuck this!" I hiss before storming from the room. If my mates wanna hang with me, then they fucking know where to find me.

Not fucking here, that's for sure.

I rush out of Rhys George's house like a fucking imposter, and storm to my car, feeling nothing but used by my mates. I'm the only one that has a license, and even though Garrett turned eighteen a couple of days ago, exactly seven days after my birthday, he doesn't have quite enough driving hours to go for his probationary license yet. This means I'm their go-to guy for a lift right now and fuck them. I'm not their fucking taxi.

Closing myself inside my dad's shitty old twin cab Hilux Ute, I start it up and crank the music loud, Post Malone's, 'I Fall Apart' blasting through the speakers. I grip the steering wheel, closing my eyes and suck in a deep breath as I try to calm my building rage. I just feel so fucking angry. Like all the time.

Does it have to do with a certain blonde-haired girl that I grew up with and wished I could call my own? Yes, partly.

But as much as I am sad and disappointed that she chose another guy, this rage isn't because of that. No, this rage started the day I was beaten to a pulp by that girl's half brother.

My heart races as flashes of that day burst into my head like a fucking explosion, my breathing becoming harder as my mind summons the memories without my consent.

I tried to fight back that day. I tried to escape the brutality that Mike West inflicted, but it was no use. He was more monster than man, and I fucking hate that I was no match for him.

He came after me to show Lexi that his threat of her friend's safety wasn't idle. He wanted her, and he was going to do whatever the fuck he could to get her.

I have a scar on my upper lip where his fist burst my flesh open. I still remember the taste of blood filling my mouth, and I remember the sound of my ribs cracking as he kicked me over and over while I was laying helpless on the floor of the boys' bathroom at school.

I still don't know how the fuck he got on campus unnoticed. I guess the only reason I'm still able to walk around like I'm not nearly pissing my pants all the time, is because Lexi killed him in self-defence when he attacked her one too many times.

His death doesn't stop the nightmares, though. It doesn't stop these moments that keep slamming into me more frequently. And it doesn't stop the building anger I have at the world.

Nothing takes this fury away, and nothing eases the ache I have for Lexi West to be mine.

I've tried everything.

I've tried fucking the heartache of my unrequited love for Lexi out of my system, but the organ beating in my chest isn't interested in anyone else but her. I've been so drawn to her, aching for a moment alone to tell her how I feel, but Ayden Mitchell is always there. Always touching and kissing her and doing all the things I dream of doing.

Lexi knows how I feel, though. She just doesn't realise that I can't seem to fucking get over her. Get over something that never even began.

What the fuck is wrong with me?

Why the fuck can't I accept that she's never going to be mine?

I slam my fist against the steering wheel and growl loudly into the small space inside the cabin. My eyes fly open as my rage builds, my memory instantly going back to the day I woke up in hospital a few days after Mike West nearly beat me to death. Lexi had been admitted to the hospital too, because she was suffering her own injuries after the final showdown with her brother when she killed him. Lexi had Ayden bring her to see me, and she burst into tears, climbing onto the bed and throwing her arms around me. Even though it sent sharp pain to my ribs, I hugged her back and pulled her onto my lap. The only problem with that was that the action meant she was straddling me, and my heart ripped open from wanting to hold her like that forever.

I still remember Ayden's words.

"Enjoy that hug, Crowley, because it's the last time I let my girl straddle you like that."

And so far, he's kept his word, making sure we aren't ever alone together.

My lids fall shut again as I try to remember her scent, but I just can't reach it anymore. Three months have passed, and I can no longer remember how she smelled when I was lucky enough to get that close to her.

"Fuck, Six. Why can't I get you out of my head?"

My deep voice is pathetically pained, and I loathe myself for being such a fucking pussy over Lexi West. Fuck, I need to stop thinking of her as Six, her childhood nickname that was only used between me, Lex, Marcus and Abbey. Thinking of her as Six isn't helping my situation. I need to wipe her from my memory somehow.

I just don't know how to do that when she's the one who holds my heart.

3

———

DEE

ox Pines Catholic College has the most uncomfortable uptight school uniform I have ever had to endure. Maybe it's because I've never been to a school where wearing a uniform is compulsory, but the stiff white shirt and necktie are enough to make me want to strip off in front of everyone and walk around the rest of the day in only my bra.

Do I do that though? No. Of course not. That would draw attention that I don't need, or want, so I cross my arms over my chest, silently protesting and aware that my new foster mum, who is also the principal of this uppity school, is watching me. She insists I go to this school, even though I wanted to go to the public high school. That's the reason I'm in this town, yet here I am, not going to the high school, but being herded in with the other brainwashed sheep to start the first day of the year in a fucking Catholic school.

I'm not religious, and honestly, I'm annoyed that I didn't burst into flames when I stepped onto this bullshit holy school ground. If there is such a thing as a God who sits above us all on his mighty cloud watching, then he knows damn well I'm the devil's spawn. My presence here is not going to end well, which I am now counting on to work in my favour.

My plan, if it works, will see me annoying my new foster mum so much that she will withdraw me from this school and send me to the one I wanted to go to in the first place. To do that, I'm going to have to prove I don't belong here at FP Catholic, without annoying my foster parents so much that they decide to send me back to the group home. I need to remain in their care for about five more weeks until I turn eighteen. Then I'm going to take what I came to this town for and get the fuck out.

Unfortunately for my introvert ways, and my need to stay in the shadows, if I'm going to cause issues that see me removed from this school, I'm going to have to get people's attention. A dilemma for sure, but I'll do what I have to do, and I'll do it fast because I don't have much time left before I age out.

"Try to enjoy your first day here, Dee. Please give this school a chance." Cynthia, my foster mum, smiles warmly, waiting for me to respond. So I don't. I just walk off, heading deeper into the school as eyes land on me, while I have no clue where I'm going.

"She means well." My new foster sister, Rhys, dashes up beside me, matching my pace.

I glance up at her, and her deep brown eyes lock with mine as she flashes me her teeth. Naturally, I roll my eyes and look away, and all it does is amuse Rhys, causing her to giggle.

"We have an all-school assembly first thing, so you're heading in the wrong direction." Rhys snickers, latching onto my arm and steering me left.

I try to tug my arm free, but the girl is determined, and also a little crazy because she meows in my face and throws her head back, giggling to herself. I frown, pretending like I think she's coo-coo, but really, I know she isn't. I know more about Rhys George than she or anyone realises. I know about her past with her old foster families. About her drug addict mum, who died when Rhys was nine. About her birth father, who is currently dying from cancer in prison where he has been since he got busted for the sick games he liked to play with Rhys when she was still a child. I know about the abuse she suffered, and all about those who dealt it to her. And now I know she's in some sort of group relationship with four or five other guys, and I also know I never want to hear them going at it again.

That was… not cool. I'm no prude, but hearing an orgy coming through the door of my new foster sister's room is not my jam.

Speaking of her guys, I hear them before I see them, and Rhys does too, jumping in excitement as the crowd of students part and they come into view. Unfortunately, Rhys doesn't let go of my arm, and her jumping jerks me around, so I tug myself free and keep walking, even when the blonde long-haired dude bounds up to her like he's a fucking Labrador and lifts her in his arms kissing her.

Jesus, anyone would think it's been days since they've seen each other, but it's only been hours.

The Spanish looking guy passes by next, shooting me a playful wink before he takes the blonde guy's place and kisses Rhys like they are starved for each other.

"You'll get used to it."

I glance up to the towering height of one of my sister's fellas, his icy-blue eyes meeting mine as he smiles.

I frown. I don't want to get used to it. And I won't have to since I won't be here for long enough. The big dude chuckles at my expression and I slip past him, continuing forward towards the front of what looks like a big gymnasium. I'll give it to the Catholics. They sure have fancy facilities.

"Hey, Dee." A deep voice gains my attention, and I see one of my sister's other guys heading towards me with that blonde guy with the bright blue eyes that got pissy at me yesterday. I think he said his name is Jared. I wasn't really paying that much attention because I just wanted to get away from him. I don't normally do people and I knew that today was going to be a lot, so having to do it yesterday was always going to be too much.

The dark-haired guy doesn't go up to Rhys like the other three did. Nope. He starts walking beside me, and the pissy blonde guy squints his blue eyes at me like he's not sure if he wants to frown or shoot me daggers.

Bring the daggers, arsehole!

"You excited for your first day?" The dark-haired guy asks, and I raise my brows at him.

He's not being serious, is he?

"Save your breath, Grady. She's too good to talk to us." Blondie states before the dark-haired dude frowns at him.

"Crowley. Not cool man."

"What? It's true. She doesn't want to talk to us." Jared shrugs.

Finally. A quick learner.

"Who doesn't want to talk to you?" Rhys pushes in between me and her dark-haired lover, linking arms with both of us.

"Dee." Jared grumbles as his mate's attention is taken by my foster sister.

"Oh, that's because she's shy." Rhys grins down at me, shooting me a wink, and again, I roll my eyes and look ahead as we walk through the crowd.

There are so many students here. I've been to a lot of schools, but I don't think any have had this many kids turning up to learn. What makes it worse is there are so many eyes on our group as we walk. Some are focused on Rhys and the guys, others are focused on me, the new girl.

Hell, even if I wanted to, I don't think I could sink into the shadows with Rhys George as my new foster sister.

"Hey, girl." A blonde beauty steps into our path, throwing her arms around Rhys' neck as a dark-haired guy lingers behind her. I glance at the girl whose appearance screams sexy Aussie girl next door, her long blonde hair falling down her back in waves, and her bright blue eyes shining with happiness as she speaks to Rhys.

I ignore their conversation. There's nothing I need to know about this girl or Rhys to need to pay attention, but as I look past the blonde girl, who I overhear is named Lexi, my eyes land on Jared's face. He's looking at her, his chest rising and falling as if he's struggling with some sort of emotion, but then his eyes shift from her to me. He frowns, his dark blonde brows meeting in the middle as his breathing evens out. I should look away or hiss at him or something. Anything to get his attention off me, yet for some reason I don't. I just stare back at him.

If he wants a stare off, then he's messing with the wrong girl. I can stare any arsehole down and win.

As our eyes stay connected, his seem to darken and a look of anger dances across his face. It's the same expression he was wearing yesterday when he came to hang out with Rhys and her boyfriends. He was pissed off, and now he seems to be feeling the same way.

Did I do that? Does my mere existence piss him off?

I fucking hope it does. It's sure to steer his attention away from me.

A loud beeping sounds, and the students start moving towards the now open doors of the gymnasium. I guess that's the school bell. Even it's fancy, matching the slick buildings well.

Jared is the first one to break our eye lock, and I bite the inside of my cheek to hold back my grin. I won. He lost. Victory is mine.

Ok, so it's a pretty basic victory, but it's victory all the same. Unfortunately for my introvert ways, I'm fucking competitive. It can be a problem when I need to hide.

Rhys leads me into the gymnasium and drops her hold on me as she falls in behind one of her fellas as they shuffle into the back row of seating. I stay standing at the end of the row as her other guys rush in behind her like they will die if they aren't near her, and the blonde girl, Lexi, giggles as her boyfriend whispers something in her ear as they move into the row next.

"You gonna sit or what?"

I don't even turn to acknowledge Jared, making a point to ignore him as I shuffle in to sit next to Lexi. She smiles at me as I sit, so I turn my full bitch off for once and offer her a small smile, taking my seat before the broad shoulders of Jared bump me when he flops into the seat on my other side.

I fight the urge to curl my lip and dick punch him. That would draw too much attention. Although, it would be satisfying.

"Good morning students. Please quieten down." My new foster mum's voice comes through the speakers, and I straighten my spine, trying to see over everyone to the stage where Cynthia is standing. I can only just see the top of her head, my short height not doing me any favours in this scenario.

The crowd of students slowly falls quiet, and I have to admit, it's kind of impressive. None of the other schools I've been to would have managed such obedience so quickly.

Cynthia starts talking, and I zone out, because she is

harping on about the uniform policy and detentions that I know I'll be the receiver of before recess even hits. As soon as I get out of this crowd, I fully intend on throwing my school blazer in the trash and replacing it with the hoodie I stuffed into my bag earlier with my sports gear.

"Why aren't you on social media?"

The deep whisper comes from my right, and I flinch back as Jared's warm breath floats over my ear. I fight the urge to glance at him. That will just give him the impression that I want to talk to him. Which I don't. Even though the urge to give him attention has a strong pull on me for some reason.

"You're not on Facebook or Insta. Are you on SnapChat?" he whispers again, and I tense as I force my eyes to remain on my fingers in my lap.

Of course, if I *was* on social media, he would never find me. I'm not idiotic enough to put my real name out there. To post selfies with my breakfast or pose for a shot for all the world to see.

"What is Dee short for?" He's a persistent fucker, isn't he? "Delilah? Dena? Dianna? Debbie?"

I keep my eyes on my lap.

"How about Delicious? Devil? Devious? Deranged?"

A grin escapes and I quickly bite the inside of my cheek, hoping he didn't see.

"Ahhh. So, it's either Devious or Deranged." He chuckles quietly next to my ear. "I'm going to go with Deranged."

Fucker.

Of course he'd go with that.

Hell, I probably would too.

"What's your last name, Dee?" He leans in more, his lips nearly brushing my lobe.

Shit, that does something to my insides that I'd rather not admit to.

"Her surname is Porter." Lexi whispers over my head, and I turn and shoot her a glare.

Firstly, how does she know that? And secondly, who said she could divulge that information?

When Jared doesn't respond, I take a risk and glance up to see him frowning at Lexi over my head, as if he's annoyed that she eavesdropped on our one-sided conversation. Good, I kind of am too, even though I don't want to have this conversation with Jared, or anyone, for that matter.

When Jared's blue eyes dart down to mine, I quickly look away and focus on my fidgeting fingers once again.

"Deranged Porter. I think it's fitting." Jared chuckles quietly close to my ear again, and I can't help it. I glance back up to shoot him a dagger. He's not looking at me, though, and it's too late when I realise that he's taken a selfie with me glaring at him.

I itch to reach out and snatch his phone off him and delete the picture, but that will involve more interaction, which I'm meant to be avoiding. Especially with him. I don't have time to deal with whiny arseholes. Or the patience.

Instead, I watch him caption the picture.

Having a blast at FP Catholic!

Fuck my life.

Seriously, do I really have to put up with this immature bullshit? I should have brought Thana with me. Maybe if I flashed her blade at this fucker, he'd back off and leave me the hell alone.

I focus back on my fingers, closing my eyes and repeating an affirmation over in my head.

I will not kill today. I will not kill today. I will not kill today.

Hey. It's a legit affirmation. Don't judge.

I sit through the rest of this bullshit assembly with my eyes closed, blocking out the world to help me find some sort of peace and strength to get through the rest of the day.

When I feel the air shifting around me, my lids fly open, and I notice students starting to stand from their seats. As I join them, my eyes land on Jared, who is un-moving as he watches me.

I sigh silently, keeping my eyes forward, looking towards the end of the row, waiting for him to move. I don't give in and look at him again. I don't engage. I wait patiently, counting backwards from one hundred in my head.

"Move your arse, Jared." Rhys calls from somewhere behind me, and Jared finally gives in, standing and moving out of the row so we can all get out.

As soon as I'm free, I dart ahead, again not knowing where the hell I'm going. I have PE first, which is short for physical education. PE is a good class for me to get out my competitiveness without standing out too much. I'd been excited about getting into this class, hoping it might offer dance, cheer or gymnastics at some stage, but like a lot of Victorian schools, they keep the activity fairly mainstream and boring.

Not that I would actually participate in the cheering part of cheer. But I can flip and dance, so that would have at least been fun.

"Hey, Dee!" A familiar female voice calls before Lexi bounds up beside me. "PE is this way."

I stop walking, raising my brow at her and she giggles. "Rhys told me that we have English, Media and PE together, and asked if I can show you where they are this week while you settle in."

Of course, Rhys did. She's my foster mum's little helper, it seems.

I try not to be rude, giving her a nod and turning to walk with her back towards the gymnasium.

"We have a new PE teacher this year. Mrs Bailey. I haven't met her yet, but rumour has it she came from Redfield High, and is a hard arse." Lexi explains as we walk. "I should probably tell you that the class is male dominant. There are only six girls and eighteen boys. A lot of girls dropped year twelve sport."

Oh, fun. A sausage fest.

"But don't worry," Lexi continues as she pulls a door open at the edge of the gymnasium's main foyer. "My boyfriend Ayden and his mates are in this class too, so they will make sure the other guys in the class aren't dicks to you."

I don't know why that matters. I can handle dicks. I can handle more than most. I'm guessing my quietness and my small frame is doing its job to once again have someone underestimate me. I inwardly grin. Having this secret makes me feel powerful. I don't mind people making assumptions about me because proving them wrong, or surprising them when they least expect it, is my brand of fun.

Lexi leads me into the girls' change rooms, and instead of stripping off in front of everyone, I lock myself in a toilet cubicle to change. I don't need prying eyes to latch onto the scars on my arms. I don't need to hear their whispers of sympathy or gossip. Hiding away in here is consistent with my shy demeanour, and I like to play my role well. So I quickly strip out of the suffocating preppy uniform and slip into the navy sports shorts and white t-shirt that has FPC in bold navy letters across the front.

I don't take off my long sleeve black top that I was wearing under my uniform. I leave it on, not caring that I will get hot, or that the teacher will take one look at it and have an issue with how I'm dressed. I'm counting on it.

Once I finish lacing up my Nikes, I head out of the change rooms to find Lexi lingering near the entrance, waiting for me. Her blonde brows lift a little as her blue eyes take me in, but she doesn't say anything. She just grins and gestures her head back towards the doors.

We move outside to the quad where the class has gathered, and all eyes fall on us as we approach. All four of Rhys' fellas are here, along with Lexi's boyfriend, and the pretty boy blonde arsehole, Jared. His blue eyes flare wide as I approach, and fuck, I'm pretty sure it's excitement I see in them.

He's going to challenge me in this class. It's written all over his smug expression as he quietly chuckles to himself. I want attention so I can get in trouble and piss the teachers off, but the attention this guy is giving me is far from the type I need right now.

Great. Just great.

4

JARED

This day is just getting better, and better. I'd been dreading it. Dreading being so close to Lexi again, as we are forced to hang around each other at school because of our friendship groups. I hadn't expected to get so easily distracted from Lexi, though.

My attention had been on Lexi before school started, my eyes roaming over her face and her ever-growing beauty. Laying eyes on her had set off my emotions, reminding me that she isn't mine, and never will be, but a moment later, like the pull of a magnet, my eyes were dragged from Lexi to land on the new little pocket rocket of the school.

Dee.

She was watching me, her dark pools observing my reactions, and for some reason, I found peace from her gaze. My heart slowed to a comfortable pace, no longer aching like it had only moments before. I took that moment to really get a good look at Rhys' new foster sister since I hadn't been able to see her features that well yesterday when she was hidden under her hood.

She can't hide today, though. Not when she is forced to

wear the school uniform to make her look like she's one of us. To most, she probably looks the part, but I see more. I see a unique strong-willed female before me that has darkness dancing in her eyes. For some reason, I find myself drawn to it. Drawn to her.

She is quite beautiful. Naturally so. Her lashes are long, thick, and naturally dark. Her eyes are big, the white in them so bright they are almost tinted blue, and the two round lenses that study me are the richest of browns. Her button nose is dainty in comparison to her eyes, and her cheekbones are high but not overpowering on her heart-shaped face. Her lips are full, but not extreme, and have a deep pink tinge to them. Her brown hair is shiny, long and silky, falling past her shoulders. She's made no attempt to clip it back or tie it up. It's as natural as the rest of her.

I'd been outwardly staring at her, and she'd stared right back. Confusion had swept through me. I can't understand the pull she has on me, especially to take my attention away from Lexi. I haven't been able to find anyone to do that yet. To have the power to break the spell Lexi West has on me. That is, until this dainty creature came along.

The problem is, she seems to hate me. Dee is not a fan of Jared Crowley.

Yes, I was a prick yesterday, but she wasn't exactly welcoming. Plus, she won't fucking talk to me. Rhys can call Dee shy all she wants, but it's not shyness that stops her from speaking to me. It's something else, and it pisses me off not knowing.

The assembly gave me a chance to try to get a reaction from her. I deliberately hung back, so I'd have to sit next to her. I also didn't want to sit next to Lexi, so it worked out well when Dee took the seat next to Lex. Then I searched social media for her. First, I stalked Rhys' friends, figuring if she was friends with anyone here yet, it would be her foster sister. I came up blank, though. So, I searched Dee, only to find many Dees, and the top results weren't even close to the beauty sitting next to me.

When I leaned in to ask her why she isn't on social media, I didn't miss the way she stiffened, yet kept her eyes cast low, ignoring me.

I'd considered that Dee may be deaf. She didn't seem to react to people, and if there were any sort of reaction, it was when she'd been looking at someone. It would explain why she hasn't spoken to anyone yet. I've been watching her closely, and even though people talk to her, she never talks back.

So when she stiffened from the words I'd said in her ear, I figured she could hear me. Then again, she could have felt my breath over her ear, so I'm still confused as to what her situation is exactly.

Can she hear? Surely if she couldn't, she would use sign language or something. Although, I still wouldn't be able to understand her because I don't know how to sign.

Maybe she's just a snobby bitch that thinks she is too good to speak to us lowly Catholic students. If that's the case, then I'm sure going to have fun tormenting her.

"Today we are playing dodgeball." Mrs Bailey yells over our chatting voices, gaining my attention from Lexi and Dee as they approach us where we are gathered on the quad. Dee looks even tinier in her sports clothes. As small as she is, though, she has womanly features, like the full swell of her tits hiding under the fitted white t-shirt, and the sensual curve of her hips.

Fuuuck. My dick just woke up.

I dart my eyes away from her to focus on our butchy new female sports teacher. She reminds me more of a bulldog than a woman, and her voice is deep and gruff as she yells to get our attention.

Unfortunately, her attention snags on the latecomers, Lexi and Dee, and she bellows across the quad.

"Excuse me, young lady. That shirt under the t-shirt is not part of the uniform."

I watch Dee for her reaction. She doesn't give one, just continues forward with Lexi at her side.

"She's new, Miss," Lexi explains.

Mrs Bailey frowns. "It's Mrs Bailey, thank you very much. And I am new too, yet you don't see me violating the uniform policy."

Lexi smirks, not caring about the scolding tone from our new PE teacher, and Dee's face still remains neutral as they come to a stop to stand with the group.

"Young lady, you must go and remove the long sleeve shirt now," Mrs Bailey growls, coming to stand before Dee.

When Dee lifts her deep brown eyes to meet the glare of our teacher, her face remains neutral, although her eyes seem to harden. Much like when I first encountered her yesterday at Rhys'.

I hold my breath, waiting for her to finally speak. Waiting to hear her voice, but it never comes. Dee just glares right back at the teacher.

"Ahh, Mrs Bailey?" Lexi tries to get the teacher's attention. "This is Dee Porter. She is the principal's new foster daughter."

I smirk at Lexi's attempt to try to play the principal card. Sure that she is about to get an earful from our teacher, but her words seem to interest Mrs Bailey, and she takes a step back.

"Oh. Right, yes, I read the email about you." Mrs Bailey's tone softens, and she takes another step back. "Uh, you should really familiarise yourself with the uniform policy, Dee." Then she turns on her heel and walks off.

What the fuck?

"Form two teams. You have one minute to figure it out or I will choose for you." Mrs Bailey bellows at us again and I have to fight the urge to cringe at her manly tone.

Lexi grips Dee's arm and leads her over to us as we naturally fall into our friendship group, making up the bulk of our team. Apparently, that includes Dee as well.

"You sure that's a good decision Lex?" I ask, keeping my eyes on Dee as she glances at me. "She's pretty quiet. Probably doesn't have the backbone to be a valuable player."

Finally, a reaction. Dee's eyes harden into the daggers she sent me yesterday, and I let my smug grin free.

"Jared!" Lexi hisses in protest, but I ignore her, staying in another stare off with this little pocket rocket.

"Dude, you need to stop being a dick." Marcus nudges my shoulder, breaking my eye lock with Dee.

Fucker.

I shrug at him, not able to hide my smirk. I know I'm being a prick. I can't seem to help myself lately, especially now with this little beauty snagging my attention. It feels good. To not be pining over Lexi feels fucking fantastic. And if I have to torment this new girl in order to get Lexi out of my system, then I'll fucking do it. I'll fucking do anything to forget her.

With me, Marcus, Garrett, Simon, Shaun, Ayden, Lexi and Dee making up the bulk of our team, we accept four other guys on our side, leaving the other team to take the four other chicks in the class.

Mrs Bailey goes over the basic rules, a waste of time since we tend to make up our own rules as we go, and we get into place to start the game.

Lexi goes in the first group with me, Ayden, Marcus, and Simon, as well as Paul, one of the other guys I don't know too well. Because we are playing at school with limited time, the rules are a little different to make sure we all get a go. We dominate the first round, wiping the other side out quickly, with only Paul going out on our side. Then we swap, taking the bench so the second group can have a go.

I smirk at Dee as I pass her by, her dark eyes glaring at me in challenge as Garrett and Shaun trail her, along with our other three players. A quick glance around at everyone shows all eyes are on our new addition. Curiosity plaguing us all.

Allison May, one of Lexi's old friends turned enemies, stands before Dee, a bitchy grin contorting her face.

"What's wrong Dee? Cat got your tongue?" Allison pokes her face out as she speaks, standing tall like she is someone of importance. She isn't. She's nothing, especially after Lexi sorted her attitude out last year.

Dee doesn't react. Just keeps her neutral expression in place, staring right back.

"Can you even hear me? Are you deaf and dumb?" Allison laughs, and I hiss, bolting up from the bench I was seated on.

Marcus' hand comes to rest on my arm, tugging me back down. "Let Dee handle her. Hopefully Allison will learn the hard way."

I turn my attention to my lifelong mate, studying his face. He knows something I don't. Has Rhys told him what the deal is with Dee?

The whistle blows and I shoot my gaze back just in time to see the ball in Dee's left hand while her right fist connects with Allison's face.

A loud screech comes from Allison as she falls back and blood sprays over Dee's white t-shirt. Then Dee leaps on top of Allison and throws another punch.

I'm on my feet in an instant, running onto the court with Marcus at my heels. Garrett, who is only a few feet away from the action, gets to Dee first, wrapping his arms around her waist and lifting her off Allison, who is screaming like a banshee. The whistle is blowing wildly, like that will stop the fight before Mrs Bailey starts marching towards Allison.

Just as I near Garrett with Dee in his arms, she surprises us all by doing some sort of ninja shit which sees Garrett, who is the size of a fucking tree, get flipped over and thrown on the ground.

Dee bares her teeth at him, and his eyes widen in panic.

My heart flips and then races as I take a risk and try to calm this mad woman down.

"Dee. Stop." I growl, moving to her side, just out of arm's reach. She doesn't respond, her chest heaving as she keeps her glare on Gaz. He's a fucking hulk of a guy, but right now, he looks fucking scared. It should scare me too, right? This chick is unhinged, yet I take a step closer.

"Deranged Porter. Stop." I chuckle, because apparently, I've lost my fucking mind, too.

Slowly, and almost creepily, Dee turns her head to the side to glance up at me.

"Stop." I say again, with amusement in my tone. Then she arches a brow.

Ten fucking points to me for getting another reaction from her. Although I have to say Allison is the clear winner here. She sure as shit got a reaction from Dee, and now she's laid out on the ground with blood pissing from her nose, crying like a little bitch.

"What have you done?" Mrs Bailey cries as she kneels down to help Allison, her glare shooting to Dee, who just shrugs and turns to walk off.

"You! Boy!" I turn back to see Mrs Bailey pointing at me. "Take Miss Porter to the principal's office and ask the receptionist to send the school nurse here immediately."

My brows shoot up, but I don't argue, because now I get more time with Dee, who has already walked off towards the change rooms.

"I'll go get the nurse." Paula, one of Allison's friend's cries, already running off towards the main administration building.

I turn my attention to Dee's retreating back as she enters the gymnasium foyer and move quickly to wait for her to come out of the change rooms. I figure she must be getting changed back into her formal uniform, but a minute later she comes strolling out of the change rooms still in her sports clothes which are stained with blood, with her bag slung over her shoulder and her school blazer in her hand.

Fuck. Why does blood look good on her? And why isn't that thought freaking me out?

She eyes a trash can off to the side, walking up to it and tossing her blazer in it. When her eyes meet mine again, she gives me a shrug at my raised brow before she leaves the building.

"Aren't you gonna get in trouble for tossing your blazer?" I ask as I hurry to her side. She just keeps walking. "Don't you care if you get in trouble? You just attacked another student. Not that I didn't love every second of it. Allison had it coming." Still, I get nothing from her. "Do you want to get in trouble? Is that it?"

Her head turns towards me slightly, but then she stops, like she's trying not to respond to me. But she did move her head, so I'll take her reaction as confirmation. She is trying to get in trouble.

She picks up the pace, her little legs working hard to speed up as my long strides keep in step.

"Why do you want to get into trouble?" I watch her closely again, but she remains quiet. "I know you can hear me, Dee-ranged."

Her lip quirks.

Fuck yes.

"Was Allison right? Does the cat have your tongue? That's gotta make it hard to lick ice cream."

Again, her lip quirks.

"You certainly aren't dumb. Allison was dead wrong about that, proving she's the dumb one." She gives me nothing this time, so I grab her arm and spin her to me. "Why won't you talk to me?"

Her dark eyes glare at me, obviously annoyed that I dare challenge her, and before I can say anything else, she shakes my hand off and turns, storming off again.

"The admin building is this one." I point to the right, and she changes direction. I could have let her keep walking, but she would have ended up in the science block, and I get the feeling we should probably keep her away from the Bunsen burners.

As she walks up the back steps of the admin building, I jog up just in time to slam my hand against the door, stopping her from entering. I know I'm dancing with the devil here. She has some crazy skill that could sit me on my arse in an instant, but it's a risk I'm willing to take just to get another rise out of her.

She spins on me, her eyes wide with fury as I cage her in against the doors. She's so fucking short, I bet she's as light as a feather. I could easily throw her around the bedroom.

"Talk to me." I hiss in her face, and she bares her teeth at me, still making no sound. "Make a fucking noise. Do something." Her silence in maddening me. I don't even fucking know why. She is nothing to me. No one. A stranger.

A smug grin crosses her face then. Her glare disappearing and instantly unsettling me. She snaps her hand out, fisting the front of my t-shirt and tugging me down to her short height, bringing us nose to nose.

Is she going to kiss me? Bite me? Fucked if I know, but I'm here for it.

Her chest rises and falls with emotion she is trying to tame, her dark eyes locking with mine as her sweet scent wraps around me.

Fuck. I want to kiss her. The thought is consuming, yet I don't act on it, because I'm still not sure what she's doing right now.

As if reading my silent question, she grins wide, her face contorting into a stunning smile that I don't get the full effect of because of how close we are right now, and then with her free hand, she grips my chin, turning my head to the side before running her tongue up the side of my face.

5

———

DEE

$\mathcal{M}$y plan backfired. Not only am I *still* a student of Fox Pines Catholic, but I've only been given a warning. Like, what the fuck does someone have to do to get kicked out of the school? Surely assault is at the top of the list.

Apparently, Allison wouldn't divulge what happened, and the other students in the class remain tight-lipped, so the only person talking is the new PE teacher, who apparently has questionable judgement.

I read her file when Cynthia left me in her office to go and speak with Allison. I used my alone time to snoop on Cynthia's computer and found out some interesting facts about Mrs Bailey. She's been fired from multiple schools for false accusations and student bullying and was only hired at FPC because she was the only one that put in for the job.

That's all the info I managed to extract before I was nearly busted. Of course, Cynthia would never consider that I snooped on her computer. Before now, she thought I was relatively quiet until I walked into her office covered in Allison's blood today.

The whole process was a waste of time, and I missed recess and my first Media class. I can tell Cynthia is pissed at me, her frown more on the angry side than disappointed, as she leads me into the toilet just off the sickbay to get changed back into my uniform before I head to English. As she walks away from me, leaving me to go in the bathroom, I eye the open door of a wardrobe next to me and peek in. There are spare uniforms in there, for both guys and girls, and I grin as a new idea occurs to me.

Quickly rummaging through the clothes, I find a pair of the boys' formal shorts and duck into the bathroom. I get changed, keeping my long sleeve black shirt on under my short sleeve white shirt, and tug on the boys' shorts, leaving my shirt untucked. I slip the tie on loosely and put my socks and shoes back on before looking at myself in the mirror.

I look a little dishevelled, but it's a good look, and I feel even better now that I'm not wearing that stupid kilt-like skirt.

I quickly dash from the sickbay out of the administration building, looking at the map Cynthia gave me to figure out where the hell I have to go now. It's a big campus, spread out on a large patch of land a small distance from Fox Pines' main shopping centre. I could easily get lost if I weren't familiar with navigating maps and building floor plans, so it doesn't take me long to locate the English block on the map, and I head in that direction.

Lexi had told me we have English together, but she failed to mention that Jared was also in this class. Of course he's in this class. He's all around me, apparently. Even on my tongue.

I grin to myself. That kinda sounds dirty, and it makes me want to be bad, in the best way, but since I'm not actually all that experienced at that sort of bad, I'll have to stick to the type of bad that ends people's lives.

I have no idea what possessed me to lick Jared's face earlier. My goal was to prove that I did indeed have a tongue, but did I really have to lick his face? I could have just poked my tongue out and showed him that no cat had it.

Then again, why am I even contemplating the idea of trying to communicate with him in the first place? I don't communicate. That's my whole vibe. It's worked for the last seven years, so why the hell am I engaging now? With a pissy arsehole, for that matter.

It does kind of feel good to see everyone's shocked reactions when I stroll into class ten minutes late. I'm sure the tea has spread through the school by now about Allison meeting my fists. I bet no one thought they'd see me here again.

Yep. That reaction is satisfying, for sure.

"Oh, Miss Porter. I'm Ms Dice, your English teacher. Please come and take a seat."

The short lady, although taller than me, smiles warmly, her brown bob cut bouncing as she walks towards me and gestures to the only spare seat left in the class.

I swear he did this on purpose. Jared Crowley's goal is to rile me up, so making sure I had nowhere else to sit, but next to him, is totally obvious to me. I shoot him a dagger as I approach, and he bites his lower lip, trying to hide his shit-eating grin.

It would be so easy to smack it off his face. In fact, maybe I should. Two assaults in one day would surely see me kicked out. Although, I do risk getting in trouble with the cops if I do that, and I've worked so hard to stay off their radar over these last few years. It would be a shame to throw it all away now.

Fuck it.

I drop to the seat next to him and glance at the teacher, who is patiently waiting for my attention.

"Right. This here is Jared." Ms Dice gestures to my left, but I keep my eyes on her, ignoring the smug prick next to me. "We are currently working in pairs to read the first novel of the year. A good way to work together is to read a chapter out loud, and then discuss the chapter and make note of points that are on this list."

My shoulders slump and I glare up through my lashes at Ms Dice as she places a piece of paper on the desk in front of me, waiting for her to remember that I can't do what she's asking. After all, apparently my foster mum emailed all my teachers, so they should know.

"Do you have any questions?" Ms Dice asks and I just continue to glare at her.

She shifts uncomfortably, and then, as if she has a lightbulb moment, her brows lift in surprise.

"Oh my goodness. I am so sorry, Dee. Your situation slipped my mind for a moment there." She sighs anxiously, looking between me and Jared. "Uh. I guess you could read the chapters to yourselves and perhaps write down your discussion?"

Or, I could just work on my own.

I'm better at working on my own than with other people. I could write *that* down to tell her, but I'm not feeling very helpful right now. And the more difficult I am, the more likely Cynthia will move me to FP High.

"Thanks, Ms Dice. We will work it out." Jared offers, and I roll my eyes.

What a suck.

"Oh. Ok." Ms Dice smiles, slowly stepping away from our table.

"You have a tongue. We've established that." Jared chuckles, and I chew the inside of my cheek, forcing back my smile. "Given the way you're trying to hide your smile, I know you can hear me. So why can't you talk to me?"

I ignore him, picking up the book in front of me, and opening it to the first page.

"Hmmm. It's like that, is it?" Jared chuckles again. "You know, I'm not giving up. I'm going to keep fucking with you until I hear your voice."

I turn the page, pretending to read.

"You have a voice, right? Or are you like… mute or something?"

I slowly inhale, trying to keep my heart rate calm, because all he is doing is trying to get me to react. I hate the word mute. And I hate the white coats who think they can call my choice to not speak, selective mutism.

Yes, it's selective, but it isn't a condition. My lack of vocal speech isn't because I suffer from an anxiety disorder or have a phobia of talking to people. I simply choose not to speak, because it gives me all the power.

That, and I may have taken someone's words to heart when they said they never wanted to hear my voice again. Nevertheless, I quickly learned that by withholding my voice, I can control certain situations.

For example, telling me that I have to do something usually backfires because I simply don't respond. I don't nod. I don't shake my head. I don't in any way agree or disagree, so I usually leave people so stumped and annoyed that they don't bother with me anymore. In the end, I get what I want, which is to be left alone.

Does this mean I don't communicate at all? No. Of course not. There are times I need to, but I still don't use my voice. I don't hand over that power to anyone, and the few times I have used my voice in the last few years were for helping other people.

Is it strange for me to want to help other people if I don't want to deal with people in general? Maybe. But I do, because there are a horde of people out there who need someone to fight for them. And given my ability to be underestimated and fly under the radar in certain situations, I have perfected some important skills that I can only justify are ok to use, if I'm using them to help someone else.

"Hey." A large hand comes to rest on my thigh, and I automatically flinch.

I'm not used to people touching me. I'm not used to people getting close enough to do that. My eyes, furious and wild, dart to Jared's blue gaze as he looks down at me.

"Tell me to remove my hand." Jared smirks and my nostrils flare. "Say the words, Dee."

I narrow my eyes and I gently place my hand over his on my thigh. His eyes widen, his breathing growing deeper as he misreads what is happening here. I link my fingers with his, nice and slow, ignoring how good it feels to have his touch, and as we gaze into each other's eyes, I tighten my grip and start to pull back on his fingers.

His eyes darken as he silently grits his teeth, trying to pull his fingers back the other way, but the position of my hand over his gives me more momentum, and I keep pulling back, watching his nostrils flare as his body starts to react to the pain.

I lift a single brow at him, waiting for him to yield, and a second later, he nods, so I release him.

He leaves me alone for the rest of the lesson. My warning a success. I try to ignore the little pang of guilt inside me. There's a part of me that was enjoying our interactions, but I remind myself that I'm not here to find friends. They are distractions I don't need.

At lunch time, despite the hot afternoon sun, I slip my hoodie on and press my EarPods into my ears, shutting the world out as I close my eyes and listen to Billie Eilish. Rhys had led me here to a courtyard where the rest of her friends were, but I moved away from the group to sit leaning up against the brick wall in the cooler shade.

I pull my hood on, sinking back into it so my eyes are shadowed, and every now and then I ease them open a little to watch my surroundings.

Rhys and her boyfriends have some serious self-control issues. They don't even get halfway through lunch before two of them disappear with her into the gymnasium to do God knows what. The other two, who I think must be Garrett and Marcus, hang back with Jared, Ayden and Lexi, sitting on top of a picnic table. I can see that they are talking about me. People don't realise that it's a natural instinct to look at the person they are talking about if they are in the same vicinity. They try not to make it obvious, but they fail.

I can just imagine what they are talking about. Is she a mute or not? Is she bat shit crazy after her attack on Allison earlier? Is she a serial killer?

All three of those questions just might be true.

My eyes are drawn to a blonde girl walking behind their table, her hair in two braids, her eyes darting up to glance at Lexi as she passes by them unnoticed. I don't know who the girl is, but do know a victim when I see one.

Someone is abusing her. She seems skittish. There are dark circles under her eyes like she is having difficulty sleeping. She takes a wide berth around anyone that passes by her, and when someone says hi to her, she lowers her eyes, not acknowledging them.

The contradiction to her is that she approaches a picnic table at the other end of the courtyard, which is surrounded by guys. I watch as she slowly steps through them and takes a seat at the end of the bench before taking a book out and pretending to read it. That's when a guy moves to her side and slaps the book out of her hand. All the other guys around her laugh, but she ignores them and picks the book back up and resumes pretending to read it again.

I glance back over to where Lexi is sitting and see that her and the guys with her are now looking towards the blonde girl, too. Does Lexi know her? If she does, then why isn't she doing anything to help the girl? It's obvious that she's being mistreated.

I could do something as well. It would be pretty easy for me to fuck them up a little, but one thing I learnt a long time ago is to do my homework first. I get the feeling that whatever is going on, Lexi West knows about it. If I want to help this girl, I will need to find out what her story is first.

I'm pleased when I get through the whole lunch break without being bothered by anyone. Closing myself off to the world usually works wonders, but sometimes there are people who ignore the obvious fuck off signs and insist on getting in my space.

My last class of the day is Textiles, which I'll admit, I've been looking forward to. I manage to navigate my way to that class, and Ms Holland introduces herself as my teacher, showing me where all the equipment and supplies are. I don't have any of Rhys' friends in this class, which I'm pleased about, but I recognise the blonde girl from lunch that wears the most painfully broken expression on her face.

I cross the room, taking the sewing machine next to her and gather the items for today's simple task of sewing a cushion cover. Ms Holland is using this lesson to assess our abilities before she discusses our portfolios next lesson.

The girl, who I establish is named Abbey after the teacher calls the roll, sits quietly next to me, not making any attempt to look at me or anyone else. She speaks if the teacher asks her something, but other than that, she keeps to herself.

She's much like me in a way, withdrawing from the world

in order to be left alone. The difference between us is that I do it because I like to control my situations. She's doing it because she's scared.

6

JARED

The first day back at school has been exhausting. I should go home, but I can't bring myself to sit there and answer all of my mum's questions. I know she loves me, and she means well, but ever since I nearly died from Lexi's brother's attack last year, she hasn't stopped hovering.

I get it. She lost my brother, Tim, six years ago. It was a car accident, which has made my mum even more clingy since I got my license. She nearly lost me a few months back, so her fears are controlling her. It just gets to be a little too much sometimes, and I feel smothered.

Unfortunately, with my parents, it's either smothering me with their worry, or ignoring me as they numb their grief with alcohol. So instead of going home, I drive around for a bit running my interactions with Lexi and Dee through my head from today. It surprises me that my interactions with Lexi were minimal, and I find myself not really caring to think about her as much as I have been over the last few months. Even at lunch, I didn't feel the pull I had to her only the day before, but I did feel a pull, just to a different girl.

As if my brain conjured her, my eyes somehow find the petite frame of Dee as she walks up the path away from the town centre bus stop. I ease my car to stop at the pedestrian crossing in time for her to walk across, right past my car without even noticing me. When she reaches the other side and walks up the street, I sit patiently while other pedestrians cross, watching her like a creeper before she opens a door and slips inside the Fox Pines School of Dance.

What the?

I frown, driving forward when a horn honks behind me, and I do a blockie of the main street before pulling up in a parking spot a few doors down from the dance studio.

Does Dee dance?

Surely not. That doesn't make any sense. She doesn't seem like the sort of girl to want attention on her, so why would she dance?

I try to picture her in a tutu, dancing gracefully like a ballerina, and I start chuckling to myself. No way. That scenario just isn't possible.

I sit in my car and wait for twenty minutes, expecting Dee to come back out, so when she doesn't, I find myself getting out of my car like I'm in some sort of trance, and I head through the doors of the dance studio.

The sounds of muffled music and giggling children meet my ears, and I glance through the large windows along the wall, which look into different dance studios.

"Can I help you?" An older lady with glasses perched on her nose approaches me, and suddenly I feel like an intruder.

"Ahhh. Um. I'm looking for my, uh, friend."

Why the fuck can't I speak?

The lady grins. "If by friend, you mean your girlfriend, all the older girls dance upstairs. You can watch through the viewing windows with the other boyfriends."

She points to the staircase, and I simply nod and make my

way up them, not bothering to correct her that I'm not here to see my girlfriend. I don't have a fucking girlfriend, and I don't intend on having one any time soon.

When I reach the top, I see a few other guys around my age looking through different windows. My heart flips with guilt. I shouldn't be here. I wasn't invited here by anyone. Certainly not by Dee. I should turn around and go back to my car. But do I do that? Nope. I move forward, peering through the windows.

I glance into the first studio, seeing girls in black leotards wearing those ballet shoes that they go up on their toes in. I don't know what they are called, but I already know without having to take a good look that Dee isn't inside that room. It's just not her vibe.

When I reach the second window, I still when I see dancers moving in unison, their bodies flowing in creative movement that is nothing like the ballet stuff in the first studio. That's when I see her. In the back corner, keeping out of sight as much as she can, Dee is dancing, following the choreography with the other dancers like she has been doing this for years. My breath hitches as I take in her face, so relaxed and calm, at ease with herself as she moves with fluidity.

The way she moves is like an expression of its own. It's like she is talking to me with her body, her movements so heartfelt that I just can't look away. Her arms lift and extend with grace, and her head follows, her eyes moving to look straight at me. I gasp like a little bitch and move to the side of the window, hoping she didn't see me.

"Your girl doesn't know you're here, hey?" A guy asks as he chuckles, and all I can do is shake my head. "Don't worry, man. It's one way glass. All they can see on the other side is a mirror."

"Oh. Right." I feel like an idiot, yet I still hesitate to step back out where I was before, feeling like Dee Porter has x-ray vision.

"I haven't seen you here before. Are you here with the new girl?" The guy asks and I nod, taking in his sandy coloured curls peeking out from the black cap he's wearing. "She's one hell of a dancer. Don't tell my girl I said that, though, will ya?"

I chuckle and shake my head. "My lips are sealed." I shift closer to the window to watch Dee again. They have stopped dancing and are being directed by the teacher to split up into groups. "What are they doing exactly? Like, what sort of dance is it?"

"Contemporary dance. It's expressive dance, I think. I'm not totally sure. I try to pretend to care when my girl talks about it."

I laugh, nodding.

"So right now, they have just finished learning some choreography, and are being split into smaller groups to show the teacher what they have picked up."

Suddenly, nerves cause my heart to race, and I realise they are for Dee. She would probably hate that part, having people's eyes on her. But then again, why would she dance if she didn't want someone to watch her?

She's not in the first group, and I watch her as she watches them dance, her hands sometimes subtly moving in time with those who are dancing. When the first group finishes and moves off the floor, I hold my breath, waiting to see how Dee will react. I expect her to stay hovering in the corner, but she doesn't. She moves out into the centre of the room with confidence. There are four other girls in her group, and they listen to the teacher talk before the music plays again and they take their positions.

Then they dance.

With fewer people around her, Dee is able to create

bigger movements with her body, her arms lengthening, her legs stretching, her spine straight, yet her stance fluid and relaxed. She keeps the pace with the other girls, and when they leap, Dee rises higher than them, as if she has springs in her feet. I hold my breath, worried that she might fall or twist an ankle when she lands, but her feet land gracefully as she continues to dance.

"Her Jete is sick. Where did she dance before she came here?" the guy asks and I shrug.

"I'm not sure."

The guy chuckles. "You two are pretty new then?"

"Yeah." I chuckle awkwardly. "You could say that."

My eyes stay locked on Dee, and I watch in awe at how natural the movements come to her. Then the dancers all start doing something different, and I look at the guy next to me in confusion.

"They get to improvise the last part of the dance. Apparently, being able to improvise is an important skill for a dancer to have. It also lets them be more unique in their expression."

I nod, turning back to watch Dee express her unique self.

I'm awestruck. My mouth drops open as I watch her spin and leap, tumbling to the floor in a roll before she's up again, kicking her leg up so straight and high that it touches the side of her head. She does another leap that looks like some sort of martial arts kick, only graceful, before she spins and slows her movements, coming to stop with the end of the music.

"Holy shit." The guy next to me says out loud what my brain is thinking. "She's fucking amazing, man."

I nod. Not able to speak. I don't think amazing even describes what I just witnessed. I can't even find words to answer the guy as I watch the other girls in the class clap and smile at Dee. The teacher even looks in awe, her hand over her heart as she speaks to the class, gaining everyone's attention, and Dee returns to her spot in the back corner, giving the faintest of smiles in return to the girls that smile at her.

She doesn't speak, though. Her lips don't part to release her voice, but she does give her teacher a nod when she says something to her, and fuck if that isn't interesting.

She *can* communicate if she wants to, even if it isn't using her voice. This girl has me so intrigued. I want to know why she won't speak. I want to find more ways to get reactions from her. I want to know everything about her.

But why? Why the fuck do I want that?

Dee Porter is none of my business. She's made that clear, yet here I am, spying on her like a fucking stalker, trying to learn more about her.

It's possible I'm an obsessive motherfucker.

I obsessed over Lexi. It turned me inside out with rage that I couldn't have her. It's turned me into a different person. Angry. Aggressive. A fucking prick. But did I even care that much about Lexi West if the moment Dee Porter caught my attention, I'm suddenly over Lexi?

Nah, that doesn't make sense. Although, I've been searching for a distraction. A way to forget Lexi, and it looks like Dee Porter is it.

When I notice the dance class wrapping up, I mumble a *see ya later* to the guy next to me and rush back to my car, so Dee doesn't spring me.

I'm so fucking antsy. *That* part of my obsessive behaviour isn't disappearing, and I know I need to get my shit together before I go home.

As the dance studio doors open and groups of girls start to step out, I sink back down in my seat, hoping to lay eyes on the mysterious newcomer to Fox Pines. Predictably, she is the last one to leave, and the moment she steps out, a car pulls up and I recognise Rhys' dad. She gives him a smile as she approaches the car, and I feel fucking jealous. What do I have to do to get her to smile at me like that? To communicate with me in some way?

Taking my phone out of my pocket, I watch Dee drive away with her foster dad before I bring up my contacts and do something I told myself I wasn't going to do anymore.

I call Travis Watson.

Travis is a year below me in school and goes to Fox Pines High when he can be bothered turning up. He's not who I typically prefer to hang out with, but lately, he's been the only guy available who isn't too fucking busy with a chick, and as an added bonus, he has access to the most affordable weed in the area.

I never used to be that into drugs and alcohol, but of late, I find them calling to me more. It's a dangerous path to go down. I know that. Which is why I normally try to keep my partying to weekends, but I'm too riled up tonight. I need to chill the fuck out, and the only way I can do that fast is to inhale some MJ.

I hit call on Trav's number and it rings twice before picking up.

"Trav speaking." His voice is gruff, which matches his short but solid stature.

"Hey man. It's Crowley."

"Naw. You miss me already? It hasn't even been two days and you're already pining after me."

"Shut the fuck up," I grumble, and Trav chuckles.

"What's up, man? You wanna party on a Monday night?"

"Not exactly." I cringe at how pathetic I am right now. "You got any Mary?"

"Have I got any Mary?" he chuckles. "Dude, it's growing under my house. Of course, I do."

I chuckle, too, but it's more for show than actually

thinking it's a good thing that his family business is growing and selling weed.

"How much do you want?" he asks.

"Just a joint." I run my hands through my hair, feeling shame wash over me.

"So, no party then? Just taking the edge off?" he asks and I grunt.

"Something like that."

"Cool. Come to mine. We can hang for a bit before I gotta hit the streets," Travis suggests and I agree, because where the fuck else am I going to go?

"See you in ten." I end the call and stare at my phone, hating the loneliness that's seeping in.

If I were being honest with myself, I'd admit that I'm not just an angry prick because of Lexi. I'm also pissy at being ditched for pussy by my mates all the time. We used to hang out every day after school and spend weekends together. Now I have to invite them places and see which ones are cool with ditching their girl for the night and which ones can't go an hour without her. It's frustrating as fuck, and most times now, if I ask the guys to party with me, they give me an excuse as to why they can't.

I need to stop asking them. The disappointment is eating me alive.

I've even considered asking Abbey if she wants to catch up. We were childhood friends. Me, Marcus, Lexi and Abbey growing up together. Everything changed last year, though. Lexi found Ayden. Abbey and Lexi had a falling out. Abbey became secretly engaged to her arsehole boyfriend, Daniel Stone, after their parents came to some sort of arrangement which has to be illegal. And Marcus fell for Rhys George and decided he was happy to share her with Shaun, Simon, and Garrett.

Abbey's weird situation is why I haven't reached out to

her. That, and also because she crushed on me for years when we were younger and I never felt the same way. I'm worried if I ask her to hang out with me that she will think more of it. Not that she would hang with me now. Not with Daniel dragging her around like his slave.

I should beat the shit outta him for the way he's treating Abbey, but she told Lexi last year that any interference will make things worse. Not just with Daniel, but with her parents, too. There's some weird shit going on in her house. That's one thing I know for sure. I just don't know exactly what.

When I pull up outside Trav's, I triple check that my car is locked and secure before approaching his house. This area isn't exactly a nice part of town, and I feel like a preppie fucker wearing my fancy FP Catholic uniform while a group of guys walk by in filthy wife beaters and no shoes.

When I knock on the door, Trav answers wearing a shit-eating grin, and tugs me inside.

"You'll end up getting raped if you walk around this neighbourhood wearing that uniform," he chuckles and I smirk, rolling my eyes dramatically.

"Maybe I should be more concerned with hanging out with you, Watto. Stay away from my arse." I follow him through the small living area, and we pass a kitchen that has dirty dishes piled high on the benchtops.

Trav scoffs. "Unless you've got a sweet cunt and an overflowing handful of tits, then I ain't going near your arse, man."

I chuckle as he guides me down a passage that leads to his bedroom. I've been here a few times to get stoned with him, so this is nothing new, except wearing my uniform is probably a mistake. I'm going to need to wash it before my mum can smell the herbal smoke on me.

I close his bedroom door behind me, and he grabs a joint

off his desk, passing it to me before flopping back on his bed. I sit my arse on his desk chair and use the lighter sitting on his desk to light the joint before inhaling deeply.

"Shit man. No foreplay? Just straight to the action?" Trav chuckles and I roll my eyes before exhaling the smoke into his room.

"You want me to open the window?" I ask, my voice raspy.

"Nah, I'll sell more if it can be smelt on me." He grins, and I shake my head before taking another drag.

"Is it Lexi that has you so worked up?" Trav asks, and I draw my gaze away from his window to look at his brown eyes and the smattering of freckles across his nose.

"Nope. Not Lexi."

His brows shoot up. "Really? Who then?"

I sigh. "There's a new girl in town."

Trav sits up. "Do tell. Is she a good little Catholic girl?"

I chuckle. "No fucking way she is good. She is little, though."

"Ahhh. So she has the devil in her. Sounds like my type of girl."

I study Travis for a moment as I take another drag. Would Dee like him? He is short. Not as short as her, but still short for a dude, so maybe they would be better suited. I can't see her tolerating his immature ways, though. And I can't see him having the patience to deal with her lack of talking.

"She's mine." I claim, and fuck, where the hell did that come from?

Trav's brows shoot into his hairline before he throws his head back, laughing. "Fuck, man. How long has this girl had your nuts?"

"Like, a day."

Travis clutches his stomach as he laughs harder, and tears form in his eyes. "A day? A fucking day?"

"Shut the fuck up." I grumble, relaxing in the chair as the MJ starts to do its thing.

"She must have a magic pussy."

"I wouldn't know." I state, and Travis falls silent for a few beats before bursting into laughter again.

"You haven't even fucked her?" He laughs. "And you're claiming her? You're royally fucked, man."

I nod, blowing more smoke up into the room, watching the haze thicken. "Don't I know it."

7

DEE

My foster mum is a stubborn woman. For the last two days, I have worn the boys' uniform to school, and she has said nothing but asked me if I'm trying to make a statement. I didn't answer her, so she shrugged it off and that was that.

She is infuriating.

I realise I have to step up my efforts to get kicked out of the snobby Catholic school, so I decide to go on a strike of sorts. It's now Thursday and I have a double study period, which in my old school I would have simply stayed home until later in the day, but since Cynthia insisted, I get dressed and get in the car, and I arrive at school for a waste of time double period.

Before I go to class, I find a bathroom and take my uniform off, slipping into my black slashed skinny jeans and my cropped black Stussy hoodie. I instantly feel more like myself, and trade my uncomfortable black shiny school shoes for my black Cons before dumping every piece of my uniform in the trash.

I share the study class with Jared and one of Rhys' fellas,

Shaun. I can't seem to get away from Jared Crowley. He's like a rash. Fucking everywhere. He has, however, given me space over the last couple of days.

I should be happy about that, right? I should be happy that he isn't pestering me to talk to him, yet I find myself missing his attention. Well, I still have his attention. He just isn't talking to me. His eyes stay on me though, and he still makes sure I have nowhere else to sit in class but next to him, but he hasn't been trying to get a rise out of me, and I miss it.

When I stroll in late to class, wearing not a scrap of the regulation uniform, Mrs Brennan gasps and stands from her desk as all eyes fall on me.

"Excuse me, Miss Porter. Where is your uniform?"

I don't answer her for obvious reasons as I weave through the tables to take the only free seat left next to Jared. I risk a glance at him and notice him biting his bottom lip as he tries to hide his smirk.

"Miss Porter!" Mrs Brennan yells, so I lift my gaze to meet hers as she stands with balled fists at the front of the classroom. "I expect you must have a letter to show me explaining your lack of uniform?"

I just continue to stare at her, watching as her face turns red.

"Come here now!" She yells, but I stay in my seat, watching her cheeks practically burst on fire. Finally, she huffs, spinning on her heel and going to her desk to loudly tap out something on her laptop.

"Shit, Dee. I think you broke her." Jared whispers next to my ear and I chew the inside of my cheek as I relax. I'm being a brat to get my foster mum's attention, but did I do it to get Jared's attention, too?

Maybe.

"What's the reason behind this today? You had dudes'

uniforms on for the last two days and now no uniform at all? Who are you trying to piss off?"

Jared is so close that I can smell his spicy scent. I can feel the heat radiating from his body, and his warm breath flutters over my hair that falls over my ear.

"You can't be going to all this trouble for me. I think you totally rocked the boys' uniform yesterday, by the way. And shit, your arse looks hella hot in those jeans today."

I can't help myself. I react, but in a calm, not giving a shit, way.

I tilt my head towards him and lift my brows, shooting him a *really* look, and his face morphs into a smile, giving me a glimpse at dimples that sink in a little before his bright blue eyes dart to my lips.

Does he want to kiss me?

This moody yet pretty—in a masculine way—arsehole who gives me whiplash, is now looking at me like he's starved, and even though my heart races and my tongue darts out to wet my lips, I force my gaze away from him and rest back in the chair crossing my arms over my chest.

That's when the door flies open, and a furious looking principal fills the doorway.

Whoops. I think I've pissed her off.

My foster mum marches up to Mrs Brennan and they speak quietly before she turns her glare back to me and storms up to loom over my desk.

"Stand up, Dee," Cynthia demands. So naturally, I stay seated. "Dee, if you don't stand up right now and come with me, you will find yourself regretting it."

I continue to keep my eyes cast forward, not acknowledging Cynthia or her threat. She huffs, lowering to her haunches before me to get in my line of sight.

"Do you really want to have this conversation here in front of the whole class?" she asks, her voice low so only I can hear. And I guess Jared can probably hear too. Still, I keep my face neutral and stay in my seat. "Why, Dee? Why do you want to go to the High School so badly? What is there that you can't have here?"

Her voice is still low, but I can tell Jared hears by the way his leg stiffens next to mine.

"Why won't you give this school a go?" she asks, still getting no response from me, so she sighs, lowering her head in defeat. "I won't consider removing you from this school, Dee. Not until you tell me *why* it's so important that you go to Fox Pines High. You can continue these charades if you must, but a simple conversation will go a long way to getting what you want. I won't be blackmailed. It's best you learn that right now."

Cynthia stands then, and I feel heat prick the backs of my eyes as my emotions fight to take over. I shut them down, though. Visualising a stop sign and then pushing those weak emotions to the back of my mind. They have no place here.

Cynthia returns to Mrs Brennan, talking quietly before leaving the room, and Mrs Brennan shoots me a look of disappointment. I don't let her feelings towards me affect me, though. When I get what I came to Fox Pines for, then I'll never have to see these people again.

"I'm learning a lot about you, Dee Porter." Jared whispers against my ear, and I fight the urge to flinch away. "You can hear, and have a tongue, and can probably speak, but you choose not to. You're on some sort of mission to drive your foster mum crazy, because you want to go to the public school, and I also know what you like to do in your spare time."

My head darts around, my nose nearly brushing Jared's, he's so close. He eases back and our eyes lock as he grins like a smug prick.

Does he know my secret? But how? Surely, he doesn't

have the ability to find out something like that. Not even the cops have figured it out. He hasn't heard my voice either, so he can't possibly link me. No, he must be talking about something else.

"You seem panicked." He whispers, leaning closer as his grin spreads wider. "What's wrong, Dee? What other secrets are you hiding?"

I have to assume he's talking shit. I can't risk giving myself away, and fuck, I really hope he doesn't know, because it would be a shame to end his existence. It really would.

"Come on, Dee. Talk to me." He reaches forward and brushes my hair behind my ear.

I never let anyone touch me like this. I should dick punch him now, but fuck, my body is betraying me because I lean into his hand a little, and his blue eyes flare. "Communicate with me in *some* way at least."

Slowly, I shift back so his hand falls away from my ear, and I stare at him for a long time, contemplating if I should give him what he wants.

I don't normally have the urge to communicate with people unless it's absolutely necessary, but Jared Crowley knows how to push my buttons, and the pull to interact is getting damn near impossible to ignore.

So, I do it. I decide to communicate with him.

Standing from my seat, I take a few steps before turning back to him and flipping him off.

His laugh is loud in the quiet classroom, his head going back as he clutches his middle and then, to add a little extra, I kiss my middle finger before spinning on my heel to leave the classroom.

"Sit down please, Miss Porter. And please be quiet, Mr Crowley," Mrs Brennan calls, but I ignore her, swinging the door open wide and striding out.

I bite my lower lip as I walk, holding in the laugh that

wants to escape, while my cheeks heat. I probably shouldn't have stepped over that line with Jared and communicated with him. Now he's going to expect more, and as much as I feel the pull he has on me, I know it's pointless. I have less than five weeks to get what I came here for, and I know it will take some time, so I really need to figure out a way to start working on my end game fast.

I'm officially wagging now. Even if Mrs Brennan emails my foster mum again, Cynthia may not even bother coming to look for me. I believed her when she said she won't be blackmailed, which means I need to think of a new strategy to get what I want.

I grab my bag from my locker and leave the holy school grounds, and start my walk to the town centre. Maybe I can catch a bus to the High School and go in search of who I'm looking for. I know they wear casual clothes at that school, so I should be able to blend in for a bit without getting busted.

I pop one of my EarPods into my ear and listen to Sam Smith's 'Dancing with a Stranger' as I walk, letting myself fall into the lyrics as my mind starts to choreograph movements. I do this all the time, creating dances in my head so when I can find some time alone, I can give my body to the song and truly feel it. It's exhilarating at times, to let myself go and be so at peace and so free to just let myself feel and express. There are other times when I'm mentally in a dark place that dancing lets my emotions crash through me. It's amazing how it has the ability to provide me with therapy without even speaking words.

The loud toot of a horn makes me jump, and I spin to see a charcoal Hilux pulled up to the curb, and the smug grin of Jared Crowley as he laughs at my expense.

I shoot him a dagger and keep walking.

"Oh, come on Porter. Get in the car." He calls through the

open passenger window, but I keep walking. "I'll take you to wherever you want to go."

I stop and turn back to look at him.

"You just have to tell me where that is."

I roll my eyes, because this is just another attempt to try to get me to talk, so I start walking again.

"Ok, so you don't have to use your voice," he calls. "Just put the address into google maps and I'll take you there."

I stop again, lifting a single brow at him.

"That's a good compromise, right?"

There are so many reasons why this is a bad idea, yet I still find my feet moving towards his car before I open the passenger door and take a seat. I risk a glance at him to see his beaming smile. Fuck, he's good looking. I don't usually pay that much attention to... well, anyone, yet here I am nearly drooling over a guy that is annoying and nothing but a distraction I don't need.

After I click my seatbelt in place, he hands me his phone with the maps app open, and I search for Fox Pines High School, then hit directions. It's on the other side of town, in the rougher neighbourhood. Which is about a ten-minute drive, according to the app.

Glancing up, I meet Jared's blue eyes and hand his phone back, watching his expression as he takes in where I want to go.

"You really want to go to the public school, hey?" He glances up as if I am going to answer him, and then he narrows his eyes. "Why do you want to go to that school? Is there someone there that you know?"

I stare at him, keeping my expression neutral as he stares back as if he has the power to look inside my mind. I know he doesn't have that ability, because if he did, he'd be kicking me out of his car and going to the cops.

After a beat, Jared sighs, putting his phone in the console, and pulls away from the curb. He turns his stereo up as he drives, and the remix of 'Old Town Road' by Lil Nas X thrums through the speakers.

It's typical that Jared would listen to this song. I bet he listens to the top forty playlists and probably doesn't have a favourite band or singer. Don't get me wrong, I enjoy most songs on the charts, but I prefer my music more... depressive.

Shit. I guess that makes me a depressive bitch, although I don't feel depressed. I guess I don't feel overly happy either. I'm just me.

Jared taps his fingers on the steering wheel to the beat of the music as he drives, and my eyes are drawn to his masculine hands. They look strong, and I can see a few scars on his knuckles, so he's obviously used them in a fight before. His fingers aren't too skinny, nor are they too short, and the memory of his grip on my thigh from Monday turns my cheeks red.

"So, how do people normally get to know you? Do you talk to anyone at all? Or do you write stuff down to talk? Or sign language? Do you do that?"

He glances at me quickly before he turns a corner, and obviously, I don't answer him.

"Is it a blink once for yes and twice for no type of thing?" He smirks as he glances at me again, and I stay neutral. "Do you make any sound at all? Like when you sneeze, do you make a sound?"

I suck my lips in, trying to fight back the urge to smile at his attempts to make me cave.

"What about laugh? I know you have this whole serial killer vibe going on, but surely serial killers find things funny and laugh." He wags his brows at me, and I look away, trying to keep myself composed.

He has no idea how close I am to being a serial killer. I

wonder if he'd run screaming in the other direction like a scaredy cat if he ever found out how I make money.

"Do you snore? Or talk in your sleep? What about burp?"

I give in and roll my eyes at him, watching the smug satisfaction of getting a reaction from me spread across his face.

He focuses on the road again, turning another corner and I frown, realising we are in a housing estate that is much too nice to be near the rougher side of town. Jared flips the indicator on and pulls up outside a house before turning to look out my window at the building. I look too.

"This is my house. I thought you might want to know where I live in case you ever want to visit."

I turn back to face Jared, who is leaning closer than he needs to, and his blue eyes drop to my lips, so I shift back a little, creating more space between us.

Am I tempted to tell him I'll never be visiting him here? Sure. But do I voice that? Hell no.

"Nineteen Willow Lane. My bedroom is around the back. The code to get through the gate is 1919, because my dad is forgetful and used the most predictable numbers, but you can always jump the fence if you forget."

Damn, it's hard not to roll my eyes at him again. As if I'd need to get through his gate to go to his bedroom. Cocky fucker.

Jared chuckles, moving back over to his seat, and slowly pulls the car from the curb. As we move away, I take another glance at his house. It's a typical 90s suburban house. It has a tropical garden with yuccas and a palm tree, even though we live in the southern part of Australia, which isn't tropical at all. The lawn is cut short and looks well maintained, and the house looks like it's undergone a recent paint job, freshening up the tiled roof and eaves, while the sandy coloured brick remains a little weathered.

As we drive, I notice a lot of the houses in this area are the same, with tropical gardens and light-coloured brick. It probably would have been a pristine estate when the houses were first built. It's definitely a family neighbourhood.

Turning corner after corner, I notice the houses slowly declining in taste and design, and mostly maintenance. Old mill homes start to line the streets, sitting on small blocks that hold very little garden. Some houses have front fences and I watch young children, who should probably be at school, playing in their front yards while their parents sit on the porches smoking and drinking.

I glance at the street signs as we drive, looking to see if we pass the one I'll be visiting eventually. Mercy Court.

I take my phone out of my hoodie pocket and open my map app, finding our current location. A quick study tells me Mercy Court is a couple of streets over to the west, and then I notice the location of the high school on the map is coming up on the right.

My heart races at the realisation of how close I am to finding who I'm looking for.

Jared eases the car to a stop across from the school and looks over at the uncoiling wire fence that's meant to keep students in, or non-students out.

"Fuck. It looks worse than the last time I saw it," Jared mutters.

It does look pretty bad, but that's of no consequence to me, so I shift to pick up my bag off the floor, and Jared turns in his seat, eyeing what I'm doing.

"You can't go in there. You're not a student."

I ignore him and turn to grab the handle to open the door.

Suddenly, I'm thrown back into the seat as Jared takes off fast, and I dart my glare towards him.

"You're not going in there, Dee. You'll end up getting stabbed."

My nostrils flare as I ball my fists, and Jared darts his eyes back and forth from the road to me.

"Tell me why you need to go in there?" He hisses like he's angry, and fuck him, he's the one blocking me from doing what I need, not the other way around. He has no damn right to be angry! "Who goes to that school that you want to see? A boyfriend? Is that it? Your lover goes to that shithole?"

Crossing my arms over my chest, I stare straight ahead, not giving Jared the attention he wants from me.

"What's his name?" Jared growls, his anger more evident, and I fight back a scoff.

Why the fuck is he angry?

I realise now that I've made a huge mistake in trusting Jared to help me. Getting in his car has given him all the power. Short of diving out of a very fast-moving car, I'm trapped in here until he decides to stop. Even as he approaches intersections, he doesn't slow down very much, making it impossible for me to jump out and run.

For the zillionth time, I regret not bringing Thana with me. I don't typically carry a knife in everyday life, only when I'm working. But maybe I should rethink that. It certainly would have come in handy right about now.

I am kind of expecting Jared to drive me back to school, so I have to deal with my foster mum, but instead, the built up area of Fox Pines drops away and I find myself watching open fields dotted with cattle pass by as he takes me out of town.

I need to tell him to turn the car around, but I get the feeling that is exactly what he wants. He wants me to talk, and he expects me to give in because he's basically kidnapping me. This fucker has messed with the wrong girl.

8

JARED

Never have I met someone more fucking stubborn that Dee Porter. I have basically kidnapped her, and she still keeps her voice in, not bothering to scream at me to take her back. I really thought this little plan of mine would work, yet here I am getting proved fucking wrong once again.

I drive us out of town and only slow my car when we near the dirt roads surrounding Lake Woodall. The lake itself isn't that deep, and can only be used for swimming, kayaking, jet skiing, or small tinnie fishing boats. It's popular in the summer, the small beach coves filling with families and young adults looking to cool off. Across the other side of the lake are the towering cliffs that rise up to the old mill town of Woodall Ridge. It's one of those towns that you don't visit, as outsiders aren't particularly welcome. There are many stories about what goes on in that town, and I, for one, am quite happy never to find out in person.

I watch Dee out of the corner of my eye as I pull my car up under the shade of a tree. It's quiet here today, given it's a

Thursday and the school holidays have now finished. There is no one in sight, which is perfect because I need more alone time with Dee and I'm hoping that freeing her from the confines of my car will work in my favour.

Cutting the engine, I sit in silence for a moment, waiting to see if she'll get out, so when she doesn't, I sigh and do it first. Moving around the front of the car, I watch her watching me as I approach her door, but she stops giving me attention as I pull her door open.

"Let's go."

She doesn't move.

"Come on Dee. Get out of the car and come for a walk with me."

Still, she doesn't move.

"Fine." I huff and lean into the car. She flattens herself further into the seat as I lean across her and unclick her seatbelt, and when she still makes no attempt to move, I quickly wrap my arms around her and sweep her into my arms, lifting her out of the car.

She scrambles, and I can tell she's going to do that ninja shit on me, so I quickly drop her to the ground and laugh when her arse lands on the grass.

Her glare tells me exactly what she's thinking. *Arsehole.*

It's fair enough. I am an arsehole. I can be nice though, so I offer her my hand, but she slaps it away and gets herself up off the ground, sweeping her hand over her arse to dust herself off.

"You must be hot in all those black clothes on a day like today." I grin, and she narrows her eyes.

"We could go skinny dipping. There's no one here today."

Her eyes turn to slits.

"Or we could talk." I shrug and she rolls her eyes, walking off.

"There's no one out here to hear you, Dee. So, talk to me. Scream at me. Do something."

Her casual steps turn into long strides as she moves quickly away from me. Naturally, I follow after her, my heavy steps snapping twigs as I walk behind her in the bushy scrub surrounding the lake.

Dee glances over her shoulder before picking up her pace, so I match it, showing her she can't get away from me. Then, she starts to run.

Why the fuck is she running from me? Is she scared of me? Or just trying to piss me off?

I decide it's the latter, because I get the feeling not much would scare Dee Porter, so I start running after her. She ducks and weaves through the trees, and I have to give it to her. She's a fast little thing. I find myself grinning as I chase her, having more fun than I probably should, but when sweat starts to stick my shirt to my back, I take control of the situation and speed up.

A quiet gasp spills from Dee's lips as I catch up to her, gripping the back of her hoodie to try and stop her, but the next thing I know, she's doing some weird duck and twist and I'm left with her hoodie in my hand while the creamy skin of her bare back retreats fast.

Fucking hell. Does she even have a bra on?

As she leaps over a log, her long straight hair bounces up to reveal the strap of a black bra, and I momentarily feel disappointed. But, hey. She's only in a bra, so that's still a win.

My grin is broad as I take off fast to catch her, taking a shortcut through the trees as I see her run up behind the barbeque shelter. Slowing my pace, I try to creep the rest of the distance quietly, hoping to surprise her. I approach the shelter with caution, her hoodie still in my hand as I assess the area for signs of movement.

I make it to the concrete pad that the shelter is built on, and move quietly along the wall, coming to the corner. Slowly, I peek around, not wanting to get sprung, and my eyes land on the back of her head as she slowly backs herself along the wall towards me.

She is expecting me to have followed her through the top end of the shelter, not realising that I took a shortcut. I bite my lip to keep in my victorious laugh before I leap forward, gripping her arms to spin her to me before pushing her up against the wall.

Again, I hear the faintest gasp fall from her lips as her chest rises and falls from the chase.

"You can't get away from me, Dee," I rasp, leaning in to press my body to hers, trapping her between me and the wall. "But you can put an end to this little game by simply saying, stop."

Her large brown eyes widen at my words, and fuck yes, I finally have her undivided attention. She can't possibly ignore me now. I drop one of my hands from caging her in to press against the warm flesh just above her hip, her skin searing my hand in the best way. Dee's chest rises and falls, this time not from the chase, but from the feel of my hands on her and I shift my stance to press my thigh between her legs.

"Say it, Dee. Use your voice and tell me to stop."

Her eyes drop to my lips for the briefest of seconds before returning to my gaze, and I study her closely as I run my hand up her side, heading towards the swell of her breast.

Part of me really wants to hear her voice, but fuck if she speaks right now and tells me to stop, I'm gonna be royally disappointed. I don't know what it is about this girl that has captured my attention so quickly, but I'm not going to question it. I haven't felt this alive in a long time.

As my hand reaches the cool black fabric of her bra, I press my thigh closer, feeling the heat through the thick denim of her jeans.

"Tell me to stop," I rasp quietly. "If you don't want this to go further, you'd better say the words, Dee, because I'm not stopping for anything else."

Her nostrils flare at my words and her lips part a fraction.

Fuck. Is she going to speak? My fingers peel down the fabric of her bra cup, my eyes remaining locked with hers, waiting for her to react. I may only be giving her the option of using her voice, but I know damn well she can push me off her if she truly wants me to stop. So, does this mean she wants this? Because she won't speak to me and she's so fucking good at masking her emotions, it's been hard to read her. Yeah, I'm attracted to her, but she hasn't given me any indication that she's attracted to me in return.

My fingers finally graze over her nipple, and my dick jerks when I feel how tightly pebbled it is. I shift my thigh, causing the smallest bit of friction between her legs, and she bites her lip.

"Fuck, Dee. Please tell me to stop if you don't want this."

I'm pleading now because I need her to give me some sign if she doesn't want me to touch her like this. I can be a prick at times, but I'm not a fucking monster. I'd never do this unless she wanted it, yet she hasn't even nodded her head to show her consent.

She remains quiet, her teeth digging into the skin below her lip as her chest rises and falls in time with the way I circle her nipple.

Fuck it. If she won't tell me no, or show me she doesn't want this, then I'm not stopping.

Dropping my other hand from the wall, I ease it down between our bodies heading south, and her breath hitches when the fingers on my other hand roll and pinch her nipple. I can tell she's trying to hold back, but surely, she can't completely. Surely in the heat of the moment, she can't control the sounds her body wants to make.

As my hand moves over her jean clad mound, my ears pick up the faintest of moans falling from her lips as they part again.

Fuck yes.

I cup her covered pussy, using the heel of my palm to rub over her, and her lids flutter shut as the faintest noise falls from her again.

My grin is fucking huge, and my dick is fucking hard, and I'm fucking determined to break down the walls Dee has in place.

As I rub between her legs, I press my lips to her ear and whisper.

"Tell me to stop, Dee."

Then I lean back and drop my lips to her straining nipple.

A slight whimper sounds in Dee's chest right before her hands clamp onto the sides of my head, and at first, I think she's going to pull me away, but then her fingers sink into my hair, gripping my blonde strands, holding me to her.

My blood ignites in my veins, lust unlike anything I've experienced before shooting through me in a wave while I lick and suck her pink nipple before moving to the other one.

Finally, Dee releases a moan, not too loud, but definitely loud enough to be certain it came from her, and I pick up my pace, revelling in the knowledge that I'm giving her so much pleasure that she can't hold it in.

I can't take it anymore, my lips leaving her nipple to trail kisses up her chest, over her collarbone and up her neck. She arches her neck to give me better access, and I stop rubbing between her legs to undo her jeans.

That's when her hand comes down hard over mine, holding it still so I can't undo the button. I pull back, looking into her dark eyes, waiting for her to speak, but she doesn't. She just moves my hand back between her legs and starts moving my hand back to the rubbing motion I'd been doing.

So, she doesn't want me to go that far. Doesn't want me to touch her bare pussy, which is disappointing because I'm fucking craving it bad, but also, the fact that she stopped me shows me *what* she's consenting to.

As I rub, creating more and more friction, her hand falls away, giving me the control and we stare into each other's eyes until I am helpless not to take more. Leaning forward, I press my lips to hers, and for a moment I don't think she's going to kiss me back, her lips unmoving as I nibble at her lips.

"Kiss me," I whisper against her mouth, continuing to take, and wishing she would give. Then she does. Her lips part and her hands fist in my hair again as she lets me in, my tongue dancing with hers as I apply more pressure with the heel of my palm between her legs.

There's no mistaking the moan Dee releases then. It's loud, and husky, and I need more as I break our kiss and move to nibble on her ear.

"Come for me." I rasp, revelling in another moan falling from her lips. Her hips move against the friction I'm working before she gasps and instead of crying out, her teeth sink into my t-shirt covered shoulder as she comes apart in my arms. My dick jerks and my balls tighten with a knowing feeling, and I explode in my fucking jocks like a twelve-year-old having a wet dream. But fuck, it's worth it when she finally falls limp in my arms, her teeth releasing my shoulder, and a gravelly moan falls from her lips.

I could say something to her about her moans of pleasure. I could brag that I finally got her to make a sound, but I'm not a fucking idiot. If I do that, she will never let me get close to her again. And I absolutely must get close to her again, if for no other reason than to hear those sounds fall from her lips for me.

I've finally found a way to hear Dee's voice, and if I want to hear it again, I'll have to sex it out of her.

9

———

DEE

*J*ared Crowley is going to cause me a shitload of trouble. I should never have given into him, but my body betrayed me, taking control of my mind and only thinking about itself. It was almost like an out-of-body experience, because *I* didn't feel like myself, yet I've never felt more like me, at the same time.

I don't know how to explain it. It's confusing, and now all I can think of is how he made me feel with his hands and his thigh and his lips. Fuck, his lips are heaven. I've kissed guys before, maybe not very many, but none ever came close to how Jared kisses. I can't even explain it. It's almost as if his lips were made for mine. It was as if they fit together like a puzzle piece. Which sounds utterly ridiculous, yet that's how it felt.

No one has ever made me come until now. I've had loads of fun with my own fingers, but I don't tend to get close enough to anyone to let them do what Jared just did. I have no idea why I let him do that. I'm not even sure if I trust him. I just knew I couldn't deny the way my body burned for him.

It was something else.

I'd thought about letting him touch me bare. Hell, I fucking yearned for it. It was my brain that controlled that part, though, reminding me that getting too involved with someone is a stupid idea because I'll be leaving town soon. And honestly, if I let Jared go too far, I'm not sure how I'd handle it. I feel like he has the power to break me.

Just remembering how his blue eyes darkened, his pupils so dilated that I thought he might be high, has heat flushing over my body. I know he wasn't high, though. At least not on drugs. On me, maybe. Which is crazy, right? And it really wasn't fair how good he smelt. His scent was intoxicating, which I'm sure is why I gave in so easily.

Not to mention how it felt to have him suck my nipple into his mouth. Who knew that would feel so damn good? And his voice. There was a gravel to his voice I haven't heard before. When he told me to kiss him, my heart did a triple somersault in my chest. I liked that he didn't ask me to kiss him. He told me to. Like a command I couldn't ignore. Which is strange. I don't tend to do well with being told what to do, yet I kissed him back.

And then there were those other three words he rasped into my ear. Three words I never thought would have so much control or power, and maybe they wouldn't if they fell from someone else's lips, but when Jared said, *come for me*, I knew I couldn't deny him or myself what my body craved. Even as I let myself go, I could still hear his heavy breaths next to my ear, and the way his pelvis jerked as he pressed against my body with his own release.

It was so incredibly hot, and felt so incredibly right, which is why when I crashed back into reality, the knowledge of not being able to have more with Jared sent a dagger slicing pain to the centre of my chest.

In another place and another time, Jared Crowley could be mine.

I thought I'd feel more embarrassed about what we did together as we slowly walked back to Jared's car, taking the waterfront route. And maybe I would have, if Jared acted awkward about it, but instead, he talked to me like nothing had happened. And as we walked, he told me about the lake beside us and the town that sits up on the ridge across the other side of the water.

I already know about this area. I've kept a close eye on it for years, so the information Jared speaks of isn't new to me. But he doesn't know that, and I don't intend on him finding out. He has a few different theories on the inhabitants of Woodall Ridge. His theories come from the rumours the residents in that town leaked years ago, which helps to deter visitors. Something else he doesn't know. Most of the people in this area are oblivious to what a dark and depraved place the Timber Valley region really is.

They don't see the corruption and sinister ways of some of their higher-ranking officials, although, last year, some cracks began to form. All within a few months Fox Pines was hit with a house of Horrors that involved my foster sister's friend, Lexi West, and then the scandal with my foster sister and a secret sex club linked to a paedophile ring. What the locals here don't realise is that those events are just the beginning, and Timber Valley has an organisation gearing up to chase the sickos out of hiding. The problem is, the sort of organisation capable of doing that comes with its own outlaw-ish ways. Nothing is ever simple.

Before we left the serenity of Lake Woodall, Jared led me to a public toilet block where we parted ways to take a minute to freshen up, and I found myself smirking, wondering if he was in the men's toilets taking off his jocks to throw in the trash, or if he was attempting to clean up the mess I know he made in them from our time at the barbeque shelter. The urge to ask him when we meet up outside the toilet block is almost overwhelming, and it kind of scares me.

I don't talk to people. I don't ask them questions, because I don't care about them. Did he fry my brain with that orgasm before? What the hell is going on with me?

Once we are back in the car, Jared keeps quiet for the first five minutes as he drives his car off the dirt tracks and back onto the main road. But then he can't help himself.

"What's a guy gotta do for you to tell him why you want to go to the public school?"

Oh well, I enjoyed the peace while it lasted.

I remain silent as always, ignoring his building broody mood as he drives us back towards Fox Pines, and I turn his music up, opting to hear the pop music rather than have him trying to get me to talk again.

His chuckle meets my ears and when he falls quiet, I risk a glance to see him smirking, his eyes trained on the road as he drives. He doesn't drive fast this time. He drives like an old grandpa taking his time. I can't tell if he's doing it to try and annoy me, or to prolong our little road trip, but either way, I don't mind. I don't really want it to end.

Once we are back in town, Jared goes to the Maccas drive thru, ordering us some lunch, not even bothering to ask me what I want, probably knowing I won't answer him. Then he drives around the residential streets of Fox Pines, giving me a tour. He shows me where his mates live, plus some of Rhys' friends, including Lexi, which seems to piss him off a little just by mentioning her, and by the time he is done, we have successfully wagged the whole day of school.

"Where should I drop you off?" Jared asks, and I lean forward to grab his phone so I can put the address into the maps app, but before I can get it, he snatches his phone from the console and slips it into his shirt pocket.

Why does he have to be so difficult?

"Do you have dance classes tonight?"

I freeze, my eyes widening as I replay his question in my head.

Jared chuckles. "I told you I know what you do in your spare time."

I turn my shocked eyes to him, and he grins like he's victorious or something. How the hell does he know I dance?

"Don't look at me like that. Did you really think I wouldn't do my homework on you?"

I could slap him.

"It's contemporary dance, right?" He grins, darting his eyes from the road to me. "That's what one of the other boyfriends told me at the dance studio when we were watching. He said you're a really good dancer. I mean, I could already tell, but he seemed to know more about that dance stuff than me."

Other boyfriends?

"Your jumps are sick, too. You must have been learning dance for a long time to be as good as you are."

What the actual fuck is happening?

"I think watching you dance has to be up there with one of my favourite things to do. The way you move your body, and how relaxed and happy your face looks, is just everything."

This is too much. Dancing is *my* thing. The one thing I have to myself. It's the thing that has helped me through so many dark moments in my short life. There's no way I'd still be functioning now if it weren't for dance. It's kinda sacred. Well, it used to be until Jared fucking Crowley came barging into my life.

I should be thankful I guess that he thinks my secret is dancing, and not how I make my money. Although, I'm feeling a little violated that he knows I dance. And what? He's been watching me? Is he a fucking stalker?

I keep my lips sealed, as usual, and Jared huffs, driving me to the town centre before pulling his car up right outside the dance studio.

Shit. He really does know where I dance.

I turn to him, one of my brows rising as I shoot him an unimpressed glare, and he grins. Like my blatant show of annoyance is a win for him.

Fuck you, Jared Crowley!

I want to say the words out loud, but even if I was someone that talked, I would probably keep the words to myself just to piss him off. After all, he's just trying to get me to react.

Angry, I quickly undo my seatbelt before shoving the door open and scrambling from his car. I ignore the fact that Jared does the same, and I barge past him, my eyes cast to the doors of the dance studio as I flee.

"The best part of my day has been coming here to watch you dance."

I still at his words, my hand resting on the studio's door handle, ready to push it open.

Don't look at him, Dee. Don't show him that he affects you.

I don't turn to him, but my eyes find his reflection behind me as he stares after me, standing at the front of his car.

Why is he doing this? Why is he so fucking determined to… to… what? Be in my life?

Emotions I don't want to admit to feeling swirl through me, and I grit my teeth, holding them in as I push through the glass door of the studio. I don't look back. I keep walking towards the change rooms before locking myself in the stall and sitting on the lid of the toilet.

What am I doing? I should never have gotten in the car with Jared. I should never have put that much trust in someone. He knows too much about me already. Why haven't I been more careful?

Sighing, I push my emotions away, visualising the stop sign and taking in a deep breath. It's a mistake I won't make again. I'll wear a thicker skin around him from now on.

My mood is flat as fuck, and after I change, I make my way through the lower level and climb the stairs, recognising the familiar faces of the girls in my class, but I have no smile for them today. They are laughing, chatting about boys, and a party, something I have no care for until my ears catch the words, FP High party this Saturday night. Instinctively, I move closer behind the girls as we enter the dance studio so I can try to pick up more information. A FP High party is the next best thing to visiting the school itself.

"Girls, mark your name on the list and take your places, please," Miss Adele calls, clapping her hands to get our attention.

The girls in front of me stop chatting, scurrying forward to mark their names off the list, so I follow, doing the same before claiming my usual spot in the back corner.

We do a vigorous warm up, and I push myself hard, feeling the burn and waiting for it to take this weird ache away that's sitting in the centre of my chest. Once we are warm and already feeling sweaty, we move off to the sides to have a quick drink.

"I saw your boyfriend out there again today." I glance up with wide eyes to see a flaming red-haired girl looking at me. "My boyfriend, Caleb, said he's been coming every day. He's thankful to have someone to talk to." She leans forward, checking over her shoulder before turning back to whisper. "Some of the other girls' boyfriends are real idiots."

My eyes dart to the mirrored glass of the viewing window where Jared and Caleb must be.

"Hurry up, please," Miss Adele calls and the girl smiles wider before spinning on her heel and taking her place at the front of the class.

Shit. He's out there? Now?

I'd hoped he'd leave after dropping me off. I didn't think he'd come in again after admitting to stalking me and seeing how pissed off I was about it.

Music starts to play, and Miss Adele starts teaching today's choreography, so I move into place and mark out each move, not feeling the pull to actually dance.

What the fuck is wrong with me?

What does it matter that Jared has seen me dance? What does it matter if he's out there right now watching?

I spin and face the back wall as my eyes prick with heat.

It doesn't fucking matter, Dee.

I blow out a breath as my chest rises and falls, emotions I haven't let myself feel in a long time trying to escape.

Just dance. Pretend no one is here and just let yourself feel.

That's the problem, though. I do need to let myself feel, but the feelings I need to feel are for myself. I can't let anyone else see them. Not today. They are too big. Too out-of-control today.

As the class continues to dance, I move to the corner, pressing my back to the wall and lower myself to the floor, keeping my eyes cast low as I start counting backwards from one hundred.

100. 99. 98. 97. 96.

I close my eyes and slow my breathing.

95. 94. 93. 92.

I visualise the numbers in my head as I count.

91. 90. 89. 88. 87. 86. 85.

I twist my hands together in my lap, waiting for the tension to ease in them.

84. 83. 82. 81. 80. 79.

"Miss Porter. Are you alright?"

My eyes fly open at hearing Miss Adele's voice, and I realise the music has stopped and all eyes are on me.

Great. A fucking audience.

I give Miss Adele a small nod, hating that Jared is probably out in the hall watching me communicate with someone.

"Are you not feeling well?" Miss Adele asks, tilting her head to study me.

I shrug and silently beg for her to forget about me.

"Do I need to call your foster parents? Perhaps you should go home if you aren't well."

I shake my head, and she sighs, looking annoyed, but then gives me a nod.

"Join back in if you feel up to it."

She turns away, clapping her hands three times to gain the other dancers' attention away from me, and they give me their backs, resuming the class.

Drawing my legs up, I rest my arms on my knees and bury my head, re-starting my count. I stay that way for the rest of the class, and when it ends, I stand and gather up my things as I prepare to leave and probably face Jared. If he's still there.

"Miss Porter. A word, please," Miss Adele calls as the other dancers file out, some looking over their shoulders with curiosity as they leave.

I stop in the middle of the room and face Miss Adele, waiting for her lecture to begin, but I'm surprised when it doesn't come.

"You know dance can be very therapeutic, Dee. If you're having a bad day, dancing can help to push all those bad thoughts away."

I nod, knowing it's true, but unable to tell her that if I let myself go today, I will probably break.

"This studio is free for the next hour. You should stay. Dance. Move. Get those demons out. I'll even close the viewing curtain so you can have some privacy."

I'm about to shake my head, even though part of me wants to accept, when a deep voice comes from behind me.

"Dee would love that."

My eyes widen and I turn to see Jared walk into the room, smiling warmly at me as he approaches. "Dee had a bad day at school. She didn't really feel up to coming today, but I drove her here anyway because I know how much better she feels after she dances."

That lying fucking prick. What is he doing?

"You must be her fella?" Miss Adele smiles at Jared.

I'm about to shake my head when he wraps his arm around my shoulders and extends his hand to Miss Adele. "I'm Jared. Dee's boyfriend."

What the actual fuck is happening?

Miss Adele takes his hand, giving it a shake, her smile wide as she looks between us.

"I'm so glad you've found someone, Dee. I know it's a lot for you to communicate with people, so finding a caring boy like Jared here is simply wonderful." She claps.

Fucking claps.

Jesus Christ.

"Well, I'll leave you to it, Dee. You have an hour to yourself. Your boyfriend is welcome to stay and watch." She beams, moving to pick up her bag before exiting the studio.

The moment she closes the door, I whirl to Jared with obvious anger flaring across my face.

He grins. "Just wait a minute." He bops me on my nose and moves over to the viewing window before tugging the curtain across the mirrored glass, closing us off to the outside world.

As he approaches me again, he is still grinning like a smug prick. "Now you can show your anger. I don't think Miss Adele would have liked to see it."

I shove him hard in the chest, my small frame barely making him budge, and he throws his head back, laughing.

Fucker.

My anger gets the better of me and I grip his wrist with both hands before lifting it over my head and spinning, the action causing him to shriek in pain as he falls to his knees.

"Fuck, Dee." He hisses and I shift closer, creating more burn on the friction. "Mercy." He cries out and I bare my teeth at him before letting him go.

I spin on my heel facing the back wall, not wanting him to see my emotions anymore, and I close my eyes as I try to calm my breathing.

I can hear Jared moving behind me, and I hope he got the message loud and clear to leave me the fuck alone and go, but then music fills the room, and I spin and see him hovering near the sound system. His blue gaze is soft as he eyes me, his hand rubbing the wrist that I hurt only moments ago.

"Why would you waste the whole class being stubborn just because I was out there?" he asks softly, and I fight to swallow the lump forming in my throat. He leans down and flicks through his phone, which he has connected to the sound system, and a moment later the familiar opening piano of Billie Eilish and Khalid's 'Lovely' fills the room.

I blink rapidly as he approaches, feeling like he can somehow see into my soul.

How does he know I listen to Billie?

"I will leave if you want me to. I'll never come back and watch if that's what you want, but you have to promise me that you'll never stop dancing, Dee. You were born to do it."

The tenderness in his tone. The caring words he speaks. They undo me.

I'm not used to people caring about me. Not like this. I'm

not used to being the centre of someone's attention. It's something I've deliberately avoided. Mostly because it ensures I don't get hurt again. If I don't care about anyone, then they can't really hurt me, but fuck, for some strange reason, I've let down my barrier and I care about this guy. I know I shouldn't. It's not fair to me or him. I know I have to stop whatever this is, but right in this moment, I can't bring myself to do it.

My emotions get the better of me and my eyes fill with tears as he reaches me, his hand coming up to cup my face before he steps around me, his hand staying on my hip as he moves. When he's behind me, he slowly wraps his arms around me, and my eyes fall to our reflection in the mirror.

He's so much taller than me. We are like complete opposites. He's tall. I'm short. He's social. I prefer the shadows. He has good in him, and I... I have the baddest of bad in me.

"Dance Dee." He starts to sway to the music. "Close your eyes and just let go."

My eyes fall shut as if he commanded them to, and his arms drop away as a tear falls from my closed eye, rolling down my cheek as I continue to sway.

The click of the door opening and then closing meets my ears, and then a sob escapes me as I start to dance.

Prying my eyes open, I barely see past the blur of tears that I've held in for so long and let the haunting beauty of the song seep into my heart and wrap around it, taking over.

I bend and roll my body, my arms lengthening, my knees bending before I fall to the floor and roll before standing again and leaping. I spin, throw myself to my knees, grip my hair in my hands before arching my back.

I dance and dance, letting go. Something I haven't completely given myself over to in a long time.

I don't know why the lock on my darker parts has sprung open today. It could be from frustration at finally being so close to my goal but having constant roadblocks stopping me from reaching it. It could be my heart recognising the possibility of a friendship or someone to care for me, wanting me to drop my walls and give in. Or it could be from the orgasm I let someone else give to me.

All I know is I can't afford to be emotional right now. I need to get my shit together and keep my eyes on the prize.

I have responsibilities, of which I know I've been lacking since I moved here last weekend. I have people to check in with that I've been avoiding because it will likely lead to jobs that will distract me from my current goal. And I have plans to finalise for when I finally turn eighteen.

As the song ends, I stand in the empty studio staring at myself in the mirror before I approach it and glare at my reflection.

Toughen up, princess. It's time to put the wall back in place and get to work.

10

JARED

My heart broke as I watched Dee through the small gap in the curtains outside the viewing window last night. I was happy she was finally dancing, but I hadn't expected so much emotion to fall from her. She was definitely struggling with something serious. You don't fall apart like that unless you have experienced something life changing.

It made me second guess my pursuit to piss her off just to get her reactions. Maybe that was the wrong approach, but the moment she stepped out of the studio, I knew that I wouldn't be able to help myself and I'd continue tormenting her.

Her deep brown eyes were wild as they found me, right before she threw my phone at me, not so gently, and flipped me off as she gave me her back. At first, I felt angry that once again she was blowing me off, but then I found it hard to wipe the grin off my face, because as much as she was walking away from me, she also reacted to me, and I'm pretty certain she hasn't been giving anyone else in town this much attention.

By the time I exited the studio, Dee was climbing into her foster dad's car who must have been waiting the whole time. As they drove off, Dee kept her eyes forward, pretending not to see me, but I know she did. She knew damn well I was watching her.

Fucking hell, this girl gives me whiplash.

Still, I found myself trying to find her on social media for most of Thursday night before giving up and messaging Rhys to see if she knew what name Dee used. Apparently, Dee isn't on any platform. Almost as if she doesn't exist.

It's stupid to think like that. I'm sure there are a heap of people that don't share their lives through the internet, it's just really odd for a teenager not to. Even the introverts have accounts.

Not Dee, though.

Unfortunately, her lack of socials just makes me even more intrigued, and I find myself daydreaming about her through most of my double history class on Friday morning. I've been wracking my brain trying to figure out a way to get her to communicate with me. Sure, making her really pissed off works, but not in a good way for me.

Like yesterday at the studio, she did some ninja shit on me, twisting my arm. I thought she was going to snap my fucking wrist. I should have been pissed at her for doing that. Should have left her then and there, yet I didn't. She can push me away all she wants, but I know we have a connection. I just need to show her again, because I know she felt our connection out by the lake yesterday.

At recess, I look around for her in the courtyard, but she doesn't show.

"You alright, man?" Marcus asks, knocking my shoulder with his as we sit on the picnic table top.

"Ah. Yeah." I frown, wondering if I should tell him about my new obsession.

"Who are you looking for?" he asks and my eyes dart to his as I realise how fucking obvious I'm being.

"Do you know if Dee is here today? We have English next, and I need to know if she's here to do the classwork with me."

His eyes narrow a little as he smirks. "Yeah, she's here. Rhys said their homeroom teacher was trying to hand Dee detention slips for wearing casual clothes and Dee just kept pushing them off the table each time Mrs Monaghan wrote one out."

I nod, my heart racing with the anticipation of seeing her again. She's sure pushing the rules of the school by wearing casual clothes again. I wonder if Mrs Rogan will give in and let her go to the public school.

Just the fact that her foster mum knows she wants to go to that school tells me Dee has communicated that with her in some way. They must have had a conversation somehow. Maybe by text message or something?

As soon as the bell goes to end recess, I run off quickly, determined to get my books and get to English before Dee so I can make sure she has to sit next to me again. When I get to the classroom, I find Dee already there, sitting at our usual table, and I can't hide my fucking smile as I weave through the desks. It's so good to finally lay eyes on her again. She has skinny black ripped jeans on again, and a royal blue long sleeve cropped shirt. No hoodie today, but the fact she is wearing long sleeves in the middle of summer again leaves me curious.

She wore a long sleeve top under her PE and school shirt earlier this week, and I noticed her wearing long-sleeved leotards to her dance classes. One might think she is trying to keep her body covered, but the fact that yesterday and today's tops are cropped, at times showing the creamy skin of her tummy and back, seems to contradict that theory.

Is she just trying to hide her arms?

As I slide into the seat next to her, noticing she hasn't taken her eyes off the book she's reading, I try to think back to yesterday when I had her hoodie off. I remember seeing her arms as she ran, but I wasn't taking any notice of them. Her arms really weren't on my radar when I was rubbing the heat between her legs, either.

"Hey, Deranged." I tease as I shift my chair closer to her, but as usual, she ignores me. "How many detentions have you received for your clothes so far today?" I nudge her shoulder with mine, and still, she ignores me.

Fucking hell. I feel like each time I make the smallest bit of progress with her, something happens, and we take ten steps backwards.

"Take your seats quickly, please." Miss Dice calls over the chatter of the students entering, and finally Dee looks up to see the room filling. "We will continue working on the novel. Since it's a double class today, use the time to work with your partner and discuss each chapter so far."

I watch Dee for a minute, trying to figure out how to get her to communicate with me. I know she's not going to use her voice, but I wonder if I can get her to engage in another way.

Opening my exercise book to a blank page, I lay it on the table, pushing it towards Dee before taking my pen and drawing a series of lines.

Then I write at the top of the page.
LET'S PLAY HANGMAN.
That gets me a smirk, and Dee turns to look at me. I shrug, showing her my smile, and gesture my head to the

paper, feeling like I've already won from that basic reaction alone.

I wait patiently, hoping like hell she'll bite, and fuck, when she picks up the pen and writes the letter *A* at the bottom of the page, I have to fight the urge to leap out of my seat and fist pump the air.

Grinning, I take the pen from her hand, trying not to linger when our fingers brush, and I fill in the letter.

I offer the pen back to her and notice her lip twitch.

Is she trying not to smile?

Then she writes the letter *E*, so I take the pen and fill in the letter.

She rolls her eyes, obviously annoyed, and I chuckle as I hand the pen back.

She writes *I*.

I see what she's doing. She's going through the vowels first. Smart.

I fill in the letter again, biting the inside of my cheek to try to scare my stupid grin away.

As I hand the pen back, she studies it for a minute, before her shoulders drop and she writes the letter *O*.

_ _ A _ I _ _ O _ _ _ _ _ _ E _

Once I've snatched the pen back off her and fill in the letter, she snatches the pen back, and I chuckle at her frustration as she writes the letter *U*. She shoves the pen at me, and I bite back another laugh because I don't want to tease her too much, but I can see she's a competitive little pocket rocket that likes to win.

I fill in the letter.

_ _ A _ I _ _ O U _ _ U _ _ E _

We go back and forth for a while. Since there are no vowels left, she has to think harder about what letters to try.

I get the main part of the hangman frame drawn before she stays focused on it for a while, studying what's left.

_ _ A _ IS YOUR _ U M _ E R

I sit back, feeling fucking proud at finally finding a way to get her to do something with me that I don't have to force. I struggled to sleep last night wondering if I forced myself on her yesterday. I had told her she had to say the word *no*, if she didn't want me to go further. That was an arsehole thing to do to someone that doesn't speak. The thing is, I know she can still communicate without speaking if she really wants to, so she could have shaken her head, or pushed me back, or even ninja'd my arse. But she didn't. The only thing she *did* do was stop me from undoing her jeans, and honestly, I'm relieved she did that.

Not because I didn't want to take things further, because fuck yes, I did, but because I knew then that she would tell me to stop if she didn't want to do the things we were doing.

So eventually I gave myself a pass and fell asleep, and instead of dreaming about Mike West beating me, I dreamed about her lips and tongue and the way I came in my jocks.

Those fuckers are in the trash in the men's bathroom back at Lake Woodall.

Suddenly, Dee stiffens, and she turns her eyes to me before giving me an eye roll. Then she turns her attention back to the paper and completes the Hangman.

WHAT IS YOUR NUMBER

She flicks the pen out of her hand and shoves the book back over to my side of the table, so I pick up the pen and write.

I just want your number so we can text. We can talk like that, can't we?

She ignores me, picking up the novel and opening it to start pretending to read.

I sigh. She's not going to make this easy for me, but I'm not a fucking quitter, and it's best she learns that now.

Come on Deranged Porter, I know you wanna. Maybe we can talk about how you came apart on my hand yesterday?

Her cheeks pinken as her eyes fall over my words and she bites her lower lip. She stares at the paper for a minute, and I wait patiently to see if she'll communicate with me.

When she moves to pick up the pen, my heart about leaps from my chest and I watch as she responds to me.

Maybe we can talk about how you came in your jocks?

My eyes widen as I read over her words, and a laugh escapes before I can stop it, gaining the attention of Miss Dice.

"This book isn't a comedy, Mr Crowley."

I suck in my lips, looking up to the front of the room to where Miss Dice is frowning at me, and I give her a nod.

"Yes. Sorry." I mutter, not even bothering to give her an explanation as I turn my eyes back to the page where Dee had just called me out on the mess I made in my jocks yesterday. I hadn't been sure if she noticed me jerk while I was pressed against her, but she must have.

After a minute of pretending to do my work, I risk a glance at Miss Dice and find her attention now with a student at the front of the classroom, so I take the opportunity to continue my conversation with Dee.

Reaching out between us, I snag hold of the side of her seat and slowly drag it closer to me. A move which wins me a frown from Dee. She doesn't push me away and move her seat back, though, so I lean in and revel in her fresh fruity scent as I whisper in her ear.

"Tell me to stop, and I will."

She stiffens at my words. But fuck, I think she may have leaned in a little closer. I can't be sure. It could be my mind playing tricks on me, but I tell myself she did lean closer, and I slip my arm over the back of her chair.

To anyone in class, it would just look like a casual move for me to stretch out, but Dee knows the truth. I can tell by the way she jerks a little when I rub my thumb over her shirt, near her shoulder. A few strokes later and she relaxes again, letting me touch her in this innocent way.

My dick is instantly hard. It has a fucking mind of its own ever since Dee caught my attention. I should be happy about that since I was worried it was going to have a limp life, but with Dee giving me the cold shoulder most of the time, my dick may end up leading a very fucking stiff life with little satisfaction.

Since Dee is letting me touch her in the most subtle of ways, I keep quiet for most of the class, doodling cartoons in my workbook which occasionally induces a small smirk or eye roll from Dee.

When the bell goes, I quickly pack up my things and stay at Dee's side as we walk out of the class to our lockers. The need to touch her is almost overwhelming. I know trying will push her buttons, and since I'm all about pushing her buttons, I reach between us and link my fingers with hers.

She flinches, stopping abruptly and ripping her hand from my clasp as she glares at me. If looks could kill, then I'd be fucking dead right now. Since looks can't kill, and I'm still very much alive, more alive than I've felt in a long time, I lean over her small height so she has to strain her neck to look at me.

"Tell me to stop, Dee."

I move to grab her hand again as people rush by us, eager to get to their lockers, but Dee does more ninja moves on me, and the next thing I know, my world is the wrong way up as I flip and land on my arse.

Laughter booms in the passage, other students stopping to take out their phones and snap a picture of me, which I'm sure will be on social media in a matter of seconds.

Fucking Dee!

My eyes dart through the crowd, but she is nowhere in sight, so I drag my sorry arse up off the floor, not really feeling all that sorry. By the time I reach my locker, Dee is gone from hers, so I turn my focus to finding her once my books are away.

She isn't in the courtyard with the rest of the crew, so I check the library, since I know that was a place Lexi used to hide out to get away from everyone, but Dee isn't there either.

I walk all the way up to the back of the school, behind the gymnasium, but I only find Tillie and Dale smoking a joint.

"You look like you've lost something?" Tillie giggles at me as I approach.

She's one of Rhys' friends, and someone I've gotten to

know a little. We nearly hooked up once towards the end of last year, but she saw right through my bullshit and called me out on my obsession with Lexi. Tillie's pixie style isn't my type, and I couldn't lie to her about that. We had a good chat that night, and she told me straight out that Lexi and Ayden will most likely grow old together, so I needed to find a way past my unrequited love for her.

Tillie is honest and a good person.

"Ah… yeah." I run my hand through my blonde hair, hoping not to sound too obsessed when I speak. "Have you seen Dee?"

Tillie's brows shoot up and she glances at Dale before returning her eyes back to me.

"Yeah, actually. I noticed her walking across the oval to the tree line up the back. Either she's hiding out up there, or she's jumped over the fence and ditched."

I nod. Both are possibilities. "Ok. Thanks."

"You're welcome." She grins as I pass by, knowing the quickest way to where Dee went is around the other side of the gymnasium.

The scent of MJ wafts over me as I pass, and I have to fight the urge to turn around and join Tillie and Dale to smoke the joint in my pocket. I don't know why I've been bringing it to school with me. I've never smoked MJ at school, but for some reason, knowing it's there just in case I need it, seems to make me feel better.

When I round the corner of the gymnasium, which is overgrown with bushes, yet has a trail through it made by students trying to hide out, I look down the tree line to see a couple of different groups of people seeking the cool shade from the hot summer sun. That's when my eyes land on a pair of black Converse shoes peeking out from behind a tree not far from where I am.

Bingo!

As I approach, I notice Dee is definitely alone as she relaxes back against the tree, the tinny sound of music floating up from the earbuds in her ears.

Because she clearly can't hear me, I'm able to sneak up behind her without giving myself away, and I lean down slowly before quickly gripping one of her EarPods and tugging it free.

I was hoping she would scream from fright, or gasp and curse, but even though I scare her, she still remains silent as she darts her head around to shoot me a glare.

"You looking for this?" I tease, waving the EarPod in front of her face.

Dee leaps up from the barky ground and lunges for her EarPod, but since I'm practically a giant compared to her short height, I'm able to hold it out of her reach.

Her dark eyes turn to angry pools as she glares at me again, and I just fucking know she's about to hand me my arse yet again.

"Please don't hurt me. I'm only trying to have fun with you."

Dee stills, her arm still outreached before she drops it to her side and her shoulders slump.

Oh! So she has a heart? Noted.

She shakes her head at herself and slides back down the trunk of the tree to the cool ground, so I sit my arse down too. Right in front of her.

I chew the inside of my mouth as I pretend not to see yet another glare shot my way, and slip her EarPod in my ear so I can hear what she's listening to.

"Harry Styles, hey?"

She doesn't respond.

"He's ok I guess." I shrug, and still she doesn't respond.

"Can I put a song on?"

When Dee does nothing but continues to glare at me, I

slowly reach for her phone, which is sitting on the ground just to the side of her. She doesn't stop me, which surprises me, so I pick it up and hold the screen in front of her face for it to unlock.

She refused to give me her phone number when I asked so nicely for it in our Hangman game in English, so now I have to be sneaky.

"Take your earbud out for a minute so I can make sure I find the right song." I flash a stupid smile at her. "It's a surprise."

She rolls her eyes at me, but does as I ask, and while she thinks I'm busy searching for a song, I open her messages and send myself a text, before saving my number in her phone, and then deleting the message. Then I open Spotify and pick a song before nodding at her.

"You can put it back in now."

She narrows her eyes at me, but does as I ask, and I hit play.

"Do you know this song?"

Blackbear's 'Hot Girl Bummer' plays through the mini speakers in our ears, and again she rolls her eyes, but she listens.

I'm not sure what the eye roll was for. Maybe she thinks it's a typical song for me to like. Or maybe she was telling me that, of course, she knows the song.

I don't fucking know, so I sit and watch her face as she drags her eyes away from my gaze and relaxes back against the tree.

I guess I should be happy that she's comfortable around me. At least she seems to be with how relaxed she looks.

I'm anything but relaxed, her mere presence turning me into a fucking ball of energy I don't know what to do with. My thoughts fall to the joint in my pocket. That would calm me the fuck down. I wonder if Dee likes to smoke weed.

When the song is about halfway through, I can't help myself, and I turn the volume down before I ease the joint from my pocket and rest it in my palm, holding it between us.

"You wanna smoke this with me?"

She frowns.

"We can go behind the gymnasium. That's where your foster sister and her friends go to get stoned."

Her dark eyes lift from the joint in my hand, so I lean forward to take her hand, but she snatches it to her chest, refusing me.

"Right, so that would be a no for coming with me to smoke the joint, then?"

When Dee lifts a single brow, I instantly understand her expression. She's probably saying, *'you think'* or *'duh'*.

"You don't like to smoke weed?" I hold the joint between two fingers dangling it in front of her face, and her lip curls in a silent snarl before her hand snatches out, lightning fast, taking hold of the joint before ripping it in half and tossing it into the bushes behind her.

What the actual fuck!

"Did you really just destroy my Mary J?" I growl, letting her see and hear how fucking pissed off I am. I might have needed that.

Dee's face falls neutral, like she doesn't fucking care, and I grit my teeth trying to figure out what to do.

I could make it really fucking obvious that destroying my joint is not fucking cool. Or, I could be thankful she hasn't gouged my eyes out yet. And let's be honest. I get the feeling she probably knows how to do that.

I decide to go with thankful.

"It's pretty hot today. Why don't you take your long sleeve top off?"

No answer.

"Do you have another top under it?"

Still no answer.

"I can take it off for you."

No answer, again.

"Do you have the black bra on again today?"

Her cheeks turn red.

Finally, a reaction.

"Did you like it when I touched between your legs?"

No answer, but she shifts a little.

"Did you like it when I took your nipple in my mouth?"

Her chest rises and falls as her breathing deepens.

"Did you like it when I kissed you?"

Dee stands up quickly, but I grab her hand and tug her down onto my lap before she can escape. I wrap my arms around her small frame, holding her to my chest as I press my lips against her ear.

"Tell me to stop without assaulting me."

She could ignore my request and get out of my arms easily enough, so when she doesn't, I let myself think it's because she likes being there. Sure, people can see if they're looking this way, but I don't care, and I hope she doesn't either.

Dee shifts, and I loosen my hold before she grabs her phone from the ground to do something on it. The music cuts off, and I assume that's what she's doing with her phone, but then she holds the screen up, showing the open notes app, and the word I don't want to see.

'STOP!'

DEE

Why won't Jared Crowley leave me alone? I know I've made things worse by interacting with him, something I never do, so why the hell is Jared different? He's persistent. I'll give him that. But it's not like people haven't made it their mission to try to get me to talk before. In fact, it's one of the things that gains people's attention. They somehow think they can fix me or change me. They somehow think they are different from all the others that tried before them.

So why the hell is Jared different? I've never caved the way I do with him, and it's freaking me out. He's consuming too many of my thoughts when I should be focused on my end game.

Since it's so hot outside today, we do PE in the gymnasium. It's hot in there too, but without the harsh sun burning our skin, and with the industrial fans circulating air, it really is the better option.

"At least pull your sleeves up, Deranged." Jared teases as he eyes my long sleeves again as I pass by him to stand with the other group. "Just looking at you is making me hot. Although, maybe that has nothing to do with your clothing."

I chew the inside of my cheek, willing myself not to react to his blatant flirting. If that's what you can even call it.

Today we are playing soccer, and this time I'm on the opposing team. I have to work hard to hide the smirk that wants to burst free, my competitive nature rearing its head. If Jared comes near me, I'm going to hand him his arse.

Mrs Bailey rattles off the rules, which no one pays attention to, and we move into our positions to start playing.

Allison is on Jared's team, and I see her talking to him while they both look at me. Are they going to team up to piss me off? The thought shouldn't annoy me, yet it does, so I drag my gaze away from them and focus on Lexi, who is on my team.

We start to play, and it's only a minute before the ball goes through the other side's goal, their cheers echoing off the walls. Jared's smile is wide, and it's the first time I've seen him look so happy, as he chest bumps one of Rhys' boyfriends.

Our goalie is some guy called Marshall. He looks around at our teammates and I raise my arms up as high as my five one will let me, waving them around.

"Oh my God. That's just embarrassing, Dee. You can't even call for your team to pass you the ball."

Fucking Allison's retched voice instantly fills me with anger, but I try to ignore it as Marshall passes the ball to someone else, and the ball starts to travel towards my goal.

"You should just sit this game out, Dee. You're a liability to your team if you can't talk," Allison giggles. "Is it because you are dumb, too? Are you a bit simple?"

I know she is saying those things to get a reaction from me, and fuck, I've heard it all before, but the way she was talking with Jared before the game started has me losing my control. Did he tell her to say these things to me?

Allison is behind me, so when I stop jogging and spin on her, she nearly runs into me. She backs up as I stalk her, her dark eyes going wide, and her naturally tanned skin paling. I get in her face, rising up on my toes to get a better angle, and she balks.

When her mouth opens to call out to the teacher, she steps back, but I step with her to her side, and slam my shoulder into hers so hard that she falls to her arse in pain.

A screech falls from her lips, but by the time the teacher notices, I've moved well past her.

"Mrs Bailey. Dee hurt me." Allison dobs on me, but I pretend like I have no idea what she is talking about.

Mrs Bailey rushes up to help Allison off the floor and then glares at me. "Did you do this, Dee?"

I don't answer, of course.

"She can't have Mrs B. Dee was right by my side." Lexi covers for me, stepping closer.

"Yeah, Dee was just here the whole time." Shaun, one of Rhys' boyfriends, agrees. "I saw Allison trip over her own feet."

Some of the others in the class laugh, and Allison's face turns bright red.

"I did not! That deaf, dumb, mute girl pushed me!"

Mrs Bailey's brows shoot up, and she rounds on Allison. "Allison May! You did not just say those words!"

"W-what?" Allison stutters, her eyes going wide as Mrs Bailey puffs her chest out. I should probably feel bad for Allison, but she dug her own grave.

"Get your things and go to the principal's office. I will be there to see you after the lesson ends."

Ok. So, Mrs Bailey doesn't mess around. Noted.

Allison stomps her foot like a four-year-old before

storming off, her dark brown curls bobbing with each angry step.

Shaun chuckles next to me. "Good take down, by the way." He beams, his Spanish features turning playful.

"It's always so satisfying to see someone put people like Allison back in their place." Lexi smiles, giving my shoulder a playful nudge before she runs off.

Shit. Did I just make friends? That wasn't meant to happen. People usually see my violent side as part of my crazy and steer clear.

As I try to figure out what in the world just happened, the game resumes, and the ball finds me more often now. I revel in running faster than most, my small frame helping me to duck and weave easier. Jared decides to stick to my side, and I don't hold back, giving him an elbow here and there when the opportunity presents. I have no idea if Jared told Allison to say those things to me. I don't know why he would. He doesn't seem like a cold-hearted arsehole, but then again, he has arsehole in him, and I really know nothing about him. So, I guess he could have totally orchestrated it.

"I'm not gonna lie. Watching you take Allison down again was fucking hot."

I ignore Jared's words as he chuckles even though they send a thrill through me, and I race for the ball coming towards us. When it hits my foot, I move quickly to dodge an intercept, but I run into someone, hitting them hard before I start to fall.

Arms wrap around me before I hit the floor, and a body takes the brunt of the impact. Jared's spicy scent engulfs me, and as I push myself off the person under me, who just happens to be Jared, I see his concerned face looking over me as if checking for injuries.

I glare at him, and he frowns, clearly confused by me, which is fine. Even *I'm* confused by *me*.

I don't know what the hell I'm doing.

"On the bench please, Miss Porter," Mrs Bailey calls, and I swing around to her with a glare. "Don't look at me like that. It's a blood rule. You're bleeding through your shirt. I think you've grazed your elbow."

I turn my elbow up, and sure enough, blood is seeping through the sleeve covering my left elbow.

Damn it. I like this shirt.

I reluctantly run off and flop down on the bench, debating if I should just go get changed back into my jeans now.

"Let me take a look." Jared's voice floats to me as I feel a hand take mine.

Frowning, I glance up to see his eyes focused on his task, pulling my sleeve up. He's so close right now, his blue eyes bright, darting up to mine briefly as the gentle feel of his touch relaxes me.

That is until I feel him turn my arm over as he drags his gaze down to the scarred underside.

I rip my arm from his grip, but it's too late. He's seen.

I didn't even think about it yesterday out by the lake, so caught up in the sensations he was inflicting on me, but now I feel like the only reason he is over here helping with my elbow scrape, is to check out my arms.

"Dee." His words are a low caress that hold sympathy I don't need.

I stand up, lifting my lip in a silent snarl.

I know what he thinks he saw. And hell, I almost wish it's what he thinks, but it's not, and nothing will ever erase *that* particular day from my memory.

Before he can say or do anything else, I storm off to the bathroom to get changed, before leaving class early and catching a town bus home.

There are no dance classes on Fridays or on weekends, at

least not for my age, so when I go back to my foster home, I feel like a caged animal. Emotions I usually manage to keep hidden are right at the surface and I'm struggling to keep them contained.

Why has moving to Fox Pines already paid such a toll on me? I guess it could be because I've been planning this for years, and now that it's here within arm's reach, I'm just so desperate for it to end.

And I do want it to end. The things I've had to do to survive, to get the money to be able to look after myself as soon as I turn eighteen, are extreme. I'll admit that some of my jobs have been well worth it, knowing the heinous things that my marks did before I took their lives from them. And yes, I often get a rush from killing, something which scares me as much as I enjoy it, but yesterday, out by the lake, I got the same rush when I was in that barbeque shelter with Jared.

Wait. No. It wasn't the same.

It was more.

So much more.

Sure, I feel powerful when I'm slicing Thana across someone's throat, or driving her deep into their heart, but never have I felt as alive as I did yesterday when Jared was chasing me. When he leaped on me from out of nowhere. When he pressed his strong body against mine.

I felt trapped between the press of his body and the wall of the shelter, yet I didn't feel scared, and I didn't want to escape.

I wanted to feel.

That's new for me. I've spent so much time and energy avoiding people that I hardly remember what it's like to be touched. Not just intimately. But at all.

I need to get my head back in the game, so I slide the

drawer in my desk out and reach down to the cavity below to pull out the files I have stashed there.

I advised my clients that I was going on vacation until the end of March. That would give me enough time to get what I came to Fox Pines for, get away, and make all traces of myself disappear.

I know I've been doing important work, but it comes at a cost, and now it's time for me to steer my path in a different direction.

Even though I'm not offering my services at the moment, I still have work that has to be done, so I spend hours in my bedroom, my head buried in my laptop, only stopping for dinner with the Rogan family, and a quick toilet break. It's about 10pm when I finish gathering all the information I need and set it aside to wait until the household falls asleep.

My phone vibrates on the bed next to me, and I frown, knowing I shouldn't be getting any calls or messages from my clients, so my brows shoot up as I see who the message is from.

The guy that made you cum

What the fuck!

Confusion swarms me as I try to figure out what the hell is going on, and then my mind flashes to lunchtime today when Jared took my phone to play a song.

The fucker must have put his number in my phone… and what? Memorised my number?

No. That doesn't seem right. More like he sent himself a message from my phone to get my number. Sneaky fuck!

I open the message and see that it's the only one, so he must have deleted the message he sent from my phone.

The guy that made you cum

Hi!

The guy that made you cum
Did I make you smile?

The guy that made you cum
I did. Didn't I?

The guy that made you cum
I can see the dots, Dee. I know you're reading this.

Shit. I forgot about the dots!

The guy that made you cum
Say something. I know you want to.

The guy that made you cum
Come on. You don't even have to open your mouth. Just text me back.

The guy that made you cum
Ok, fine. I'll make you a deal.
You have a message conversation with me for like, 10 minutes, and I'll rub your pussy again until you come.

Oh my God! He did not just say that!
And why does that make me feel all funny down there? Like I need him to do exactly what he said and rub me until I come. Again.

The guy that made you cum
You're thinking about it, aren't you?

The guy that made you cum

Oh man, are you touching yourself?
Fuuuck, what I'd do to see that!

I'm not touching myself, but hell, it's getting really hard not to. This guy is a wizard or something. He knows just how to ignite my blood.

The guy that made you cum
Oh, come on! I know you secretly want to talk to me.
Just let down that iron wall and let me in.
I'm not that bad, am I?

Shit. I want to let him in, but that's the reason I don't. It's not right to feel like this. If I'm not careful, Jared Crowley will destroy me and what I came here for.

The guy that made you cum
You know your silent treatment is doing a number on my ego.
Give me something, please.
How about an emoji?
Can you give me an emoji?

Dee Porter
*** Middle finger emoji***

The guy that made you cum
Yes!
Thank you.

I should tell him it's not a compliment, but then I'd be giving him what he wants. For me to interact even more.

The guy that made you cum
How about a picture?

Pleeeeeaaaassseee!

I consider that for a moment, and then grin as an idea comes to mind.

I open his contact and edit the name before taking a screenshot and sending it to him to show his new name in my phone.

Dee Porter
***IMAGE – The guy that can't take a hint*

The guy that can't take a hint
Ouch. You're brutal!

Dee Porter
FYI, you need a lesson in spelling.
You had your number saved as: The guy that made you cum.
But the word cum should have been spelt, come, because YOU are the guy that gave ME an orgasm.
Now, had you been the guy that made me squirt, or in fact the guy I made spill his seed in his pants, then the correct spelling is cum.

The guy that can't take a hint
Fuck, you really are brutal!

I don't respond, because really, I shouldn't have responded in the first place.

The guy that can't take a hint
You sure do know a lot about come and cum.
It makes me wonder what else you know a lot about.

I could be honest and tell him, not a whole lot, but that's just more information about me he doesn't need.

Frustrated, I shove the phone under my pillow, trying to ignore its existence as my mind fills with everything Jared Crowley. I shouldn't be letting myself think of him. I shouldn't be remembering the way it felt to be caged in by him out at the lake yesterday. I shouldn't be wishing he was here with me right now, in this bed, pressing his soft warm lips to mine, and kissing me thoroughly. And I really shouldn't be letting my hand wander over the swell of my breast as I close my eyes and imagine his lips closing over my nipple.

Heat washes over me as I give in to the feelings I've been trying to hide. I rub my thighs together, causing some friction, and my other hand travels down to rub gently over the fabric of my panties. It felt so good when he did this to me. When his large hand cupped my jean clad pussy and rubbed.

Never have I had an urge to want something inside me so much. I was hungry for him. It felt like I was starved for his touch, just like right now, as I focus on rubbing circles over my clit. If he were here right now, would I let him go underneath my clothing this time to touch my bare flesh? Would I let him slip his fingers through my folds, just the way I'm doing now?

My back arches off the bed as I hold my moan in, not wanting to be heard by anyone. I press the tip of my finger to my entrance and spread my legs wider, my mind picturing the heated and lust filled gaze of Jared as he rubbed with fast friction out by the lake. Then I slowly sink a finger inside.

I've done this a number of times before, easily finding that magic spot as my thumb works over my clit, but never have I had such erotic images in my head of the blonde-haired blue-eyed guy that has, for some reason, set his sights on me.

As my rhythm picks up, I grind my clit against my hand

as my finger presses into the wet, warm flesh inside me. Out of nowhere, my climax hits, instantly clamping around my finger as I convulse as quietly as I can in my bed.

When I drift down from the high I took myself to, my eyes flutter open to my empty bedroom, reminding me that I'm alone, and that's the best way for me to be.

Since I'm weak and my control over Jared is lacking and extremely out of character for me, I reach under my pillow and pull out my phone, going into his contact, and I block him.

Conjuring up thoughts of me and Jared together will do nothing but hurt in the long run, so the easiest way for me to shield myself is to show him he is wasting his time with me.

JARED

My car smells like Dee. I'm not sure why. I thought her lingering scent had disappeared yesterday morning when I got in my car, which was left from driving her out to the lake. I remember feeling fucking devastated that I couldn't smell her in here again. So why the hell can I smell her now?

It's almost as if she had been in my car just now. Or sometime in the last few hours. Which doesn't make sense. She was in my car on Thursday, not yesterday or today.

Maybe I'm addicted as well as obsessed.

I try to shake all thoughts of Dee Porter from my brain as I spend my Saturday delivering pizzas for Uncle Sam's Pizza Palace. The only problem is everything reminds me of her. When Blackbear comes on my radio, I think of Dee, and the brief moment of her attention she gave me under the tree at school yesterday. When I drive into the houso area near the High School, I think about how she so badly wanted to go there to see someone, and how she wants to be a student there instead of FP Catholic. When I drive through her neighbourhood to make a delivery, I make a detour to drive past her house, hoping to catch a glimpse of her.

It's safe to say my obsession with Dee Porter is getting out of control. Much like the way I was with Lexi. Maybe I'm one of those people who are more likely to get addictions. Do I have an obsessive personality?

Shit. If I keep smoking weed, am I going to become a stoner?

The thought makes me think of the FP High party on Berry Road tonight.

I've already reached out to Trav to get some more weed off him. I've been thinking about trying something stronger tonight. Something that will make me forget how easily I let some particular girls get under my skin, but what if I'm one of those people with addiction tendencies? As much as I need a night full of feeling good and no obligations, I'm not sure it's worth the risk.

FP High parties can be fun without the addition of substances. The attendees are all pretty fucking crazy as it is. It's always a good laugh, and the night tends to end in fights and a police invasion. The girls at these parties aren't as clingy as the ones that go to the FP Catholic parties. Hell, I could probably hook up with five different chicks at tonight's party, and they wouldn't get possessive or jealous. They would probably high five each other.

My gut drops just at the thought of that.

Fucking hell. Why can't I be that guy? Why can't I have meaningless hook-ups and just move the fuck on?

Because you have a heart, douchebag!

By the time night falls, I'm in a shitty mood.

Marcus and Simon have been trying to get me to go out to Bossi's for the night and get pissed with them. The problem with that is, Bossi lives out of town, so once I have a drink, I won't be able to drive home, and I'll be stuck there with them. Which brings me to the second problem.

Rhys George.

She is going to be there, so as if they aren't all going to end up in a fucking orgy before midnight even strikes.

Fuck that.

I give my mum an hour of my time and have dinner with her and my dad before the bottle of wine she keeps at her side most nights turns her eyes glassy and she doesn't notice when I slip out the door.

I walk across town, drinking a can of beer as I walk to get my night started. All alone, like a fucking loser. I have a cola stubbie holder over the can to disguise it, so any passing cops don't pull over and bust me for drinking in a public place. That would just top my week off.

By the time I hit Berry Road, the entire street is alive with music, cars, and a shitload of underage drinkers.

It has no appeal to me. Maybe I should man the fuck up now that I'm eighteen and go to a bar. Maybe an older woman is what I need.

I shake my head at myself, knowing damn well I won't go to a bar. Hell, even coming to this party is making my skin crawl, because no matter how much I've tried lately, no girl has appealed to me, or my dick, until just this week.

If I'm being honest with myself, there's only one place I want to be, and that's spending time with a girl that has no interest in me.

When I drag my sorry arse up to the house that is throwing the party, I enter through the front door, which is practically hanging off its hinges. The blasting music is almost too much, causing those trying to chat, to have to yell. I feel eyes on me instantly, and as I rake my gaze over the mass of bodies already dancing in the front living room, I notice the lust drunk gazes of girls trying to get my attention. One chick even palms her tits as I walk by.

No thanks.

I head straight for the kitchen, knowing that's where Trav will most likely be. He's just started dealing some new stuff. Pills. He was telling me the other day that now that he's nearly seventeen, and with one of his older foster brothers in prison, his foster parents—who are also his fucking dealers—have started to give him more responsibility.

I felt fucking bad for him when he said it, but he doesn't seem concerned. If anything, he's happier. It's all pretty screwed up. A sixteen-year-old selling drugs for his parents.

What the fuck is the world coming to?

"Hey man." I shoot Trav a smile as I approach the kitchen bench just as he hands a lolly bag to someone. One day an actual child is going to pick up one of his lolly bags, and when they get to the pill, they won't know the difference between the pill and a lolly.

"Here he is. The guy all the chicks are drooling over."

I chuckle. "Not all of them."

Travis grins. "So, the devil girl still has you caught in her spell?"

Sighing, I nod before downing the rest of my beer.

"You want some candy, Crowley?" I frown at the bag Trav holds up, considering if I actually want to go there and pop a fucking pill. "Or I got some good Mary if you wanna come for a walk?"

"Yeah." I nod. "I think Mary is all I should have tonight."

"Hey Travis." A raspy voice interrupts us, coming from the back fly screen door before it swings open, and a ratty-looking dude with stringy dark hair and a missing front tooth appears.

"Oh. Hey Pike. How are ya, man?" Travis asks, slipping the lolly bags that are on the bench back into his backpack.

"Ah, yeah. I'm ok. I need some gear, though." Pike fidgets in the doorway, his eyes darting around with paranoia.

"Shit man. I don't carry *that* stuff. You need to see my older brother for that." Travis frowns and the ratty guy starts to get agitated.

"Nah man. Don't fucking lie to me. I know you got some."

"Hey." I snap, gaining Pike's attention. "He's not lying. This is a fucking teen party, man. That shit isn't dealt here."

"Nah. Nah. Don't fucking lie to me, man." Pike steps forward like he's going to lunge but pulls back before doing it again. He's skittish as fuck.

"Just calm down, Pike. I'll see what I can do." Travis raises his hands in a calming gesture. "Let's go to yours, and I'll figure something out."

"Yep. Yep." Pike nods over and over as his hands start trembling.

Moving up to my side, Travis speaks quietly. "I have to get him outta here. He lives next door. Must have come through the gate in the fence. I'll get him sorted and come back soon."

I glance over at the jittery fucker in the doorway and shake my head at Travis.

"Dude, you're not going alone. I'll come with you."

Travis shrugs. "Suit yourself, but you really need to admit that you have a thing for me." He bats his eyelashes at me, a look of innocence sweeping over his face. "My knight in shining armour."

"Fuck off, idiot." I chuckle and Trav grins before turning his attention back to Pike.

"Ok, Pike. My man, Crowley is coming with us. Lead the way."

Pike frowns, and I think he's going to have something to say about me coming too, but then he nods and turns back out the door, so I follow behind him with Trav on my heels.

The backyard is weirdly empty, with most people inside

the house or out the front, so there are no eyes watching us. It's most likely why this Pike fucker came this way.

Fucking drug bag.

I follow him through a rickety gate in the fence and across an un-mowed yard where he leads us into an old shed. It's large enough to hold two cars, but instead, it's filled with junk. Like hoarded junk that's useless to anyone.

Closing the door behind us, Travis weaves through the piles of mess to approach Pike, who looks even more jittery than before.

"You got my gear?" Pike asks and I frown.

Hadn't we already established that Travis doesn't deal Heroin?

"Like I said before. My brother is the one that deals the gear. I can call him now and get him to drop some off." Travis takes his phone out, but before he can do anything else, Pike leaps forward and hits the phone out of Trav's hand.

"What the fuck?" I hiss and Pike starts jumping around before turning to the workbench behind him.

I eye Trav, who just shakes his head at me, silently telling me something, but I don't fucking know what.

"Look, Pike. If you want some smack, I gotta call Adam. I don't carry that stuff." Travis tries to explain but Pike ignores him, leaping around from the workbench and lunging for Trav with a long screwdriver in his hand.

"No!" he yells, stumbling forward as Trav dodges him.

"What the fuck, Pike!" Trav hisses and Pike snarls.

"Your brother won't fucking deal to me anymore. He's a fucking lying cunt!"

"Whoa." Trav holds his hands out. "Dude, if Adam won't deal to you, then you obviously owe him money. If that's the case, then I can't help you either. Put the screwdriver down."

"No!" Pike screams, lunging for Travis again, this time running into him as the screwdriver swings wide.

I leap into action, trying to pull Pike off Travis, but this Pike guy, although scrawny as fuck, is fucking crazed. He's wild, his teeth snapping as he tries to bite Trav's face, while both Trav and I grip Pike's hand, which is wrapped around the screwdriver.

Suddenly, we are falling as a pile of junk gets knocked over and the three of us tumble hard to the floor.

I try to right myself, but still as my weight crushes Pike between me and Trav, Trav's eyes wide with panic as Pike stops moving.

"What's wrong?" I ask as I try to pull my hand free, but it's stuck in between Pike and Trav.

Travis' eyes grow even wider, and he starts to shake his head.

I roll off Pike then, contorting my arm so I can try to get it free. Gritting my teeth, I tug a couple of times before it comes free, only to see it covered in blood.

Fuck!

I leap up, my eyes wide this time as I look down over Pike's back, and Trav's face peering up at me.

"Whose blood is this?"

Trav shakes his head again, not talking, and I see a pool of blood oozing out onto the concrete floor.

Fuck. No. Shit.

This can't be happening.

I lean down and grip Pike's shoulders before rolling him off Travis.

Blood.

There is so much fucking blood.

It's all over both Pike and Travis. The only difference between the two is the screwdriver protruding from Pike's chest.

13

DEE

By the time I arrive at the Fox Pines High party, it's in full swing. The last thing I want to do is come to a stupid party, but since I'm getting high school blocked by my foster parents and Jared, this is the next best thing.

I dressed to blend in, wearing black pleather short-shorts that hug my curves, and a black cropped long sleeve mesh top with a black pleather bra underneath. Rhys lent me these clothes, even though she doesn't know she did. I'll have them washed and put back in her wardrobe before she even notices them missing.

I added a little makeup tonight. Not something I usually do, but since I want to blend in, I suffer through the task of applying some foundation, blush, eyeliner and mascara. The eye makeup makes my big eyes stand out even more. I kind of like the look, but it's not something I'll be getting used to any time soon, since I prefer my life makeup free.

I'm surprised to see the party has spilled out on the street. It's unruly and seems like the surrounding houses are joining in, age not mattering.

I'm here for one reason, so I scan the crowd as I approach

the front door, looking for the one person I came to this town for.

I can feel eyes on me as I walk in. No one knows me here, so my presence is most likely confusing them. That's a *them* problem, though.

My short stature makes it really hard to find anyone, even when I stand on my tiptoes. I'm nowhere near close to seeing over the top of the crowd, so it looks like I'm going in.

I suck in a deep breath, preparing myself to endure feeling like a packed sardine, and then I step into the thick crowd of dancing bodies. I've barely made it past three people before some bitch spills her beer down my left arm.

"Oh my God. Sorry!" Her whiny voice doesn't sound sorry at all as I glare up at her, and the bitch just giggles.

Fucking hell. Where's Thana when you need her?

Gritting my teeth, I push further into the thick of the crowd, my eyes darting to each face I pass, looking for familiar eyes.

"Dee?"

My name being called has me turning back and my eyes land on the girl from my new dance class that tried to talk to me on Thursday.

"Hi Dee! It is you." She bounds up to me, smiling widely with a guy practically attached to her hip. "It's so good to see you. I saw your boyfriend before and wondered if you might be here." My brows shoot up and she grins. "Caleb is glad to have him to talk to during our classes."

The guy next to her nods. "Yeah. Jared is cool. You two make a really cute couple. Don't they, Ruby?"

Again, I frown as the girl, who must be Ruby, grins wide and nods.

"Oh, are you looking for him?" When I don't say anything, she continues. "I saw him a while ago in the kitchen. He was talking to that guy that," Ruby leans in closer, "supplies the candy."

Bingo!

I nod, offering them a smile as they continue to smile back, and I spin on my heel, not wanting to waste any more time. The fact that Jared is here is a problem, so I'll have to sneak around without him spotting me.

After I free myself from the idiots jumping around more than dancing, I stumble to the entry to the kitchen, being careful in case Jared is still there.

Damn it. It's empty.

"You waiting for the tuck shop, too?" A guy's voice draws my attention as a tall, dark-haired guy steps up to my side, peering in the kitchen. His use of tuck shop is code for the candy seller, so I nod, and the guy gestures his head to the back door. "He went out that way. Tell him to hurry up and come see Nathan in the front bedroom. Me and my girl want some E."

I nod, as if I'm gonna do what he asks, and he smiles and turns his back on me before disappearing into the crowd.

Eager to get the hell out of here, I rush to the door and step back out into the cooler night air. I'm drenched in sweat, and it has nothing to do with the temperature in the house, and everything to do with the anticipation of coming face to face with the reason why I'm here.

I glance around the backyard, quickly finding it empty, but my feet move to the opening in the fence. I peer into the neighbouring backyard on high alert for threats like dogs or drunken dickheads. I don't see anything, but noise coming from the shed has me moving forward again, taking big steps through the over-grown grass.

As I reach the door, I hesitate to listen, but when I hear a familiar voice say 'It's not my blood' and register the panic in their tone, I pull the door open and step inside with eyes wide.

What the fuck?

"Dee?"

"Ell?"

The words are said at the same time, and I come face to face with two familiar faces.

"What?" They both say in unison, turning their eyes from me to each other.

"You know, Dee?" Jared asks, and the boy that looks so much more man than the last time I saw him frowns.

"You mean Ell?" Travis snaps, his furious eyes darting to me before turning back to Jared. "Ell is my sister."

"What?" Jared's brows shoot up, but I can't focus on meaningless things like expressions right now, not when my baby brother is covered in blood.

I step forward, panicked, and I start signing. *"Whose blood is that?"*

Travis frowns. "You have to be fucking kidding me. You're still doing this bullshit, not speaking thing?" He grits his teeth, hissing at me. "You know, when I said I never wanted to hear your voice again, what I really meant was I never wanted to see you again."

"Hey man. Calm the fuck down." Jared snaps at Travis as I fight back the heat that pricks the back of my eyes.

"You stay the fuck outta this." Travis turns and hisses in Jared's face this time, and while he's distracted, I dash forward and lift his shirt, trying to see where the bleeding is coming from.

"Hey!" Travis snaps, slapping my hand away. "Don't fucking touch me."

I roll my eyes and point to his chest, where the dark crimson is soaked through his clothes.

"It's not his blood." Jared answers for my brother, and I

frown, turning my eyes to him in confusion. That's when I notice blood coating Jared's hand as he gestures his thumb over his shoulder.

My brows dart up as realisation hits, and I push through the two of them to find a man lying lifeless amongst a pile of junk.

In the snap of a second, I go from being Dee to being someone else, my eyes darting over the scene to take everything in.

There's been a struggle involving three people. One looks like he might be dead, killed by the tool protruding from his chest, and the other two seem unharmed, but covered in the victim's DNA.

The surrounding scene is chaos. Mess absolutely everywhere, making this a really fucking hard place to wipe clean and remove any traces of evidence.

Shit!

Noticing a box of rubber gloves on the end of the workbench, I carefully manoeuvre around the body and ease two out of the box, taking care not to touch anything.

"What are you doing here, Dee?" Jared asks as Travis huffs.

"Does it matter why she's here? She's about to leave. Isn't that right, sister?"

Ignoring the guys, I slip the gloves on before leaning down and trying to find a pulse on the lifeless body, but after a few tries, I confirm he is dead.

I pull my phone from my pocket and open my notes app and text what I need to ask.

'What happened?'

Holding my phone out in front of me, both guys lean forward to read the screen, but Travis rolls his eyes, turning his back to me.

"I'm not fucking talking to you."

Jared frowns again, looking between me and my brother, before sighing.

"Drug deal gone wrong. This Pike fucker came at Trav with the screwdriver, and we struggled before we fell... and well... you can see the result of that." Jared's frown deepens as he takes a step closer, his eyes looking down at the corpse on the ground. "He's alive, right? We should call an ambulance."

"We can't call an ambulance." Travis swings around to glare at Jared. "I'm on a bond. Once they know I was involved, they will throw me in the slammer. And that's assuming Pike is still fucking alive."

I text another message and hold it up.

'He's dead.'

"He's... dead?" Jared's brows shoot high on his forehead, his face paling as he takes a step back. When he goes to grip a stool that's behind him, I leap forward and grab his arm to stop him while shaking my head.

"What?" he asks.

I respond with text. *'Don't touch anything. You'll leave your fingerprints behind.'*

If I thought his face was pale before, then I was wrong. He's as white as a ghost now. "But... this was an accident. We didn't mean to..."

Travis chuckles dryly. "As if that fucking matters, man. One look at me and I'll be put on trial for murder, and you, well, if your olds have enough money for a good lawyer, then you might be lucky to get a reduced sentence."

'Travis is right.' I text and Jared reads it, looking like he's going to pass out.

"Why the fuck aren't you freaking out about this?" Jared's voice is high pitched as he visibly starts to spiral. "And why didn't you tell me Travis was your brother?"

"Oh, she's used to being around dead bodies. Isn't that

right, Ell?" Travis snarls before frowning and looking at Jared. "Wait. How do you know my sister?"

'None of that is important right now!' I text, holding my screen up for them to read, but once their eyes glance over it, they turn back to each other.

"You can't be serious." Travis hisses, stepping closer to Jared. "This is her, isn't it?" He points to me. "This is the devil?"

The devil?

Now my brows are shooting up, but I shake that shit away, because there's a dead body just by my feet, and his blood is smeared on the two guys standing before me.

I turn my back on them as they start bickering and try to focus on what has to be done now.

The body needs to disappear.

And the evidence needs to be destroyed.

Simple, right?

Ugh, not simple. Especially because I'll need to call in a fucking favour for the first time ever.

Shit. This isn't how it was meant to go.

I open the black app with the Angel logo and key in my pin. Instantly my screen goes black, locking my phone's regular motherboard, and connecting it with the darkboard to basically turn my phone into a separate device.

Scrolling through the contacts, I bring up the Angels' number and type out a coded message.

821198
My food was off.

Angels
I don't have you down for an order.

821198

This was a walk in.

Angels

Please confirm you didn't eat the food.

821198

No. I'm fine.
Two of my guests are a little upset.

Angels

We will send a customer care team to your location.
Please await further details.

I wish I was actually ordering food instead of a clean-up crew. I don't normally have to order a clean up like this. Normally they are already booked in and waiting because my jobs are typically planned. I also don't tend to have people with me when I go after my marks, so I needed to let the Angels know I'm not alone. This entire situation is messy as hell.

Part of me feels better knowing we will get the help needed to make this disappear, but the other part of me is reeling because there is a price for everything, and I know I'll have to pay steeply.

"What the fuck are you doing here, Ell?" Travis asks, gaining my attention again, and I roll my eyes.

Right now, I'm trying to save your arse.' I respond in text, and when I hold it up, he refuses to look at the screen for a moment.

Stubborn shithead.

His eyes squint as he reads it finally, and this time it's him who is rolling his eyes. "What exactly are you going to do, Ell? He's already dead, so your expertise isn't needed."

My face heats in anger at his words, which have nothing to do with how I make my money. He doesn't know that about me. He's referring to how we ended up separated and living the lives we have been in for the past seven years.

"How about you stop being an arsehole to your sister and help us figure out what to do?" Jared snaps at Travis, and once again, they start fucking bickering. Jesus, these two are exhausting.

My phone vibrates, and I check my new message.

Angels
Local and neighbouring teams are nearby.
ETA ten minutes.

821198
Thank you

Angels
Please ensure you schedule a face to face with me soon.
We pride ourselves on delivering the best service.

821198
Will do.

I know who runs the local team. I made sure to know that before I moved here. Griffin Marx watches over the Timber Valley region from his Redfield location, specialising in property development and adult entertainment, but also oversees the criminal underworld in this area. I've been working with him to help find the sick fuckers that were involved in the Vixen's Lodge Illicit Porn Syndicate, and he may have helped me get all the information I needed to get into the Burns Clinic in December to end the life of the man that took advantage of and raped my new foster sister.

I've been planning my entry into Rhys' family for over two years, so even though she doesn't know me, I know her more than she'd be happy about. I know her whole family more than they'd be happy about.

As for the Angels' mention of a neighbouring team also joining the local team, I am hoping like hell that it's not who I think it will be. Griffin's older cousin, Devon Marx, recently took ownership of the whole town of Woodall Ridge. None of the old residents live there anymore, and all the current ones are part of his crew, or people sent there by the head of the Marx family to be kept hidden and protected.

Fox Pines hasn't officially been introduced to the legendary Marx crew yet, but they have been slowly working their way into this community, and are about to take over in a way that will either see people flee this area or accept that they are all owned by the Marx Crew.

That's why I need to get Travis and get out of here soon, because once they take over, they won't sit back and let Travis' foster family continue to supply most of the illegal drugs to the area.

Nope. Once they take over, they will either own them or kill them, and I need to get my brother out before any of that happens.

14

JARED

What the fuck is going on? Am I dreaming? Did Trav and I really kill a guy? And is Dee really Trav's sister, who for some reason, he keeps calling, Ell? What about how Trav is treating her? He like, legit hates her for some reason, but she keeps ignoring that and is laser focused on the whole dead body situation. Which, by the fucking way, isn't freaking her out.

Why isn't she freaking out?

My heart is about to burst through my fucking ribcage as Dee approaches the shed door and opens it, nodding to two tall motherfuckers wearing suits that don't fucking blend in with this houso neighbourhood.

"Hu-." One of the guys stops talking quickly as Dee shakes her head vigorously at him, and he frowns before turning his gaze to me and Trav. When he turns back to her, she holds up her phone, and he reads something on her screen and then nods.

I've learnt a fucking lot tonight about this girl I have an obsession with, which includes that she knows sign language, which is only beneficial if someone else knows it too. And also, that she can communicate a hell of a lot if she has to.

"Ok, *Dee*. Good to see you again."

"Are you fucking serious, Ell?" Travis hisses, gaining everyone's attention. "The Marx Crew? Are you trying to get me killed?"

The two suits glare at Travis, before recognition lights their faces.

"You need to start talking, Dee," the first suit says, "Because it looks a helluva lot like you've just asked us to step over enemy lines."

Dee shakes her head, typing something out on her phone before holding it up for the men to read.

"This is bullshit!" Trav hisses. "Get the fuck out."

Dee swings her furious glare in her brother's direction, and I swear she's never looked scarier. Or sexier. Fuck, is she wearing makeup?

"Travis Watson is your brother? And you want us to let him live?" The second suit growls.

What the actual fuck does he mean by that?

"Hey! Fuck you, Marx!" Travis goes to lunge for the suits, but Dee steps in between them and does more of her ninja moves, sending her brother to the ground as he clutches his shoulder in pain.

Dee furiously types out something on her phone, before holding it up for Trav, and I lean to the side to read it as well.

'If you don't shut the fuck up, they will kill you! This is the only way I know to help you get out of the fucking shit you've gotten yourself, and your mate in. So, stay the fuck quiet and let me handle this!!!'

Man, I'd do just about anything to hear her voice spit those words.

And why the fuck am I thinking *that* instead of focusing on the dead guy?

Dee turns back to the guys, who are looking more amused than anything, and texts more words she's not willing to speak aloud.

"Wait, so let me get this straight." Suit number one crosses his arms over his chest. "Your brother is Travis Watson, the foster son of Douglas and Bianca Kerr, who have been dealing bad product in the area?"

"Hey! Our product isn't bad." Travis hisses, but no one pays him any attention.

"And you are in town to find him, but instead, come across him and his mate, who have just stabbed a known druggo and killed him. And now you want us to help you make it all just disappear?"

Dee types on her phone again before holding it up.

"Yes, technically you asked the Angels for help, and we are it, sunshine," suit number one says, looking almost amused.

"The Angels? What the fuck are you involved in, Ell?" Travis hisses, still on his arse, cradling his shoulder.

The second suit, who looks older than the first, starts chuckling. "So, your brother doesn't know what you do? How interesting."

Dee stamps her foot, and I notice her left hand balled into a tight fist at her side.

"Dev, you'd better be careful. She'll make you dead before you can even blink." The first suit chuckles, not taking his eyes off Dee.

What the fuck? Is he insinuating Dee would kill him?

Fuck my head hurts. This is too much. The need to flee is fucking prominent.

"Yeah. Yeah. I know all about this one, Griff." The second suit, Dev, chuckles.

"I hate to do this to you, Dee," Griff turns serious, dropping his hands to his sides, "because you know I like ya, kid. And I fucking respect the fuck out of you, but this is gonna cost a fucking lot."

Dee nods, like it's that easy before typing out another message and holding it up.

Dev chuckles. "Money ain't gonna cut it, sweetheart. The only way this works is in favours. We do this for you, and you work directly for us until the debt has been paid off."

Dee types and holds up her screen again.

"Why four weeks?" Griff asks with a frown and Dee types some more.

When she holds up her phone again, and they read it before their eyes dart to Travis.

"You think you can convince him to leave the area in less than four weeks?" Griff asks and Dee nods.

"And what if you can't? You know we will have no choice but to kill him and his family if they don't join us," Griff deadpans.

"Fuck you, cunt! My family will never join you!" Travis spits, somehow understanding what the fuck is going on.

I honestly have no fucking clue what I've got myself into here.

Shit! I just wanted to party a little, and instead I've aided in killing a guy and become entwined in some sort of underworld drama.

Dee spins to face her brother, falling to her knees before him as she types out a message. When she holds it up, I zero in on the words.

Please cooperate, Travis. It's not just you involved here. It's Jared, too. He's a good guy in the wrong place at the wrong time. If the cops nail you for this, they will nail Jared, too. Do you want that? Does he deserve that?'

"No, he doesn't. But how can you expect me to let these fuckers walk in and take over everything that my family has built? I can't do that, Ell. I *won't* do that."

"Let's make a deal." Dev grins, clearly finding Trav's situation funny. "Dee is the one that asked for help, so you can go back to your life knowing your sister is paying for your mistakes, but," Dev steps forward, lowering to his haunches so he's eye level with Travis. "If you haven't left town with your sister in four weeks, you won't make it to five. And just so you understand how fucking serious we are, and to make sure you keep your trap shut, your buddy here will go on our books, too."

I frown at his words, trying to figure out what he means as Dee's eyes go wide, and she leaps forward quickly, grabbing the big dude by his collar, causing him to fall back on his arse.

I take a step forward, ready to fight this fucker if he does anything to hurt Dee, but the other guy, Griff, laughs, holding his hands out.

"Let's all just calm down." He looks down at Dee. "Kid. Let him go. You know the way things work."

Dee shoves Dev back with force, causing him to laugh like a crazy fucker, and Dee taps out more words on her phone before showing Griff.

His dark eyes read over her words before he shakes his head. "Sorry, Dee. The friend works for us, too."

Again, she taps out more words before Griff answers.

"Fine, I get that he's not from our world, so I'll just make him an errand boy. But we own his arse for the next four weeks, and if brother dearest doesn't leave town, or fucking bow to us, then your friend won't make it to the end of March."

"Hold up a minute. I have no fucking idea what's happening here," I rasp, feeling my freak out right at the surface. "I'm getting one side of the conversation because Dee won't fucking speak. Tell me what's happening."

"Huh. I think I like this one." Dev chuckles as he drags himself up off the floor, dusting off his arse.

"Let me explain," Griff nods. "We will make this," he gestures to the lifeless Pike arsehole on the concrete floor, "disappear in exchange for payment in favours. Basically, it means that we own your arse, and Dee's as well, for the next four weeks, until she turns eighteen. In that time, when we call, you drop everything and do exactly what we ask of you. No fucking questions. If you don't, we can make your life really fucking difficult."

Dev nods. "Yeah, and not just for you. Your family, too. How close are you to your parents?"

Dee hisses. Like actually hisses, taking a step towards Dev.

"Anyway. I'm sure you get the picture." Dev chuckles, eyeing Dee like she's going to pounce at any moment.

"And at the end of the four weeks, if your buddy, Trav, hasn't left town and disappeared with his sister, he will have to make a choice of whether to stand down from his family business and help us in ours, or he dies. Your cooperation will determine if we let you live or die, too."

"What?" Did he really just say I will die?

"What about Dee? What happens to her if her brother doesn't comply?" I snap, my anger towards the situation, and Dee, building.

"We will own Dee for the rest of her life." Griff admits and I look at the little pocket rocket that so easily caught my attention earlier this week.

Own her? Like a possession? What the actual fuck!

I don't fucking know her at all. How the fuck is she associated with these men?

"Dee is much more valuable than either of you two. Her skill set, especially for her age, is basically unheard of." Griff glances at Dee, who looks down at her feet. The first sign I've seen since this whole situation occurred, of her confidence wavering.

"What sort of jobs? I don't kill people. Or deal fucking drugs, so I don't know how I can help you." I snap, feeling trapped by this whole situation. I almost feel like it would be better to risk getting arrested than being owned by these fuckers.

Dev grins, coming to my side and throwing his arm over my shoulder. "To put it simply. You'll do what we tell you to. And if you don't know how, you will learn really fucking fast."

"And if I don't do what you tell me?"

"You know, the best women to fuck are mums. They are fucking wild. I bet I could make your mum scream real good."

"What the fuck!" I roar, shoving Dev off me and leaping at him. Before I can even get close, Dee ninjas my arse, and I find myself on my knees next to Travis.

"What the fuck, Dee!" I snarl and she glares back at me. "Whose fucking side are you on?"

She doesn't respond, keeping her thoughts and words to herself as usual.

"Really? You have nothing to say to me? You call these fucking psychos to come and take care of something that was none of your fucking business, and now they own us?"

Still, she glares, not responding.

"My mum, Dee! He threatened my mum! He's going to hurt her!"

She flinches while Dev laughs, throwing his head back.

"Oh boy. There won't be any pain involved on your mum's part. She's going to fucking love it."

I leap off the floor again, only to have Dee get in my way again, blocking my access to Dev. Even with her five foot height, I can tell I won't be able to get past her.

She's something else.

Deep down, I know Dee is only trying to help, but in actual fact, she's made the situation worse. I can deal with these fuckers bossing me around for five weeks, but the mention of involving my mum has me ready to take the screwdriver from Pike's chest and drive it into someone else's.

15

DEE

Staying in bed all day has never been my thing. I have too many thoughts inside my head to sit still for long. Yet today, I can't find it in me to drag myself out.

Last night was unexpected and has totally messed with my plans. I'd never imagined walking into that shed to find my brother and the guy I've been trying to ignore together. Let alone standing over a dead body that they both had a part in putting there. I never expected Griffin Marx to twist the situation so I had no choice but to pay him in kills instead of cash. And I really didn't expect to feel the pain in the centre of my chest when Jared looked at me with so much hate in his eyes before he walked away from me last night.

Isn't that exactly what I wanted, though? For him to give up on his pursuit to do whatever it was he was trying to do with me. For him to ignore me.

I've never really cared if someone hated me before. I've never really cared for any connection with another person, except maybe Travis, which is just another worry swirling in my head today, because even after all these years, he still hates me for trying to save him and our dad.

It's about 1pm when a tap sounds on my bedroom door. I don't bother answering it, instead pulling the blanket up over my head.

I just want to be left alone.

The sound of the door opening irks me, but I stay hidden under the blanket, hoping whoever it is will get the hint and go away. They don't.

The bed dips beside me, and I think someone has sat on the edge, but then, whoever it is, lies down, putting their head on the pillow next to me before peeling back the blanket.

Chocolate eyes peer in at me before the blanket is pulled back further to reveal my head.

"You know it's just occurred to me that you've been here a little over a week now, and I haven't had a sister-to-sister conversation with you yet." My foster sister, Rhys, grins wide, and I know it's useless pointing her in the direction of the door. This chick will do whatever she wants. Especially in her own home. I'm the newbie here. Not her. So I wait for her to continue. "That's on me. I've been a little tied up lately. Literally." Her lips spread even wider as her face turns almost wicked.

Yeah, I know what she's been doing. I've heard it every time her boyfriends come around.

"We should go over some rules." She continues. "First and foremost. Stay away from my guys. And yes, I know you've got this whole quiet vibe going, but in my experience, it's the quiet ones you need to look out for."

I can't help it. I grin.

"Ha! I thought so." She giggles. "Anyway, I know you're not going to do me dirty like that. So, moving on." Her face turns serious. "Don't fuck with my friends."

I don't blink or show any signs that her words are a surprise. Because they aren't. I already know who Rhys

George is, and aside from being upfront and a little too open about certain aspects of her life that make most people uncomfortable, she sure as shit is fiercely protective of those she holds dearest.

"And especially don't fuck with my family," she deadpans.

I remain neutral, waiting for her to elaborate, because she didn't come in here just to say that. No, I can tell she has more she wants to get off her chest.

"So, in saying that, I'm going to need you to explain to me the situation with Travis Watson, who apparently is your brother, and the fact that you're using my parents and my home for a place to stay so you can do them dirty and ditch out once you turn eighteen." Rhys' dark brows are high on her forehead as she waits for an explanation. I could give her the silent treatment, but she knows I have ways of communicating, and to be honest, I don't want to make an enemy of her.

Sliding my hand under my pillow, I pull my phone out and type out my conversation in the notes app.

You spoke with Jared?'

"He didn't really give me a choice when he busted into Marcus' bedroom while we were mid fuck, not even batting an eyelid at how I was completely naked riding his best mate reverse cowgirl. He just started ranting and pacing and, honestly, I ignored him until I came, because I ain't depriving Kitty like that, but then I realised he had a whole lot to say about my new foster sister."

Jesus, her Kitty? Is this chick for real?

"So? How much of what he said was true? I like Jared. Sure, he's been an angry fucker over the past few months and could probably do with showing more girls that pretty cock of his so he can get laid and fuck his anger out of his system, but Jared is a good guy, so I'm inclined to think he didn't interrupt my Marky Marc time to spit lies."

My cheeks heat at the mention of Jared's dick. Not that I've seen it, but I felt it pressed up against my body out at the lake a few days ago and I remember wanting to touch it without the barrier of clothes. Which also freaked me out.

I shake that thought off and let myself feel the guilt I've been wallowing in all night. I never dreamed in a million years that I would drag anyone into my world. Especially Jared. But now he's in it, and I hate knowing it's because of me. Maybe he would have been better facing the cops rather than being dragged into Australia's underworld.

Knowing I need to be as honest as I can with Rhys, I tap out my response on my phone.

'Travis Watson is my brother.'

"And?"

'And yes, I'm hoping he will leave with me when I turn eighteen.'

Rhys' dark eyes narrow as she studies me for a few moments, and I find it hard to fight the urge to squirm under her scrutiny.

"You're more than my parents think you are. I can see that. You obviously have mad manipulation skills to have fooled them into thinking you needed a safe, stable home. While I think they are sick skills to have, I'm not fucking happy you chose my parents to use them on."

'Yes, I manipulated my way into this home, but I do respect Cynthia and Will. Through all their visits with me last year, I learnt what loving and caring people they are, but I had no other option. I needed to come and see my brother.'

"Why couldn't you just wait until you turned eighteen? Wouldn't that have been easier?"

'There are other factors at play here. It's not that simple.'

I can't tell her about the trouble Travis is getting deeper in each day he spends with the Kerr family, or the fact that if I don't disappear the moment I turn eighteen that the work

I've been doing will multiply and I will no longer be shown the leniencies I've been given because I'll no longer legally be a child.

"What factors?" Rhys frowns and I shake my head, holding up my phone.

'I can't go into that.'

She rolls her eyes. "I can't decide if I still like you."

I shrug. It's a bummer, but of no consequence to my situation. I don't have time to build a relationship with my foster sister. I won't be here for long enough to put in such effort.

"I'm curious about something else." Rhys squints her eyes this time, fluffing the pillow under her head like she's getting comfy to stay awhile. "What did you do to Jared? I've never seen him hate on someone so much before. Not even Ayden, who, if you didn't already know, swept Lexi off her feet before Jared could man up and try to do it himself. It's a whole dark story. It's like really… Heavy." Rhys smirks and even though I'm not sure why she's smirking, I'm fast learning that her mind works differently than most. So, I don't ask her to elaborate.

'Things between me and Jared are no one else's business.' I text.

Her brows hitch before she grins. "So, there is something? I thought I was getting a vibe."

'There's no vibe.' I text.

"Oh yes, there most certainly is a vibe. Did you guys fuck? Or is he so pissy because you denied him? Didn't you think his cock was pretty? I haven't seen it hard, but I reckon it must be big. Not Garrett big, because his cockzilla is H.U.G.E! But Jared Crowley is packing a long, thick salami. Definitely a pussy pleaser."

I'm fairly certain I look like a stunned fish right now.

Cockzilla? Thick salami? Pussy pleaser?

"Oh my God, are you a virgin? Did you tell Jared, and it pissed him off?" She frowns. "Dudes don't normally get annoyed by that, though. You know," she shrugs, "because of the extra squeeze."

I tap out a message on my phone and hold it up.

There's nothing going on with me and Jared.'

Her eyes narrow as she studies me again, and then she shrugs. "There is. But keep denying it to yourself if it makes you feel better." She sits up and swings her legs over the side of my bed before turning to look back at me. "A word of advice. My parents are understanding, so you really should try communicating with them about why you're really here. They won't throw you out. That's not their MO. But they may help you."

And just like that, my new foster sister skips out of my room, and I let a smile spread across my face. It's not something I do often. Certainly not while people are around, but I'm alone again in my room, and no one can see how my new foster sister has affected me.

She's a character, that's for sure. I would have loved to come into her life years ago before my life turned down a path of no return. We would have been great sisters. Maybe even the best of friends.

I consider what she said about Jared. About how angry he was. How he didn't even care that they were in the middle of… stuff. How he paced and ranted and spoke with hate about me.

I sit up in bed, clutching my phone and doing something I never do. I unblock Jared's number and open the message app and send him a message.

Dee Porter
I'm sorry.

I hold my breath as the little scrolling dots appear, and then disappear, but then reappear. When they disappear again, they stay that way and I let myself feel the full ache as my heart sinks.

I need to feel it. To remember that I'm not here to make friends or fool around with guys. I'm here to convince my baby brother to ditch his criminal family and run away with me.

Thinking of Travis, I do something else I never do. I open my Instagram app and search his name. It's the top search since I've done it almost daily for the last four years since I've had access to my own phone.

Even if he was somehow able to see who stalks his account, he would never know it was me. My account handle is @hush_tiny_dancer, so he'd simply think it's just some random girl that likes to dance. And my profile is full of inspirational dance quotes.

I don't have the account to gain followers. I have it so I can stalk. Something that I've become an expert at.

I have the same Facebook account, but TikTok is different because I use it for a different purpose.

I open an Instagram message to @trav_theman.

@hush_tiny_dancer
Hey.

@trav_theman
Heeey! What sexy little minx am I talking to right now?

@hush_tiny_dancer
Ew. Trav, it's Ell.

@trav_theman
Fuck off!

My heart sinks at his words, but I kind of expected him to be difficult after all this time, so I need to give him time to wrap his head around me being here.

@hush_tiny_dancer
I'm not going anywhere, Travis.
I came to this town for you and I'm not leaving without you.

He doesn't respond.

@hush_tiny_dancer
Fine, if you won't talk to me, then just read this, please.
Your foster parents aren't who you think they are.
Douglas and Bianca Kerr aren't small-time dealers. They have built a small empire by taking in foster kids and grooming them to be their puppets. It starts out with small things like stealing a lolly from the store, the escalates to picking pockets on the street, then to breaking and entering to steal large quantities of cash, jewellery, or even drugs. They make a living off sitting back and enjoying the riches from the work their foster kids do.
I know you have an older foster brother in prison. Dean. He got busted for dealing, possession, and carrying an illegal firearm which was linked to a death on the other side of the state. He's doing time because your parents let him take the fall. He didn't even give them up. He took the rap for the whole lot, didn't he? And what happened when he went away? Your parents asked your other older foster brother, Adam, to step up in his place. There was hardly a disruption to the supply chain, was there? Because you stepped up too, to take over what Adam had been doing. You went from dealing marijuana, to selling ecstasy as well. And I bet your olds have made it seem like a real honour to graduate to something stronger, haven't they?
What's next? Heroin? Coke?
How about the fact that most of your foster siblings are male? You

know why that is, don't you? Girls aren't physically tough enough to take being jumped, which I know you know all about, Travis. I've seen your hospital records.

No. The girls, when they take them in, get whored out. Just like your foster sister, Cassie. Have you ever asked her how she got started in whoring? I guarantee you it wasn't her idea, and I bet the first time she got paid was when she was barely into her teens. There is so much more you don't know about your foster parents, Travis, but you need to decide if they are worth going to prison for, or dying for, because they are the only two options if you don't come with me.

I'm in Timber Valley for you because I already knew the Marx Crew were moving in, and I'm not leaving without you.

I get no response, but I can see he has seen it, so hopefully he reads it, and he considers my words. I get that my sudden appearance is a shock to him. He probably thought he'd never see me again, just like he wished. I can give him a bit of space to wrap his head around things. For now, anyway.

I've missed him so much over the past seven years. I watched him from afar through social media, wishing I could go back in time and somehow fix things. I'm not sure how I could have, but I'd give it a go if it were possible.

The rest of my Sunday I spend staring into space. When I join the family at the dinner table, I zone out, only picking at my food, and only really responding with a smile when little Connor and Archie try to get my attention by rolling peas across the table to me.

I pretend I don't see the worried glances of Will and Cynthia, or Rhys' narrowed eyes, and I don't have to worry too much about Charlotte. She has done nothing but pretend I don't exist since I arrived, so out of everyone, I'm most comfortable with her.

After dinner, I finish some of the work on my side project

before shutting the lights off and staring at the ceiling well into the early hours of Monday morning.

Since my whole purpose of wanting to go to FP High is no longer a thing, I forget my uniform strike and dress in the uptight Catholic uniform, much to Cynthia's surprise. For some strange reason, I look forward to going to school, which doesn't make sense because my attendance or even finishing secondary school isn't even a factor, given I'll be fleeing in a few weeks.

I quickly learn that the real reason is Jared. I must have been looking forward to seeing him on some level, because as soon as I realise he's not at school today, my mood plummets and I simply want to slap myself in the face for letting down my wall the slightest bit and letting this guy affect me like this.

It's only going to cause me pain.

Monday is like the longest day in history. Like with dinner last night, I zone out of all my classes, especially English, as I remember the Hangman game Jared played with me last week. I can't believe I actually caved and played with him. Something else I don't normally do.

I get a message from Cynthia at the end of the school day, asking me to come to her office, so I drag my feet, wondering if Rhys has told her why I scammed my way into their care.

"Oh Dee. Good, I'm glad you got my message." Cynthia smiles as she stands from her desk as I hover in her doorway. "Let's take a walk."

A walk? That doesn't sound good.

Cynthia stays quiet as we make our way through the administration building, but speaks as soon as we are outside and away from prying ears.

"So, Travis Watson is your brother?"

My brows shoot up and Cynthia smiles, trying not to laugh at my reaction.

"Things are starting to make sense now. Like how badly you wanted to attend the public high school. You wanted to go to school with him?"

I give her a nod and she nods in return.

"Travis is still enrolled at the school but hasn't attended since the middle of last year. The principal gave up trying to contact his parents, unfortunately. Sadly, it happens a lot in the senior years of public schools in certain areas."

I follow Cynthia's lead as she turns past the library, heading towards the back of the school where the music centre is.

"I just want you to know, Dee, you have a place in our home for as long as you want it. We don't believe in aging out in our house. Whether you're five years old or twenty-five years old, when we invite you to be a part of our family, it doesn't end just because you turn a certain age, or even move on and get married. Will and I will always have a place for you in our family."

Shit. Her words hit deep in my chest, something I really wasn't expecting.

"And if Travis Watson is your brother, then he is a part of our family, too. He may live somewhere else, but our door will always be open for him. I'm sorry you were separated in the first place. I understand that you've been through quite a lot, especially those first few years after..." She doesn't say the words, obviously knowing how we came about being orphaned. "Well, anyway." She stops, offering me a warm smile. "I'd never stop a brother and sister from reuniting, so..." She gestures her hand down the path, and my eyes follow to land on my brother Travis, standing with Lexi at the end of the path, both of them wearing navy overalls.

"Travis and Lexi do community service here each afternoon to make up for vandalising the school last year. They work for an hour or two depending on the weather and time of year." I look back at her smiling face. "You should go and say hi."

I struggle with the golf ball sized lump in my throat from the kindness this woman is offering me, even after clearly finding out how I weaselled my way into her home to get closer to my brother.

Cynthia gives me an encouraging nod, so I step forward slowly, approaching Lexi and Travis as they use rakes in the garden bed. I should have probably told Cynthia that I've already reunited with Travis, and that he's likely to start yelling curses at me as soon as he realises I'm there. Cynthia doesn't know things between us aren't good, but I approach as she calls to Lexi, who looks towards us confused, frowning as she passes me, and Travis turns to see me there.

"What the fuck do you want?" He hisses through gritted teeth, and I risk a glance back at Cynthia, who is trying to give us privacy by turning her back and chatting with Lexi.

Turning back to Travis, I shrug.

"Just fucking speak." He hisses again and rolls his eyes.

I stay silent, taking this moment in the bright daylight to really look at him.

My baby brother has grown up so much. He was nine when we were separated. Even though there's less than a year between us, I've always felt protective of him.

We have the same big brown eyes and smattering of freckles across our noses, picking up those traits from our dad. Our hair is different, though. He has his mum's sandy blonde hair, and I have my mum's mousey brown hair.

Travis is sixteen now, turning seventeen in July. He's on the shorter side for a guy, but he's taller than me. I wonder what it would have been like if we hadn't been separated. Would he have rubbed it in when he finally grew a centimetre taller than me, and then again when he was an inch taller, and then half a foot taller?

I can imagine he would have. And I can imagine I would have pouted about it, but secretly liked that he was growing into a man.

"Look, you need to stay the fuck away from me, Ell." Travis hisses, leaning in closer. "Not just because I hate everything about you, but because if my olds find out you're here, they will make your life hell."

I tap out my words and hold up my phone.

'My life is already hell, Trav. I can handle it.'

He smirks, "No, you can't. You think you have them all figured out, but you're not even close."

'So you read my message?'

He rolls his eyes. "Yeah, so?"

My brows shoot up.

'So? You need to leave. Get as far away from them as possible before it's too late.'

"It's already too late, Ell. There's no leaving for me."

Shit. I'm too late. I should have come years ago, but I couldn't. I didn't have the means then.

"Look, I appreciate you helping me and Jared out. Fuck knows, I didn't mean to get him tangled up in my world. He's a good bloke. As for how you helped…" He glances around as if waiting to find someone nearby, but no one is there. "Shit just got ten times fucking harder for me. If my olds find out that I let the Marx Crew help me, they will fucking kill me, Ell. The best thing for you to do is leave this fucking toxic place and move on. I can't come with you, not just because of my family, but also because I will never forgive you for killing my mum."

JARED

The last thing I fucking wanted to do is come to school today, but my mum, who's too fucking perceptive, knows I'm not really sick, and she hovers over me from 7am, bugging me until I get dressed and drive myself to school, where the fucking Principal is waiting for me, on the phone with my fucking mum.

I'm eighteen, for fuck's sake.

I've missed Tuesday morning homeroom because of dragging my feet, but I have no choice but to head to PE with my mates when Marcus links arms with me like we are a pair of pre-teen bitches going on a fucking picnic.

And yes, I may have laughed. Once. For like two seconds.

Of course, as soon as I leave the change rooms and enter the gymnasium, my eyes fall on Dee Porter. Or is it Ell Porter? Fucked if I know. Both names are probably fake. This chick is not who she seems, and I don't for a minute believe her shy, innocent act.

She probably knows how to seduce thirty-year-old men and fuck them like a pro.

Fuck.

I rake my hand through my hair, turning my eyes from her, feeling like a fucking prick for having those thoughts. I don't really believe that. I'm just so fucking angry. Like all the time, but it seems to be worse right now. I guess being involved in a murder and cover up on top of what Lexi's brother did will do that to a guy.

My patience is practically non-existent, and the slightest annoying thing pisses me off more than it should. I should probably go and see a counsellor like my mum has been begging me to, but what will talking help? It will only bring up shit I don't want to think about and piss me off even more.

Dee is back to wearing the regulation uniform today, with the exception of a long sleeve top under her sports shirt. Mrs Bailey doesn't even look twice at the infraction, and my mind wanders back to last week when I pretended to help her with her grazed elbow and I took a peek at her arms. She had scars on the underside of her arms. At first, I thought maybe she's a cutter, but these scars seemed too thick and jiggered somehow.

But then what do I know about cutting?

Not that I care.

Because I don't.

It just pisses me off that she's breaking uniform policy and not getting called out for it.

"Ok class. Today we are going to play Aussie Rules Football out on the oval. Grab your water bottles, please." Mrs Bailey's bellow echoes through the gymnasium, sounding more manly than woman, and Simon starts doing an impersonation of her as we walk.

Simon is always clowning around and has the energy of a Labrador puppy and the blonde hair to match. His antics usually make me laugh. But not today.

"Hey."

I look to my side to see familiar blue eyes looking up at me with concern.

"Hey, Lex."

"You ok? You seem off."

I peer past Lexi to see her always watchful boyfriend, Ayden, walking not far from us, looking our way.

"I'm fine," I mutter, and she scoffs.

"Actually, you're not. So do you wanna answer me truthfully this time?"

I shoot Lexi a glare, only to see her smirking.

"I'm tired," I snap.

"Yeah-nah, I've used that term before as well. It's a bullshit phrase to steer people away from the fact that something else is wrong." Lexi smirks, "So how about you do both of us a favour and tell me what's going on with you?"

I stop in my tracks, nearly causing Garrett to run into me, but he leaps out of the way just in time.

"A little warning, Crowley." Garrett snaps, but then smiles as he passes by, something I've noticed him doing a helluva lot more since he started seeing Rhys.

"Sorry, man." I mutter, sucking in a deep breath to try to tame this raging beast inside me.

Lexi stops walking too and her brow quirks as she waits for me to answer her truthfully.

"I got a lot going on right now. That's all."

"Like what?" she asks, crossing her arms over her chest as the rest of the class passes us by. Including Dee.

I don't miss the way she sneaks a glance back at us.

"Like stuff that doesn't concern you," I snap, and Lexi frowns.

"Come on, Der. Talk to me."

I chuckle under my breath at her use of the old code name Lexi, Marcus, and Abbey used to call me back when we were kids. We took the last three letters of our names and put them backwards, thinking we were so fucking cool.

Der is not fucking cool. Neither was Abbey's, which was Yeb, and Marcus', which was Suc. Fuck, I still tease him about that.

Lexi's was the best. Her real name is Alexis, so her code name was Six. I started calling her that again last year, and Ayden had a problem with it. Didn't like the pet name I had for his girl, I guess. Naturally, I rubbed it in his face for a while, but I've stopped referring to her as Six, mainly for my own benefit. Calling her that just seems too personal. Probably because she always meant more to me than I did to her.

I consider calling her Six now, either to annoy her or piss Ayden off, which will most likely get me into a fight. Both options seem pretty fucking good right now, yet I don't use that name. Lexi and Ayden haven't done anything wrong. It's me with the fucking issues. I know that much. I just can't figure out how to get a handle on this fucking anger.

"I can't talk to you, Lex," I answer truthfully. "I've only just started *not* looking at you like you should be mine. Talking about personal stuff with you might just fucking confuse me even more."

Lexi is quiet for a beat as she studies me, before she gives me a nod. "You gotta talk to someone, though."

I nod, knowing I do. I just haven't figured out who the right person is yet. Or even if I should be talking about anything.

The stuff that went down on Saturday night isn't exactly a casual conversation. I fucking killed someone. Even if I only played a small part, and it was an accident, I helped to end someone's life. The knowledge of that is eating me up. So too is this fucked up shit with the gang I've found myself tangled in, and the fact that Travis and Dee are siblings.

Maybe I'd be in a better place to cope with all of this if the nightmares of Mike West beating me to a pulp would just fuck the hell off.

"Come on then. Let's go take our aggression out on the other team." Lexi grins wickedly, and I feel my sinister smile widen across my face.

That sounds like a brilliant idea.

Unfortunately for Dee, it's not. She's on the opposing team, and I've set my sights on her.

She isn't who she says she is. She's put me on my arse more than once, using some sort of ninja skills. She spends her spare time in the criminal underworld rubbing shoulders with some sort of Australian mob, or mafia, or whatever the hell they are. And she didn't even balk at all the blood, other than obviously thinking her long-lost brother had been injured.

Even though Dee Porter is quiet and likes to hover in the shadows, she's not shy or withdrawn. I can tell she doesn't like attention, but she is also competitive. Something I noticed comes out more in PE class.

"Try to keep tackling to a minimum. I don't need to spend the rest of my day writing up incident reports for injuries or handsy teenage boys." Mrs Bailey bellows as Lexi and I join the others. Most of the guys snicker, and some of the girls giggle, but me, my mates, Lexi and Dee remain serious. Any one of us are likely to deck a handsy dickwad that tries anything on Lexi.

And maybe Dee.

Not that I care.

On the oval, I jog across the ground approaching Bossi, who is standing near Dee.

"Trade places with me?" I ask him, and his dark brows hitch.

"You don't normally play half back flank."

I shrug, keeping my focus on him and not the girl hovering nearby.

"I wanna give it a try."

Shaun narrows his eyes at me, his Spanish heritage looking more prominent. "You wanna give up the position of kicking goals to stop the other team from kicking goals?"

I nod, Shaun's dark eyes studying me for a moment before he smirks and sneaks a look over his shoulder to where Dee is also pretending to ignore us. "Sure thing, man. Have at it."

Grinning, Shaun slaps my shoulder as he passes by before running to the other end of the oval to take my regular position.

As the whistle blows, I turn to the centre to watch the football go up as Marcus and Paul jump up for the ball. My job is to try and keep the ball away from Dee and get it back down to the other end of the oval so Shaun and the other forwards can work on getting some goals. If Dee thinks she's going to get a goal on my watch, she has another thing coming.

The ball stays down the other end for a bit, and I keep Dee in my peripheral at all times. I wouldn't put it past her to play dirty and ninja my arse.

When the ball comes our way, I wait, assuming Dee will hang back and let the ball come closer, but she has other ideas, sprinting off towards the incoming ball before I know what's even happening.

"Shit," I hiss, taking off in a sprint to catch up to her.

She jumps, catching the red ball against her chest before darting to the left and sprinting back towards her goal. She's fucking fast. I'll give her that. She bounces the ball once as she runs, like a pro I might fucking add, and then she lines up her shot, dropping the ball to her right foot as she kicks long and fast, the football bulleting towards the goal.

I stop running only a few feet from her, knowing I'm too fucking late, and watch the ball sail through the goals.

Cheers ring out across the oval from Dee's team and when she turns around, I'm almost knocked on my arse by the huge fucking smile spread across her face.

Shit. She really is beautiful.

Not that I care.

I harden my resolve, shooting her a dagger as her deep brown eyes lock with mine.

"That's the only goal you'll get." I hiss at her, and she smirks, shrugging as she passes me.

Fuck. Shit. Why does this girl rile me up so fucking much?

The ball comes our way a lot. Clearly Dee's back line are good at defending, getting the ball back down to her and the other forwards more often than not.

I'm determined to stop Dee from kicking another goal, so I stay hot on her heels, hip and shouldering her out of the way, knocking her small frame to the ground. I tackle her numerous times, slamming her hard to the cushioned grass, and other times swinging her so forcefully around that she practically goes flying.

I'm relentless and brutal, and not once does she look hurt or angry.

"Hey, man. You might want to take it down a notch." Marcus pants as he jogs up to me.

"What?" I ask innocently. Like I have no clue what he's on about.

"Dee's only little man. You're gonna hurt her." I glance back at Dee, who just shoots me a dagger.

"Nah. She's alright. She's tougher than she looks." I smirk, looking back at my mate.

"Bro." Marcus leans in and whispers. "What's your problem? You're practically attacking her."

I scoff. "It's a game, Grady. Chill." I turn back to Dee. "I'm not hurting you, am I, Dee? You can take it, can't you?"

I expect an eye roll, or a simple cold shoulder. What I don't expect is the sinister smirk that crosses her face, or the words she mouths.

'Bring it.'

"Fuck." Grady hisses and I turn back to him, grinning so hard that my cheeks fucking hurt.

The game is over quicker than I would have liked, and I walk behind Dee, following the rest of the class back to the gymnasium to get changed. It's easy to forget just how little she is when she's such a fierce competitor. She doesn't let her height get in the way when she's playing sports against tall arseholes like me, and she didn't let it be a factor the other night in Pike's shed. She put herself between two walls of raging males, for fuck's sake.

Just remembering how brave she was that night sends blood rushing to my dick, and my eyes fall to her arse as she walks. What I wouldn't give to bury my face in her arse.

Wait. What?

My eyes widen and I glance around at the other students walking nearby as if they can hear my thoughts.

Where the fuck did that thought come from? I've never buried my face in anyone's arse, and I don't fucking intend on starting to, either. Especially with Dee Porter, or Ell Porter, or whatever the hell her name is. She's bad news.

My eyes travel down the creamy flesh of her legs and back up again, and my dick jerks in my shorts.

Fucking hell. I have a fucking boner. At school.

Making sure my t-shirt is hanging over my noticeable bulge, I beeline for the guys' change rooms, snatching up my clothes and ducking into the toilet section, locking myself in a stall.

The sounds of banter from the other guys in the class

float through to this section, but as I dump my clothes on the ledge above the toilet, I tug down my shorts and free my dick, wrapping my hand around it with a squeeze. The sounds of the other guys in my class fade as my thoughts turn to a certain little pocket rocket with big brown eyes, and I remember how she felt pressed against me out by the lake last week.

My hand starts pumping my dick slowly as I savour the feel of the building pleasure, images of Dee's deep pink nipples flashing through my mind, my tongue instantly remembering the feel of how they pebbled into tight peaks as I sucked on them.

Faster I pump, from my tip to the base of my shaft, pressing my thumb harder as it glides back up and over the rim of my head.

"Fuck." I whisper, my mind remembering how hot it was between Dee's legs. How her jeans almost felt like they might burst into flames with the heat oozing from her core.

I bite my lip, trying to hold in a moan, and my mind flashes to how it felt to finally kiss her. For her lips to part and let me in, my tongue dancing with hers as she gave her trust to me. Fuuuck, her lips were so fucking soft. What I wouldn't give to see my dick slide into her pretty little mouth.

I pump faster.

What I wouldn't give to have her fall to her knees and look up at me as she lets me fuck her mouth.

My balls tighten as I go rigid and I jerk as my orgasm hits, my muscles contracting as hot jets of cum shoot from my dick and into the toilet below. I bite my lower lip, trying to hold in my moans and wait for the waves to subside.

"Fuuuck." I whisper again, not giving a shit if anyone is nearby and can possibly hear me.

Slowly, my muscles start to relax and the blood drains back out of my dick, leaving it lifeless.

Well, that's a first. I've never needed to jack off at school before, and like all the recent changes in my life, the reason behind it points to one particular little brunette.

17

DEE

My body is already starting to ache, but in the best way. I feel like I've had a brutal workout, and I guess in a way I have. Jared made sure of that in PE class this morning.

Something is different about him today, which has me on edge. Yeah, he seemed like a loose cannon last week, struggling with some sort of demon while trying to get my attention, but now he's not trying to get my attention at all.

Sure, he paid me attention in PE this morning, but I quickly realised he was taking his aggression out on me. I had to let him. If I didn't, he'd deliver it to someone else who couldn't handle it and he'd probably end up in more trouble than he's already in.

Because of me.

At recess, I did the cowardly thing and hid in the girls' toilets. I figure I owe Jared that much. Hopefully out of sight, out of mind applies here, and he was able to spend his spare time laughing with his mates, instead of seeing me and being reminded of Pike's dead body, or the fact that I've managed to get him fast tracked into the Marx Crew.

In English, I arrive to find Jared sitting with Marcus, leaving Lexi to sit at my table. He didn't even look up as I walked to sit down, and he stayed quiet the whole lesson. So, naturally, I went back to the girls' toilets to hide again at lunch.

I guess he's finally getting the hint that I'm not the right girl for him to show an interest in. He knows now that I'm only here for a short time. He knows I'm not a good person. So now, he can move on and find a nice girl. Someone he deserves.

The only other interesting thing about today was Abbey in our Textiles class. Normally, she's so withdrawn and as quiet as a mouse. It's hard to remember she's even there half the time. Today, however, she looked distressed. She very publicly wore a split lip, and if I'm not mistaken, a slightly swollen eye that makeup is working its magic to hide a bruise, I bet. She was also paying no attention to her work, instead texting frantically on her phone, and when the teacher asked her to put her phone away, she packed up her things and ran out of class.

Whatever is going on in her life, it seems to be escalating. I can't help but feel worried about her. She seems like she would be a nice person, but something is going on that is killing her on the inside.

Maybe I should look into her a little more.

Since I skipped dance last night, deciding to take the extra time to chat with Travis, and then feeling unbelievably spent afterwards, I jump on the town bus after school and arrive at the studio with plenty of time to spare. I take my time getting changed, wearing black leggings and a black long sleeve wrap crop. It's old, something I've had for a couple of years that I was given out of the lost property bin at one of my old dance studios, but I love these clothes. They are me, and since I'm attending classes on a casual basis,

Miss Adele doesn't mind that I'm not in their regular studio uniform.

As I walk into the contemporary studio upstairs, I see Ruby kissing her boyfriend, Caleb, goodbye before she joins us in class. She offers me a small smile as I position myself in my usual back corner, and we all turn our eyes to Miss Adele as she starts to explain that today we will be doing partner work.

I've done partner work before. I don't hate it, but I'm a solitary person, and much prefer to dance on my own.

As the girls around me get excited and start partnering up, I wonder who the unlucky one will be that is the odd one out and has to partner with me.

"Can I be your partner, Dee?"

I glance up to see Ruby's smiling face, her green eyes looking vibrant against the backdrop of her ivory skin and flaming red hair. My brows shoot up and I look around before glancing back at her and giving her a nod. She beams.

"Yay." She claps excitedly. "This is going to be fun."

I offer her a small smile, trying to hide my lack of enthusiasm before Miss Adele proceeds to explain, and demonstrate today's partner work.

We are given a ball to share, and instructions that we are to improvise using movement by rolling the ball between our bodies. We mustn't let the ball touch the ground and must stay connected to each other through the ball at all times.

This sounds like hell.

I hang back when the dancers move to the corner, and music starts to flow through the room. Ruby beams at me, excited about the task as we watch others try, and fail, to stay connected. I analyse what they are doing wrong and right, pointing to them and showing Ruby with a thumbs up or down which things we should try or avoid. She nods, seeming to understand my communication.

"So, I think most of the girls are trying to rush. It's not a race." Ruby leans in to whisper, clearly as competitive as me. "We need to feel the music and feel each other."

I nod, knowing she is right and pushing any discomfort I have about this task to the back of my mind.

When it's our turn, Ruby places the ball to her belly and gives me a nod.

Right. Now it's time to get up close and personal.

I step up to Ruby, pressing my body to the ball and close my eyes briefly to feel the music. Then I snap them open, and she gives me a nod before I move.

The ball rolls between our bodies as we bend and arch and turn and stretch, focusing on the connection and balance, and the ways our bodies talk to each other without words. It's a gentle push and pull, helping me to get lost in the improvisation and the music.

When we reach the other corner, it takes a moment for me to hear past the music, to the clapping and Miss Adele's praises. Even though it wasn't a competition, I feel like I've won, and I can't hide the smile that forms on my face.

"We did it." Ruby singsongs as I turn back to her, and she engulfs me in a hug. I stiffen for a moment, and if Ruby notices, she doesn't say anything. "We make a great team."

I nod and smile, happy that she's happy as we move to the end of the line and go through the whole process again.

After class, I wait for the other dancers to filter out before I leave, coming across Ruby and Caleb again in their little love bubble.

"Oh, hey, Dee." Caleb calls after I turn my back to head down the stairs.

Stopping, I hover on the top step and turn back to him.

"Where was your fella tonight? I was hoping to catch up with him."

I offer Caleb and Ruby a smile as I shrug, trying to ignore

the pang of disappointment at knowing Jared wasn't here watching me tonight. I don't know what's wrong with me. I don't like being watched. And I don't like Jared. So… Yeah.

I'm very aware of my childish thoughts as I leave the studio and climb into William's waiting car. He asks me how my day was and as usual I stay quiet, feeling exhausted from interacting so much today.

I don't know how people do that all day, every day.

Or even why they would want to.

When we get home, the aroma of delicious food engulfs me, and I make my way into the main living area to where I hear Cynthia chatting away.

Then I stop dead in my tracks.

Travis, my brother, is sitting at the island bench.

What the….

"Oh good. You're home." Cynthia smiles warmly as she takes me in.

I'm sure right in this moment I look like a fish, my mouth in an O as I look between my foster mum and my brother. He looks like he's had a shower, his sandy hair slightly damp, but he's still wearing the clothes he obviously wore to community service at the school.

Travis frowns and I close my mouth before pointing to my brother.

Cynthia instantly picks up my silent question.

"I invited your brother to dinner."

"She insisted." Travis advises not sounding all that happy.

"It's great to have you join us." William says from behind me, and I nod before darting out of the room to get changed.

I take my time, having a shower to wash away the sweat, before dressing in a long sleeve green crop and black baggy trackies. I don't bother with my hair, opting to pull it up into a messy heap on top of my head, before I rejoin the family for dinner.

Since the weather is still warm, and the table is bigger outside under the alfresco area, Cynthia insists Travis take the seat at the opposite end, before sitting me to his left, and Rhys to his right. The twins are sitting next to me, Archie closest, while Charlotte and Cynthia sit across from them.

It all feels very family-like. Formal, yet informal at the same time. I guess I'm feeling weird about Travis being here. I know how much he would have wanted to say no to Cynthia.

"If you're Dee's brother, why don't you live with her?" Connor asks, and Cynthia frowns at him.

"Connor, that's a personal question, which is none of our business."

"Why?" Archie asks, and Cynthia sighs.

"It's ok, Mrs R." Travis speaks up, drawing everyone's attention. "I don't mind."

My gut twists. Of course he minds. Travis has obviously kept my existence a secret over the years. Now, all of a sudden, I invade his life, and he's having to explain our situation. A situation I'm sure he sees differently to me.

"When Ell and I had to leave our home, she needed to go to a hospital, and I got put in a foster home."

"Who's Ell?" Rhys asks, her chocolate eyes darting between me and Trav.

Travis frowns. "Oh, that's right. You call her Dee." Travis looks at me. "Should I call you Ell..." He smirks smugly. "Or Dee?"

I glare at him, not answering obviously, and he leans closer.

"What's that? I can't hear you."

William audibly clears his throat, his eyes hard as he glares at my brother. "I'm sensing a little tension here. I'm sure it must be very emotional to see each other after all this time, perhaps bringing up some memories that are hard to think about. But let me make one thing clear." William places his knife and fork down, forgetting about his grilled chicken as he glares down the table at Travis. "We are respectful to each other in this house. Even guests, so you would do well to apologise to your sister for the rude remark, or I can show you the door now."

My eyes go wide as I glance back at Travis, who has a neutral expression on his face as he stares back at William. Crunching turns my eyes to Rhys to see her eyes also wide, but not with shock. With excitement as she chews on her salad, her eyes darting between Travis, me and William.

"I'm sorry, Mr Rogan." Travis straightens his spine, surprising me by taking the higher road.

"Don't apologise to me. Apologise to your sister."

I gulp as I draw my eyes away from William again, my face heating as I glance down at my food instead of my little brother.

"Uh… Sorry Ell." Travis' apology actually sounds genuine. Maybe he means it, or maybe he's a good actor.

I glance up at him and give him a nod before turning my focus to my food as the twins start chatting away about having to make Valentine's Day cards in art at school today.

I zone out for a bit, my end of the table staying silent as we eat. Silent doesn't mean inactive, though. At least not on Rhys' part.

I feel her kick me gently under the table and my eyes dart up to see her grinning. I frown and her eyes gesture down to her plate, so I glance down to see she's made a smiley face with her cherry tomatoes and sticks of celery and carrots.

I hear Travis' quiet chuckle next to me and I can't hold in my smirk, my eyes meeting Rhys' again as she beams before a mischievous grin spreads across her face again, and she starts to rearrange her vegetables.

I have no idea what she's doing, but she looks like she's

having fun, so I wait patiently, eating some of my own salad before she spins her plate to face me.

I nearly choke on the carrot in my mouth as my eyes make out the shape of a dick on her plate. Again, Travis chuckles quietly, and I sneak a glance at Cynthia and William to see if they are paying Rhys any attention. Thank God they aren't! Charlotte is, though, rolling her eyes at her sister's antics.

Rhys kicks me under the table again and I look back to see she's now made an arrow above the dick with her carrots and it's pointing to Travis.

A small giggle escapes me before I can stop it, and all eyes turn to me, while Rhys quickly messes up her artwork so the twins and her parents don't see.

"Did you just giggle?" Archie asks from next to me and I suck my lips in, trying to hide the smile that wants to break free.

Bloody Rhys. She makes it easy to like her, and hard to keep quiet, apparently.

Even though all eyes are on me, I lean into Archie conspiratorially and hold my finger to my lips in a silent *shhhh* before shooting him a wink.

Both twins giggle then, helping to lift the mood in the room.

Well, maybe it was really Rhys who did that, but she seems content not taking the credit.

"How was your dance class tonight?" Cynthia asks me, so I give her a nod and thumbs up.

"You still dance?" Travis' voice draws my attention again, and I take in his face, his eyes genuinely curious.

"She sure does." Cynthia smiles, looking between us. "She's been dancing for years, I believe. She's joined up at the local studio here in Fox Pines."

Travis nods at Cynthia before turning his brown eyes back to me.

"That explains your Instagram handle." He chuckles, focusing back on his food. Meanwhile, I feel the piercing dark eyes of Rhys from across the table.

One look up tells me everything I need to know.

She knows I have an Instagram account, and that it has something to do with dancing.

Shit.

18

JARED

I can't fucking sleep. When I do, I'm either having a nightmare about Mike's fists slamming into my face, or about thick red blood oozing from Pike's dead body until the entire room is like a pool of crimson and Pike's eyes snap open before maggots start slithering from his mouth.

My emotions are fucking shot. They are all over the place, either angry, exhausted, confused, or just plain fucking scared.

One thing I can't seem to do is get Dee out of my head.

It should be a no brainer. That girl has managed to get me tied up in some sort of underworld shit, something that became ever clearer last night when I received a text message from Griffin Marx. I don't even know how he got my number.

Griffin Marx
Job: Wednesday, February 12th.
Drive to the Fox Pines Train Station car park at 11:55pm.
Get into the black Audi – plates ending in 391 (Keys in glove compartment).

Drive around the town for an hour to make sure no one is following you.
Pick up package from Firelane Park at 1am.
Give package the envelope from under your seat. (DO NOT OPEN)
Drive package to 5 Element Way, Redfield.
Go dark upon approach.
Keep the motor running while the package completes the task.
Upon package's return, deliver to the corner of Eden Place and Sunny Avenue, Fox Pines.
Do not ask the package any questions.
Return the car to the place of pickup and put keys back in the glove compartment.
It goes without saying that you must NOT speak of this to anyone and delete this message once the job is complete.

I'm guessing the package is a person and going in dark means no headlights.

Fuck. What am I getting myself into? Should I just go to the cops now? Turn myself in and hope for the best?

No. I can't. Devon Marx made it clear that my family is at risk if I don't comply. Fucking hell. My mum. My old man. They don't deserve this shit. Their hearts are still aching with the loss of Tim from six years ago.

As my heart rate picks up and anxiety makes itself known, I turn my thoughts to Dee. She's both the rage and calm in my storm right now. Confusing as fuck, that's for sure.

I knew she would be at dance class last night. I watched her go in from where I stood like a stalker across the street. I have no idea why I ended up there. One minute I was driving around. The next I was watching her walk from the bus stop to disappear through the doors of the studio.

For some reason, even though I'm pissed at her and her

brother, I feel weirdly protective of her. Hell. Even of Travis, too.

The Marx Crew treated her like she was the one to be scared of, and maybe they are right to an extent, but they didn't see her tears and anguish in the dance studio last week. She carries deep pain. It's the only reason I can come up with as to why I went to the studio.

I want to protect her.

I had to fight the urge to go in and watch. I really fucking wanted to. She's mesmerizing to watch, which is exactly why I didn't go in. I need space from her. She's messing with my head and my heart.

I haven't seen her yet today, but I know she's here because Rhys was talking about her at recess, saying she's surprised Dee is even at school. Rhys seems to think Dee was up all night. Apparently, she went into Dee's room at 3am to find her doing push-ups.

It worries me that Dee isn't sleeping.

Is she upset with how I treated her in PE yesterday?

Was my aggression too much for her?

I hated myself for being such a prick, but also enjoyed the class because my interactions with Dee just seem to set me alive. I'm so messed up right now.

I actually enjoyed pushing her around. Not because I'm a prick.

Ok, because I'm a prick, but also because she seems to like it. Or at least enjoyed the challenge I was offering her. She gave as good as she got doing her ninja shit on me when the teacher wasn't looking. Made me fucking hard as a rock.

I'm in double Maths now, a class I typically like, but today our teacher, Mr Thompson, is away, so we have a sub teacher. It's almost as if there's an unspoken rule that students must give the sub teacher hell. I swear every time we have a sub, our normally well-behaved class turns into a bunch of bratty ten-year-olds hyped up on red cordial.

Gaz and Bossi are at the table next to mine at the back of the room, and they've been helping each other with the work we are meant to be doing. Bell, Dale and Tillie are sitting a couple of rows in front of mine, watching the latest episode of some weird YouTube show they follow, ignoring the sub teacher's attempts at getting them to turn it off.

Everyone else is pretty much playing up, giving the sub hell, and probably helping her decide to choose a different career path after today, which is pretty much confirmed when a pen hits her in the side of her head, coming from the other side of the room and her bottom lip starts trembling.

Sighing, I sit back in my chair and watch her come undone, her face turning red with humiliation right before she grabs her things and runs from the room, leaving us unsupervised.

It's in that moment that I hear Dee's name. My eyes snap to the row just in front of me, to the backs of the heads of three dickwads I really don't fucking like. Daniel Stone's voice floats to me, Dee's name being spoken again as he chuckles with his mates, Craig and Michael.

I fucking hate Daniel Stone with a passion. Yeah, he's a tool, but he's also Abbey Delany's fiancé. Correction. Forced fiancé.

Even though Abbey is on the outs with us after turning her back on Lexi when she needed her the most, I still fucking care about her. We grew up together. You can't just turn that shit off.

So yeah, when Daniel says Dee's name again, I fucking pay attention because Daniel Stone is the scum of the earth, and he shouldn't be talking about *my* girl like that.

I mean, my friend. Dee's not my girl!

"I bet I could make Dee scream. One thrust of my cock

and she'll be singing my name." Daniel chuckles, and I ball my hands into fists as my heart rate picks up.

"Dude, she'd probably kick your arse for touching her." Craig grins like it's a show he'd enjoy watching, and my lip curls.

"There's an easy fix for that." Michael grins. "She'll be helpless if we hold her down."

I see red.

My seat flies back as I leap up and over the table before my fist slams into the side of Michael's head. Commotion breaks out as I feel Craig leap on my back, but I pay him no attention as I lay into Michael, his words going over and over in my head.

She'll be helpless if we hold her down.

When Daniel tries to defend his mate, I turn on him, my rage giving me the strength of ten men as I slam my fists over and over into his face, this time while I hold him by the front of his shirt.

People are yelling, the sounds muffled against my rushing blood as I attack like a madman. The overgrown monkey on my back disappears as Shaun and Garrett step in.

"Crowley, man! Stop! He's had enough!" Garrett's loud voice penetrates the haze of fury blanketing me, and I still my fist, mid-air, ready to deliver another blow if I need to.

My chest is heaving as I suck in oxygen, trying to calm my rage, and as it begins to work, my eyes awaken to the brutality I've just inflicted.

"Do not fucking speak Dee's name ever again! Do not even think about her." I hiss at Daniel, pulling him close so I can see his eye under the swelling. "And if I see one more fucking bruise on Abbey's body, I will fucking kill you."

19

DEE

*A*t this point, I think I should just stop trying to sleep. It's truly hopeless, especially after receiving the message from Griffin Marx last night.

Griffin Marx
Job: Wednesday February 12th (Technically Thursday) 1am.
Be at Firelane Park before 1am.
Wait for the black Audi to collect you.
Ask the driver for the white envelope.
Study the contents while driving.
Do not share the contents or discuss with the driver.
Complete the task set out while the driver waits in the car.
Once the task is complete, the driver will return you to the corner
of Eden Place and Sunny Avenue in Fox Pines.
Delete this message once the task is complete.

I'm used to getting jobs, just not from the Marx family, so I'm too damn anxious to sleep, and I spend the night working out and practising my skills in the confines of my bedroom. I could have tried to get the day off school, but given the fact that Cynthia thinks I'm trying to tank year twelve at FP Catholic, I knew it wasn't worth the energy.

My concentration levels are practically non-existent, so I sat like a zombie through Textiles and Media, and avoided the courtyard at recess and lunch. Instead, opting to hide in the end stall in the girls' toilets inside the gymnasium. They aren't used as much as the other toilets, and are newer, making hiding out in them a little less awful.

There's only about ten minutes left of lunch when I hear the door squeak open and Rhys and Lexi's voices float to me.

"Gaz and Shaun said he went crazy and flogged the absolute fuck out of them." Rhys' voice is high pitched.

Who is she talking about?

"Shit. Was it something to do with Abbey?" Lexi asks. "I know Jared is just as pissed about the way Daniel treats Abs as the rest of us."

Wait… Jared?

"That's what I thought too at first." Rhys drops her voice lower. "I know you and Jared grew up with Abbey, so it makes sense that he'd want to protect her, but Garrett said he laid into Michael first. Apparently, Michael, Daniel and Craig were talking smack about Dee."

What? Did I hear that right?

Jared beat up some guys because of me?

"Shit." Lexi says, her voice sounding stunned.

"Shit is right. I think he has it bad for Dee." Rhys giggles and Lexi hums.

"Maybe. Or maybe he's just a good guy that sticks up for his friends."

"Lexi West. Are you jealous?"

"What? No!" Lexi hisses, which makes Rhys laugh louder.

"Yeah, you are. I thought you wanted Jared to move on?"

"I absolutely do. I'm not jealous, Rhys. I'm worried. I

know Dee is your foster sister and all, but I don't think she's good for Jared."

My spine straightens at Lexi's comment.

"Why? Because she doesn't talk?" Rhys asks, and I wait for Lexi's response.

"Why the hell would it be because of that? You know I'm not that sort of person, Rhys."

"Then why?"

"Well, you told me yourself," Lexi responds. "Dee is going to leave soon. What happens to Jared then?"

My heart sinks lower in my chest as the truth of Lexi's words wrap around me.

"You've seen how fucked up he is lately," Lexi adds.

"He was like that before Dee came here. You can't blame her for that, Lex," Rhys remarks.

"No, but he's gotten worse. I can't help but feel like there's more going on."

"Yeah, I agree. He's stopped talking to the guys. Stopped trying to hang out with them. Something more is definitely going on."

The bell blares through the small speaker in the toilets, and I startle, the loud noise thankfully drowning out the shuffle of my foot.

I wait a minute after Lexi and Rhys have left before I exit the stall and come face to face with my reflection in the mirror. I look like shit. And not just because of the lack of sleep. Coming to Fox Pines is really taking a toll on me. I thought I'd prepared myself, but I could never have predicted Jared Crowley, or covering up a murder for my brother and Jared or getting myself tangled up in Marx Crew shit.

I really should try to hide the evidence of how this place is affecting me. Maybe a little concealer under my eyes to hide the dark circles, or some blush to give my cheeks some life. Maybe even a little mascara to help wake up my big brown eyes. Even my mousy brown hair looks lifeless today.

Not that I care. People are more likely to shy away from their intrigue about me if they feel the discomfort of seeing me look like shit. Most people veer away from getting involved in others' problems, so hopefully it will help me start to fade into the shadows until it's time for me to leave.

I drag my feet as I walk to English class. I'm late, so I'm surprised to see that Jared isn't there already. Although, if what Lexi and Rhys said was true, Jared could well have been suspended by now. Or worse.

Miss Dice doesn't say anything about my tardiness, just tells me to work through the questions on the worksheet she places on my desk. As I sit and scan the questions, my eyes blur, and exhaustion slams into me. Since getting good grades isn't a priority with me leaving in a few weeks, I lay my head in my arms on the desk and shut my eyes.

I doze, kind of awake, but not. I can hear the class, but it lulls me, helping to keep me captive just below the surface of consciousness. I'm not sure how long I stay like that, but a while later, my lids flutter open to see hands on the desk next to me, writing on the worksheet.

I know those hands. I've studied them before, only this time, there are grazes on the knuckles. A little bruising, too.

Keeping my head resting on my arms, I glance up to see the familiar blue eyes of Jared Crowley looking back at me. His face is neutral, not portraying what he's feeling right now, and I have the urge to reach out to him. To take his battered hand in mine and ask him if he's alright. Not write it down. Not make a gesture. But use my voice and speak the words.

The thought sends a slice of fear through me. Since the day I decided not to speak anymore, I've never actually had the urge to want to use my voice to communicate with another person.

Jared frowns slightly, and I'm almost certain I've let my brief moment of panic show on my face. Still, he doesn't speak. He doesn't pester me to talk to him or try to coax me to interact with him. He just sits next to me staring, not looking happy, or sad, or angry. Just neutral. And I stare right back.

It's a little unnerving if I'm being honest. I've gotten used to him trying to get a reaction from me, so his silence is throwing me off. Is he done with me? Or is he trying to beat me at my own game by using silence to gain the upper hand?

Thankfully, the class only lasts ten more minutes, so our calm stare off ends before he manages to hypnotise me or something, and I watch his back as he leaves the classroom, disappearing into the swarm of students hurrying to get their bags and leave for the day.

I feel flat. Lexi and Rhys' conversation floats through my mind as I get my bag and leave the school, walking with heavy feet to catch the bus to dance class.

I wish Lexi wasn't right, but she is. I'll be leaving soon, leaving them all behind. Jared's future depends on my brother, but no matter what, he's going to be wrapped up in Marx Crew shit from now on. All because of me.

I never thought it would be this hard to move here and do this. I never expected to care about my foster family or make 'kind of' friends. I never expected to be so drawn to a guy. I'm here for Travis, though. I'm here to take him from his life, from a future of crime, and hopefully give him better opportunities.

I just have to convince him to come with me.

At the dance studio, the girls are hyped up about something, and it's not until I notice a flyer on the wall that I see what they are talking about.

Fox Pines Performing Arts Dance Competition: Easter School Holidays – Friday 27th March
Entries open Friday 21st February

"Have you done a dance comp before?" Ruby's voice gains my attention, and I notice her standing next to me. "I love doing comps. It helps me to train harder and be more disciplined."

It sounds like something a mother would tell her daughter to try and keep her focused, but Ruby's green eyes are bright as she looks back at me. No hint of anything but truth in them.

I shake my head, and her brows shoot up.

"Really? You've never competed before. But you're so good. You would clean up."

I shrug and she offers me a warm smile.

"You know, I'm looking for a new duo partner. We should totally team up and compete together. I'm sure Miss Adele can make time to teach us." Ruby's smile is hopeful, and I hate that I have to let her down, but I shake my head, offering her an apologetic smile.

I won't be here when the competition is happening, and I also don't dance for anyone but myself. I have no desire to compete, even though the competitive devil inside me rears its little head and nudges me.

"Well, if you change your mind before next Friday, let me know because I can enter us. We would win the contemporary duo section for sure."

Miss Adele starts the class, and I move to my usual spot in the back corner. Today, she wants us to close our eyes and feel the music while we lie on the floor. Then she gets us to slowly start moving the way our bodies feel the music, but we aren't allowed to stand up.

This is something I've never done before, and even

though I nearly get kicked in the head numerous times by other dancers who are flailing about more than moving with grace, I find myself enjoying the task.

Halfway through the class, Miss Adele teaches us a short routine which consists mainly of floor work, and by the time we are done, I feel lighter than I did when I walked through the studio doors earlier.

That's what I love about dancing. It has the ability to lift my mood.

When I get home, I fall on top of my bed and pass out, only to be woken an hour later by Connor and Archie jumping on my bed to tell me dinner is ready. I'm nowhere near ready to wake up, but I'm thankful for the boost the nap gave me, since it's made me more alert. A skill I will need around 1am.

"You know, for a brother that seems to be pissed off at you, he's sure loyal."

My brows hit my hairline as I turn to Rhys, who is settling in her seat at the dinner table.

"You look surprised. Or confused. I'm not sure what that look is." Rhys squints her eyes at me as I lower myself into my chair.

I give her a pointed look, and she gives me one back before grinning.

"You want to know why I said he's loyal?"

I nod at Rhys, and she continues.

"He won't divulge your Instagram handle. What's the big secret?"

I shrug like it's no big deal and twirl my fork through the spaghetti in my bowl.

"Who has a secret?" Archie asks from next to me, and Rhys turns her eyes to him and smiles.

"No one, buddy."

"But you said-."

Rhys cuts Archie off. "I say a lot of things that don't make sense. Remember?"

He considers that for a moment, and then nods, before he turns his focus on his own bowl.

"I'll find out." Rhys whispers across the table to me, and my heart sinks, because I have no doubt she will.

Dinner passes by relatively fast. I help with the dishes, and then cleaning up all the water the twins managed to get outside the sink. Rhys is hovering, no doubt wanting to interrogate me, but the ring of the doorbell, followed by a couple of familiar voices, saves me, and she disappears into her bedroom with Marcus and Garrett.

Before I pretend to get into bed for the night, I slip on an old pair of black jeans that look like they've been painted on, and a fitted long sleeve black top. My black backpack is packed with a change of clothes and my black hoodie is resting on top. I get Thana out from her hiding spot at the back of my bed head, and I lay her in bed with me, like she is a cuddly teddy bear. Then I turn out my light, lie down, and wait.

I wait for the house to fall silent, and then I wait some more, keeping my breath steady, my heart calm, and my mind free of chaos as I prepare myself for tonight's task.

At 12:30am, I quietly slip out of my bed, strapping Thana on before easing my hoodie over my head and grabbing my backpack. I don't want to risk running into anyone out in the living area, so I quietly remove the flywire on my window which I unlatched earlier to avoid extra noise, and I slide open my window before climbing out and easing it nearly shut.

I step quietly over the bark garden bed, and when I reach the lawn, I run on my tiptoes, making as little noise as possible as I make my way off the property and down the road.

Firelane Park is about four blocks away from my street. Not too far. I arrive with plenty of time to spare, so I sink back in the shadows of a tree and wait.

At exactly 1am, a black car with no headlights on pulls up to the curb. I rush from the shadows towards the car, which I confirm is an Audi as I get closer, and I pull the front passenger door open.

I freeze as familiar blue eyes look back at me with just as much shock.

"You have to be fucking kidding me."

Well, I guess he's not happy to see me.

I roll my eyes and slide into the seat before closing myself inside the car with Jared.

"Did you know I was the one picking you up?"

I shake my head, and Jared huffs, tossing an envelope onto my lap. "Here."

As Jared returns his focus to the road and pulls away from the curb, I turn my focus to the envelope.

I could stress about my driver. About the fact that Jared has been forced into this position. One which he likely has no idea what it fully entails. But I need to keep my head in the game if I want to be successful and not get myself killed tonight.

I read the contents of the envelope, absorbing the information and committing it to memory.

Mark: Jeremy Dalton.
Address: 5 Element Way, Redfield.
Age: 62.
Lives alone, has a chihuahua named Princess.
Occupation: Bank Loans officer – Victoria Bank – Redfield Branch.
Violation: Exclusive membership with Carnal Unicorn.

I was a little concerned who my mark might be as I'm not used to working directly under Griffin or the Marx Crew, but in all honesty, I'm pretty happy that my mark is a sick fuck that needs to be dealt with. The name of a site on the dark web, Carnal Unicorn, tells me all I need to know. I'm already familiar with it as it's linked to the Vixen's Lodge live streams that my foster sister Rhys was tangled up with.

It takes twenty-five minutes to drive to the house in Redfield. It's only a couple of blocks from the Red Room Strip Club, which I'm sure is where Griffin is waiting patiently for the call to say the job has been done.

As we approach the house, Jared turns the headlights back off, easing the car to the side of the street, in front of number five.

"What do you have to do?" Jared asks, even though I'm almost positive he would have been told not to ask.

I stare at him for a long moment, taking in his frown that doesn't quite hide his worry. I'm not meant to tell him anything, yet the urge to tell him everything is strong. If he only knew how fucked up I really am, maybe it would be easier for him to turn his nose up at me and ignore me. He should be aware of the monster that sits inside this car with him, which is why, when I open the door and get out, I toss the open envelope on the seat, knowing damn well Jared will read it.

Putting all thoughts of Jared Crowley to the back of my mind, I approach the house along the shadowed garden bed, placing my backpack behind a tree before sliding on my gloves and advancing on the house.

Sneaking up alongside the generic brick house, I scan the area for cameras or anything else that will need to be taken care of, thankful when there are no obstacles. I spot a window slightly open in the back living area, which just makes my life ten times easier, and I quietly pull the flywire off and slip inside the house.

It smells of stale cigarette smoke inside, and I push the vile scent away from my thoughts as I scan the space, taking in the chew toy on the floor off to my left that I'm sure will squeak if I step on it. I can't see anything else that may cause issues, so I creep into the kitchen, making my way to the fridge with the thought of sorting out issue number one.

The chihuahua.

The yappy little dog hasn't made itself known yet, but it's only a matter of time, so I crack the fridge open and grin as I find a tray of raw sausages.

Bingo.

Carrying the sausages through the house, I tiptoe to the front bedroom where I can hear the loud snores of my mark. Peeling the plastic off the tray of sausages, I pick one up before easing the ajar door open, just in time to hear the faint growls of the little rat-like dog.

I don't waste any time, tossing the little thing the sausage and grinning when Princess starts gnawing on the raw meat.

The snores of my mark, Jeremy Dalton, cut off as he chokes on his own saliva, and I turn my focus on him as I draw Thana from her hiding place.

Sometimes I feel bad for the death I deliver, but as I take in the two child sized sex dolls on the bed next to Jeremy, I feel sure and just about ending his existence tonight.

Little Princess starts growling with satisfaction as she devours the sausage, effectively stirring Jeremy awake. His eyes blink open as they adjust to the room's darkness, and I type out a note on my phone and hold it up to his face as I rip back the sheets and toss a sausage onto his naked lap.

"What the fuck!" he yells, and I shake the phone in front of him, urging him to focus and read.

'Wrap your sausage with this sausage.'

"W-what?"

I shake my phone in front of him again.

"What? No!" He moves to sit up, and I silently sigh, lifting Thana up before pressing her sharp tip to Jeremy's exposed nuts.

"Whoa. What the fuck. What is this? Who are you?"

They always ask that. Right before they remember I'm a small framed girl that they think they can overpower. Sometimes I like the challenge, but not tonight. I'm too tired to play that game. I want this over with, so I dig Thana into the sensitive flesh that hangs between his legs until a bead of blood rolls down the wrinkled skin.

"Fuck. Ok. Mercy!" He hisses, picking up the sausage with shaky hands and wraps the raw meat around his dangly limp dick.

As he does that, I pick up his phone from the bedside table, happy that the idiot doesn't have a passcode to protect it, before I whistle to Princess.

The little white creature barks once before leaping onto the bed via a little step at the end, and immediately hones in on the raw meat his owner has wrapped around his dick.

"No, Princess. Back." Jeremy tries to instruct his dog, but the little thing has a taste of sausage and wants more. She leaps up in between Jeremy's parted legs before dragging her long tongue over the area.

I take a few snaps with Jeremy's phone, the flash picking up the detail clearly, before closing the phone and placing it back where I found it.

"What's going on? Please. I don't understand." Jeremy pleads, but I just rest my hand on my hip and wait for little Princess to stop licking and start biting.

It's not too long before Jeremy cries out.

"Ouch. No, Princess!" His face contorts in pain as beads of sweat dot his forehead. "No biting!"

He lets out a guttural screech as little Princess ignores her owner, gnawing on his package, and he goes to move. I whip Thana up, pressing her to Jeremy's throat this time and shaking my head as his eyes widen in fear.

"P-please. I don't know why you're doing this. But I have m-money. I can p-pay you to stop."

This is a common plea from my victims as well. They think I'm doing this for money.

Well, I mostly am, but I'm also here because I enjoy delivering sick fucks like this to hell.

He cries out again, not able to help it as his dog starts gnawing on his sausage wrapped dick. I watch Jeremy's face contort in horror and pain as his little Princess turns on him, ravenous for the meat, her white fur starts turning red as she draws blood from her owner.

The fear in Jeremy's eyes is what makes me finally end his suffering. Not that I care, but knowing he died in absolute fear is my ultimate goal, so I let Thana take her kill, slicing her across Jeremy's neck.

His cries turn into familiar gurgles as he chokes on his own blood while it rushes from his arteries, quickly ending his life.

There's no turning back for Princess now. She has the taste for human blood, so I toss the rest of the sausages onto Jeremy's lap and close her inside the bedroom with him, before I sneak out the way I came in.

JARED

Griff is fucking with me. He has to be, to have made me drive Dee around like this. She was silent as always while we drove from Fox Pines to Redfield to a strange house in a middle-class suburban area. I can't for the life of me think why she has to go to this house. What 'job' is she doing in there for the Marx Crew? Even after reading the contents of the envelope, I'm none the wiser. There are no instructions, just details about some dude named Jeremy who apparently lives at this address. There was something about this guy being a member of Carnal Unicorn. I have no idea what that is, but it doesn't sound good. Yet, still, I have no idea what that has to do with Dee being here.

Is she going inside to steal something? Is that her specialty? Maybe there's classified documents inside that Griff wants. This guy works at a bank, so maybe they are planning a bank robbery.

Fucked if I know.

I wait for about twenty-five minutes before I see Dee's small frame emerge from the back of the house as she creeps along the fence line, hugging the shadows. She stops at a tree, and I squint my eyes to try to see better through the dark, but I can't really tell what she's doing until she steps out from the shadows a few minutes later wearing different clothes with her backpack slung over her shoulder.

When she gets in the car, my eyes widen as I take in her face, and the red smears over her skin.

"Is that blood? What the fuck happened?" I hiss, reaching out to her, but she draws away, turning her focus out the front windscreen.

The interior light fades, blanketing us in darkness, so I reach out, gripping her shoulder with one hand to turn her to face me, while my other hand turns the interior light back on.

"That's blood, Dee." I hiss again, and her big brown eyes glare at me as she quickly flicks the interior light off again.

Then she points out the windscreen, indicating for me to drive.

"Are you hurt?"

Nothing.

"Dee? Are you fucking hurt?"

She shakes her head.

"Then whose blood is that?"

Slowly, Dee turns her head back to me, shooting me a glare, which I return. She has smears and speckles of blood on her face, but she seems fine. She isn't shaking and doesn't seem scared or the least bit rattled.

"Dee?"

She frowns this time and points aggressively out the windscreen, so I do my job and turn back into her chauffeur and drive her back to Fox Pines without another word being spoken.

It's safe to say I didn't sleep a wink once I snuck back into my house in the early hours of Thursday morning. My mind conjured up so many different scenarios as to why Dee went inside that house and came out with blood on her face. Most of them were unthinkable.

When I decide to give up on sleep, I drag my exhausted arse out to the kitchen where my parents are already going through the motions of their daily routine, both quiet as they try to figure out how they have to go another day without Tim being here.

It should have been me. I fought over shotgun in the car that day. Tim was older, so he should have been in the front, but I knew it pissed him off getting shoved in the back seat, so I did everything I could to steal the front seat from him.

My parents had laughed, mum waving from the front door as Dad drove us away, taking us to the Monster Truck show in Redfield.

We never made it.

An approaching truck was speeding and took the bend too wide. It tipped and rolled. We were too close to stop in time and the rear part of our car ended up colliding with the truck as my dad tried to swerve.

Tim never stood a chance in the back seat. Crushed to death. Literally.

Nausea rolls my stomach as I let my brain go back to the day that changed my life forever.

"Oh, my goodness."

My mum's gasp draws my attention, and I come to stand behind her and my dad as they watch a breaking news story on the TV.

Mr Jeremy Dalton, local loans officer at the Victoria Bank in Redfield, has been found dead in his home this morning. Sources say, a neighbouring dog walker dropped by this morning to pick up Princess, Mr Dalton's chihuahua, only to find the poor little dog locked inside Mr Dalton's bedroom. What makes this case disturbing is that it looks like little Princess had been feasting off Mr Dalton's dead body throughout the night, but authorities have confirmed it wasn't the cause of his death. Authorities have confirmed that the cause of death was a knife wound and are investigating if Mr Dalton's death is linked to the disturbing images found on his phone of him and his dog. There were also a number of paedophilic dolls found in Mr Dalton's bedroom, as well as illegal video files on his laptop that investigators believe is linked to his death.

If you have any information that can assist the police, please call Crime Stoppers.

Holy fucking shit!

The image on the screen is the house that I drove Dee to last night. A house that Dee went inside and came out of with blood on her face.

Fucking hell. Dee did that. Dee killed that man last night while I waited in the car. What the fuck have I gotten myself into?

Not only did I have a hand in killing Pike, but now I'm an accessory to another murder. How the fuck did my life end up like this?

I turn on my heel, locking myself in the bathroom as any thoughts of food dash away. I feel like I could hurl. I feel like I could scream and punch something.

My parents are oblivious to my inner turmoil as they call their goodbyes and head to their jobs for the day, while I stay slumped on the cold tiled bathroom floor wondering what the fuck to do with this information, and if I should do anything at all.

I decide to ditch school. There's no way I can walk in there and pretend like I didn't have a hand in a man's death last night, so I throw on some clean clothes and drive out to

Woodall Lake where I sit under a tree and stare out at the water for the majority of the day.

When I decide there's nothing for me to do but pretend I know nothing about what happened, I go back to my car, passing the barbeque shelter I had Dee bailed up in only last week.

She seemed so innocent that day. Almost like she'd never been touched that way before. But it must have been an act, right? For her to know key players in Victoria's underworld, and to have murdered a man last night, she must be well experienced at just about everything.

I get a fucking semi from thinking about my hand rubbing between Dee's legs, and I want to punch myself in the face for feeling… what? Turned on?

Am I turned on even while knowing she killed someone last night?

I'm fucking sick in the head.

Driving back to Fox Pines once I know the school day has finished, I find myself pulling up outside the dance studio. I don't know why. It wasn't my intention to come looking for Dee, yet here I am, getting out of my car and entering the studio.

As always, it's busy inside. I climb the stairs to the second floor, noticing Caleb turning to me as I approach.

"Hey, man. I wasn't sure if you were gonna come back," Caleb states, wearing a grin.

I shrug. "I've had a few things going on. Made it hard to get here."

"Yeah. Year twelve is hard work."

I nod, not really agreeing, because in comparison to the rest of the shit I'm dealing with, school seems like the easiest thing right now.

I subtly ignore Caleb, turning my attention to the viewing

window, my eyes instantly locking onto Dee. I try to watch her through new eyes, through eyes that know she's a killer, but all I see is a seventeen-year-old girl hiding in the back corner as she does the one thing that seems to bring her a slither of happiness.

She looks like she hasn't slept, darkness shadowing under her eyes. Maybe she is a killer, but it's possible it brings her nightmares. Perhaps she has a heart, or perhaps she's just a good fucking actress. Or perhaps she has no other choice, and like me, she's just doing what she has to do to get through another day alive.

After the class, I'm about to leave when I see Dee approach her dance teacher and hold up her phone. Her teacher looks at Dee's screen before nodding, saying something to her, and Dee gives her a nod in return before the teacher leaves Dee alone in the room, closing the door behind her.

I stand close to the glass, watching Dee approach the viewing window. It looks like she's looking straight at me, but I know she can't see me as she draws the curtain shut, blocking my view.

I take that opportunity to leave, not wanting Dee to know I was there.

I don't even know why the fuck I went there in the first place.

21

DEE

Things have been quiet for the last couple of days. Jared was a no show at school yesterday, and when he doesn't show again today, I cave and ask Rhys to find out if he's ok. It turns out he's been ghosting his mates too, and they are on a mission to find out what his problem is.

I could have sworn I felt his eyes on me while I was in my dance class yesterday afternoon. But that's stupid, right? He hates me, so why would he even bother coming to watch? Which is a good thing, isn't it? It's what I wanted, yet it hurts the centre of my chest, and I don't understand why.

Surely, he's put two and two together and realised what I did when I went inside that house the other night. Soon enough, he won't even bother thinking about me or my existence, which is what I wanted. He's a distraction I don't need.

I've been messaging Travis, trying to get him to talk to me, but he won't message back, so after school I decide to hunt him down while he does community service with Lexi.

Today they are working in the garden beds outside the art block. It's been a hot day, and the mountains surrounding

Timber Valley are lined with angry clouds, while distant thunder rumbles roll across the sky.

"What the fuck are you doing here?" Travis hisses when he glances up to see me approaching.

I raise a single brow at his less than cheery mood and hold up my phone.

"I thought the fact that I haven't replied to your thousands of messages was a fucking clear message, Ell."

Inwardly sighing, I hold my screen up towards him to show him my note.

'Have you asked your sister how she got into whoring? Have you asked her if she keeps all the money for herself?'

I'd gone over this topic in my messages, trying to get Travis to see what's really going on with his foster family. Trying to get him to see that they aren't a real family and he's on the wrong side.

"Mind your own fucking business." Travis hisses again, but the interesting thing is, he doesn't turn away from me. He could totally end this conversation by giving me his back, but he doesn't. He waits for me to respond, so I hold up my phone with my response.

'Ask her.'

Travis glares at me, clenching his jaw tight like he wants to call me every name under the sun.

I hold up my phone again. *'Just ask her. What do you have to lose?'*

"How about my fucking balls?" he hisses, his face turning red in anger.

'If you ask me, you have no balls since you're too chicken to ask her.'

He growls.

I tap out another note and hold it up.

'I have enough money to look after us, Travis. You can go back to school and get your diploma. Go to Uni if you want.

There's still time for you to choose a different path. We can disappear and have new identities. A whole new life, anywhere in the world. All you have to do is agree to come with me on March sixth.'

Travis frowns. "The day you turn eighteen?"

I nod.

"Why would I go anywhere with you after what you did?" Travis' voice still sounds angry, but he's not yelling now, and he almost seems less hateful.

'You know I had no choice.'

He scoffs. "You had a fucking choice, Ell."

I tap out my response. *'You're right. I chose our dad and you.'*

"Yet all that was left was me. You fucking took everything from me." Travis throws the spade he's holding across the grass with angry force.

'I had to stop her, Travis.'

"You didn't have to kill her."

His words almost make me break. Not from what he says, but the way he says it.

He sounds everything like the nine-year-old boy I left behind.

'I never meant that. You know I didn't. She was killing Dad. She would have turned her rage on us next. Hell, she did turn her rage on us. If I hadn't stepped in, we'd all be dead.'

"No. You're wrong. She would have turned her rage on *you*. Not me. She would never have hurt me."

I frown. Doesn't he remember?

'But she did hurt you. All the time. Don't you remember?'

"Stop spitting your fucking lies and fuck off!" Travis sneers in my face, his hot breath hitting me with his rage. But then, as if he's flipped a switch, he sucks in a breath, and strolls off across the grass to where he threw his spade. "I have work to do."

I watch him for a moment. I watch how he ignores me, moving back to the garden bed to continue his work, just as Lexi rounds the corner, her blue eyes looking concerned.

Shit. Did she just overhear that conversation? Or at least the part of it that Travis spoke?

I decide to play dumb and dash off quickly to find my foster mum, hoping Lexi only heard Travis telling me to fuck off. My foster mum, Cynthia, is leaving early today. Apparently, she has a date night with William for Valentine's Day, and she needs to get the twins ready and dropped off at their friend's place for a sleepover.

As I go through the motions of Cynthia driving me home, I think back over my conversation with Travis to establish what Lexi may have heard. The words *'you didn't have to kill her'* cause my heart to sink, not just because of the possibility that Lexi may have overheard them, but because Travis still thinks I did it on purpose. I guess it's possible he's repressed the memories, which means I have to find a way to dig them out of his brain if I'm ever going to have a chance of getting him to leave with me.

When we get home, we find the house in some sort of Valentine's Day chaos with red balloons everywhere, some floating and butting the ceiling, while others skitter across the floor as we walk by.

"What on earth?" Cynthia asks as we enter the living room to find William and the twins packing some food.

"Don't ask." William grumbles while the twins giggle.

"It's Rhysie's boyfriends. They are celebrating Valentine's Day," Connor offers.

"Of course they are." Cynthia grumbles, but still smiles, shaking her head.

"And we aren't allowed to go to our room because they are giving her a present in our lounge room," Archie explains, brushing his dark hair back off his forehead.

Cynthia's brows shoot up as she makes eye contact with her husband, and they have a silent conversation with their eyes.

I could risk it and go to my bedroom. I'm pretty confident that I could find my bedroom with my eyes closed. My ears, however, will pick up every sound, and from the muffled noises I can hear coming from the kids' end of the house, tells me I don't want to risk it.

While Cynthia and Will continue to get things ready for the twins, I gesture for the boys to follow me outside, and we spend some time hand balling the footy while the twins *ooh* and *ahh* each time they see a flash of lightning in the distance or hear a rumble of thunder.

By the time Rhys and her group of boyfriends emerge, Cynthia and William are ready to leave, the twins packed and ready for their sleepover. I give them a quick wave and dart out of the room, desperate to get some alone time in the confines of my bedroom.

Rhys and her guys hang around the house for a bit, their voices floating to me through the closed door as they discuss which of the many parties they are going to go to tonight, or if they should just spend the night fucking.

I really want to tell them to go to a party. Anything to avoid having to overhear their intimate sessions together, but I realise I'm too late, as Rhys announces rather loudly that she wants to turn off all the lights in the house and fuck through the storm which has finally made its way to settle over the top of us.

While they go at it once again, I slip my earbuds in and listen to music as I settle in to do some work on my side hustle. I've barely made a dent in my work when I get a message from the one and only, Griffin Marx.

Griffin Marx

Really? Sausages?

Dee Porter
What? Princess was hungry.

Griffin Marx
Stop it! I can't unsee what I saw!

Dee Porter
You saw? How?

Griffin Marx
I have my ways.

Dee Porter
Right. Corrupt cops. Got it.

Griffin Marx
I wouldn't say corrupt exactly. He knows the right side to work for. That's all.

Dee Porter
Corrupt.

I know we need people on the inside in order to get things done and keep certain things covered up, but it doesn't mean I have to like it. Most of the cops that help us under the table are only doing it for one thing. Money. If someone comes along with a higher offer, they will take it and turn their backs on us without a second thought.

The Marx family has connections in high places, though. I'm sure whoever is helping them has a secret the Marx family is holding over their heads should they choose to be disloyal. It's the way of the underworld.

Griffin Marx

How's your boyfriend? Did he ask any questions?

Dee Porter

Not my boyfriend! And no, he didn't ask anything.

It's a lie, but I'm not about to throw Jared under the bus. He's not meant to be in the world Griffin and I are in. He's naturally curious, and he can't hide the part of him that has a big heart and cares. He was genuinely worried about me when I showed up with blood on my face. I'm not going to punish him for that.

Griffin Marx

Good. I notice he hasn't been at school for the last couple of days. Do you think he's a flight risk? Or has a loose tongue?

Dee Porter

He's processing. Definitely not a flight risk and doesn't have a loose tongue. He knows the deal.

The deal being that his family will suffer if he steps out of line.

My heart sinks at that knowledge. His family has nothing to do with this, and I hate that they are involved now, even though they don't know it. It's not fair to them or Jared. He never asked for this.

Dee Porter

How do you know he hasn't been at school?

Griffin Marx

I have eyes everywhere, kid. That, and I've had one of my guys tailing him.

Interesting.

Dee Porter
So where was he instead of being at school? At his house?

Griffin Marx
Nope. He drove out to Lake Woodall. He spent the last two days staring out at the water.

My heart sinks.
Jared is hurting.
Because of me.

22

JARED

I've been driving around for hours. There are three different parties tonight and all I've done is drive past them about five fucking times. How can I go into a party and pretend like I didn't have a hand in killing two guys in the last week?

Travis has called me every day and, like a fucking wimp, I've ghosted him. What the fuck am I meant to say to him? I like Travis, I do, but because of my involvement with him, and his fucking sister—which still blows my mind—my life is no longer my own. Not if I want to keep my family safe.

I make another left and notice the car behind me doing the same. Shit. They've been behind me for a while now. I turn right up the next street, and the car behind does the same, so I slam on the brakes in the middle of the road and throw my car into park before leaping out.

The other car has stopped behind me and it takes me a moment to glare past the headlights to realise it's Garrett's car. When the hell did he get his license?

He gets out.

"You ready to talk to us yet?" Garrett's big frame steps in front of the headlights, giving me a better glimpse.

"What the fuck, man? Why are you following me? And since when do you have a license?"

"Got it a few days ago, and I'm following you because something is up with you, and you keep fucking dodging us." Garrett frowns, looking at me with disappointment.

Shit. I fucking miss my mates, but I feel like there's this big void between us these days. I didn't even think they would notice my absence. Still, I can't help but be reminded of the main reason I stay away from them. That reason being the girl they share and seem to only have time for.

"Shouldn't you be celebrating Valentine's Day with your bitch?" I hiss, letting my anger come to the surface.

Garrett's lip curls. "You wanna fucking rephrase that, man? Don't fucking talk about my girl like that."

"Fuck. Sorry." I shake my head, looking down at my feet, feeling like the fucking arsehole I am.

"Let's drive up to the lookout." Garrett suggests and I glance back up at him.

"The lookout? I'm not into you like that, bro." I try to joke and Garrett laughs.

"Just follow me arsehole. Let's get out of this stuffy town for a spell."

"That actually sounds like a good idea." I nod, feeling something like relief as Garrett nods back and makes his way back to his car.

I take the lead, Garrett following behind in his car as we drive out of town to Timber Valley Lookout. During the day, you can see the entire Timber Valley region below, including the towns of Redfield and Fox Pines, as well as the beautiful shimmering water of Redfield Lake, and Lake Woodall, and the surrounding fields and rolling hills.

At night, it just looks like a blanket of lights in some

sections, and total darkness in others. The lookout is a common spot for couples or groups of friends to meet, as long as someone has a license to drive up there.

Tonight, on Valentine's Day, it's busy. Cars line the lookout, some in the more open car park, while others are hiding under the trees. Some cars are bouncing, some have steamed-up windows, while others have couples laying back on the bonnet and windshield, chatting and enjoying the view.

Music floats in through my open window as I drive further along, trying to find a free space for two cars. It's the first time I've been up here since getting my license. My dad used to drive us up here sometimes for Sunday drives when I was a kid. Back when Tim was alive. He stopped after Tim died.

Everything stopped after Tim died.

I find some vacant spots finally, so I pull in and Garrett pulls in next to me. Getting out of my car, I suck in the fresher air up here, although it's still a little humid after the storm earlier.

"So, Grady is freaking out." Garrett doesn't waste any time getting straight to the point. "You've been best mates ever since you were kids. Why are you avoiding him?"

Sighing, I mumble, "like he's even noticed. Just like the rest of you, he's too wrapped up in Rhys' pussy."

Garrett growls. "I'm not going to fucking ask you again to respect my girl, Crowley. Are you feeling left out? Is that it? Are you pissed that Rhys didn't include you, too?"

"What?" I shriek, turning my eyes from the lights of the valley to my mate. "No! Fuck." I shake my head. "I *am* feeling left out, but not like that."

"Then what is it like?"

I fall quiet as I struggle to hold back my emotions, trying

to swallow the golf ball sized lump in my throat before I speak. "I'm fucking lonely, man."

Garrett's brows shoot up as he studies me.

"I miss my mates." I whisper as my eyes start to heat. "I'm struggling. I've been struggling. The Lexi stuff. The Mike stuff. Now…"

"Now?" Garrett asks and I sigh, shaking my head as I turn my sights back to the lights below.

"It doesn't matter." I can't tell him about the Dee stuff. I can't tell him that I have blood on my hands now.

"It does matter. Something has happened. Does it have to do with Dee? Rhys told us what you told her about Travis being Dee's brother and that she's only here to get him to leave with her soon."

I stay quiet.

"You lost your shit because Daniel and his mates were talking about Dee." Garrett observes. "You like her? Is that it?"

"No, I don't fucking like her. She's a fucking psycho." Even as I say the words, they taste sour on my tongue.

Garrett frowns. "Why do you say that?"

"Never fucking mind." I grumble, crossing my arms over my chest like a pissy toddler pouting. *Jesus, I'm lame.*

"Why won't you tell me?" Garrett nudges my shoulder with his, and I risk glancing back at him.

"Because I can't, ok. Just forget it. I'll be fine. I'm gonna go hit up a party." I stand from the car.

"You mean one of the parties you've driven past ten thousand times already?" Garrett smirks and I narrow my eyes.

"Yes."

I don't wait to hear if Garrett says anything else, instead I get back in my car and get the hell out of there. Garrett doesn't follow.

I drive back to each party I've been past tonight, and still, I don't pull over and go in. I can't bring myself to face the hordes of drunk or high teenagers. I can't bear the thought of the girls coming on to me, or guys forcing beer down my throat.

After driving around for another hour, I somehow find myself pulling up across from Dee's house. I don't even remember driving here, but as I turn the motor off, I feel like I finally wake up.

For some reason, I want to see her. I have no idea why, but I find myself getting out of my car, crossing the street and sneaking through her back gate. Sticking to the shadows along the fence line, I creep deeper into the yard until the warm glow of light flows out from a window. Dee's window.

There, on the other side of the glass, is Dee. She's wearing a singlet tonight, her creamy arms exposed as she sits at a desk doing what I assume is homework. She always has her arms covered, so it's nice to see them bare. I'm too far away to get a good look, though. Too far away to see the scars lining the underside of her forearms.

I can hear muffled music coming through her closed window, and her head bobs with the beat for a few moments before her head lifts and she turns in her chair.

Wait. Are her lips moving?

I take a step closer, trying to stay in the shadows, but also trying to see if my eyes are deceiving me. Is she singing? I can't hear her singing, but the way her throat moves as her lips part tells me she is.

She looks back down at whatever she is writing, and then she puts the pen down and stops the music on her phone, getting up from the chair before music starts playing again. Then, she starts dancing.

She doesn't have much space in her bedroom, but she still moves about her room like she isn't confined to its walls.

Watching her dance is mesmerizing, and for a moment, I'm in awe. That is, until I remember the situation we are in, and I feel nothing but fucking pissed off.

How can she be so fucking calm after what has happened this week?

I can't understand it, which just reminds me that I know nothing about this girl that I seem to be so infatuated with. As annoying as her carefree mood is, I can't make myself look away. As she moves, letting her body express how she feels with the music, I watch her lips move every so often.

What I'd give to hear her voice.

Fuck, I feel like I'd sell my soul to the devil at this point.

I linger like a fucking peeping Tom for a little longer, before giving up and going back to my car to drive home.

I can't deal with anyone else tonight, so the best thing for me to do is lock myself away and hope that tomorrow is better.

When I get home, I find my mum snoring on the couch with an empty bottle of wine on the table next to her while dad watches the golf channel in his recliner, smoking a cigar. He doesn't even notice me there.

I wonder if it had been me that died in the car accident if they would have walked around like the zombies they are after losing Tim. I know they love me. Hell, mum was frantic after Mike put me in the hospital. But love isn't enough, apparently.

Pain seems to outweigh it.

Fuck it. I'm going to bed.

23

DEE

Another storm rolls in around eleven when Cynthia and William get home. I'm the only one here, with Rhys off somewhere with her boyfriends, Charlotte with her girlfriend, and the twins at their friend's house. Cynthia and William come and see me briefly before retiring for the night, and if they were my real parents, I'd probably cringe at the lusty eyes they are giving each other, knowing too well what they will be doing once they go to their bedroom. But since they aren't, all I can see is two people who love each other unconditionally. Even after all this time.

I wonder if I'll ever be lucky enough to have something like that with someone. It doesn't seem very likely given I don't like to speak to anyone, but stranger things have happened… right?

I've never liked Valentine's Day, but I have to say, I especially don't like it this year. Even though I'm a solitary person, I can't help but wish I had someone to share the quiet moments with. It must be nice having that person who stands by your side facing the world together.

At around 1am, I slip on some black denim shorts and a

long sleeve mesh top over my black bra, before grabbing Thana and clipping my sheath in place around my waist. Given the situation with the Marx Crew and Travis, I'd be stupid to leave without it at this time of night.

I sneak out of my house, needing to complete some work on my side hustle, and I need a place that is enclosed and free of interruptions. I could use my foster parents' car, since it's right there in the garage, but I risk them hearing me, so I sneak away from my house and find myself outside Jared's a little while later.

It's not the first time I've used his car to finish off the work for my side hustle. I can't explain why I use his car and not someone else's. Maybe it's because it smells like him. Or maybe it's because I feel safe there.

Whatever it is, I try not to analyse it as I focus on the task I need to complete.

It's an older car, so it's easier to break into, and once I'm inside the cabin, I set myself up and get to work.

Jared's car is parked along the side of his driveway, under a tall tree, so it's relatively shaded by shadow, making it the perfect place for me to hide away.

I'm about ten minutes into my task when my phone vibrates with a message.

Griffin Marx

Need you at the Red Room.
Your driver will pick you up on the corner of your street in five minutes.

My eyes go wide as I realise what that means.

My driver is Jared, and I'm in his car.

I rush to quickly pack up my equipment, shoving them in my backpack as fast as I can before I open the car door. It's in that moment, that a grumpy-looking Jared rounds the corner of his garage, and I freeze, deer in headlights with half my body in, and half my body out of his car.

His eyes narrow as he skids to a stop. "What the fuck are you doing in my car?"

I clamp my lips tight, keeping silent as usual.

"Right. I forgot. You don't fucking talk. To me anyway." Jared glares, stalking up to me.

Gripping my arm, his eyes fall to my backpack, which is still on the seat behind me.

"Show me what's in there."

Shit. He can't see what I have, so I shake my head.

Pushing me away as he takes a step back, Jared hisses. "Fucking whatever. Get the fuck in so I can drive you to Redfield."

He's so angry. Bitter. Is it because he just got woken up? Or is he still struggling with what happened a few days ago?

As much as I'd like to think it's because his sleep got disturbed, I know it's not. Maybe it's not helping, but his anger has everything to do with knowing I killed Jeremy Dalton.

Jared rounds the car and climbs in, so I ease back into the seat, shutting myself in the space. As we drive to Redfield, the cabin remains quiet, so much so that I look over at Jared a few times to make sure he's still breathing. He is obviously, since the car is still driving, but not once does he look over at me or acknowledge me.

I have to admit, I hate how that feels.

Jared pulls the car around to the side parking lot at the Red Room, and we both silently get out. I quickly shift my sheath around, so Thana sits along the small of my back, and tug my mesh top down over it, hoping it's concealed enough not to be too noticeable.

Joining Jared at the back of the car, we walk side by side,

approaching the entrance and the bouncer on the door nods like he was expecting us.

We walk through the strip club, my eyes remaining above the crowd, hoping to avoid an eyeful of snatch or nipple, and I'm happy to see in my peripheral that Jared is doing the same. Not that it matters if he takes a look at the girls swinging on the poles or grinding on patrons' laps, but he needs to stay focused and alert, because if we've been called here by Griffin, then we are officially on duty.

At least that's what I'm telling myself.

At the end of the main room, Griffin is waiting for us by a door. As usual, he's wearing a suit and is impeccably groomed. It's a little too out of place for a seedy strip club, if you ask me.

Griffin doesn't say anything, just gives each of us a nod as we step through the door and follow him down a passage that has private rooms off each side.

The moaning coming from behind most of the closed doors is an indication of what's going on behind them, and my body betrays me, my cheeks flushing with a blush. I'm thankful Jared is behind me right now. I don't need him witnessing how my body reacts.

At the end of the passage, we go through another door and veer off to the left, taking the staircase to the second floor.

It looks like some sort of corporate private bar with a large conference table in the centre of the room and a moody lit bar off to the side.

I don't take in much more of the room, though. Not when my eyes are scanning the people sitting at the table. On instinct, I freeze, which doesn't give Jared any warning as he crashes into my back. His strong hands grip my shoulders as he steadies us, and then he gives me a little shove, urging me to keep walking in an abrupt way.

His attitude is really starting to piss me off.

"Come and take a seat." Griffin gestures to the two seats at the end of the table, while he continues up to the other end to the head of the table.

All eyes fall to me and Jared then. Angel eyes and Marx eyes.

Shit. This can't be good.

Even though the Marx family outnumber us here, I'm not concerned by their presence. I'm more concerned by the presence of Bec and Amanda Angel. Sisters and CEOs of Angel Org. The two women who are basically my bosses, or close enough to it if I had one.

Not able to handle seeing the serious looks on Bec and Amanda's faces, I glance at the other people sitting around the table as Jared and I take our seats. I don't miss the way Jared shifts his chair further away from mine like he can't stand to be near me.

Ouch.

At the end of the table, Griffin sits in between his cousin Devon, and his older brother, Conrad, while Griffin's younger brothers, Liam and Oswald, sit across from the Angels.

Jesus, it's always a shock to see how similar the Marx brothers look, even though they have three mothers between them. Their looks must come from the Marx side, which is why Devon, their cousin, also looks like he could be their brother.

"Hush." Amanda's voice gains my attention, and I cringe at her using that name. "We were a little surprised to find out you accepted Griffin's terms to work off your debt. It's very unlike you, and also, I thought you were on *vacation*." She shoots me a pointed look.

Fuck.

I hold up my phone. *'Please call me Dee.'*

Amanda's brows shoot up. "But you aren't *Dee* in this circle. You're Hush. I'm surprised you're being so reckless, which leaves me to think there's something else going on here."

I look to my side to see Jared frowning before I tap out my response. *'Jared doesn't know I'm Hush. No one in FP does, and I'd prefer to keep it that way.'*

Devon chuckles. "Well, kid. Jared is one of us now, so there's no point in keeping *that* part a secret."

"Wanna clue me in?" Jared asks from beside me, and I stiffen.

Griffin grins. "I really do like this one. He's got spark."

"What I've got is a lack of fucking patience." Jared hisses and they all laugh.

"Jared. Since you are new, let me introduce you to everyone." Bec offers him a warm smile. "I'm Bec, and this is my sister, Amanda. We are the Angel sisters." She gestures to the head of the table. "You know Griffin, of course, and his cousin Devon. On Griffin's other side is Conrad, and across from me are Oswald and Liam. Griffin's brothers."

"Me, Griff, Os, and Con are four of the nineteen Marx heirs." Liam offers, smiling at Jared as he leans back in his chair and loosens his tie.

"Eighteen." Oswald corrects, and Liam scoffs.

"Oh, come on. Grace is one of us."

"She's not an heir." Oswald turns in his seat and shoots his brother a dagger.

"None of that matters right now," Griffin grumbles.

"Am I meant to know who the Marx family is?" Jared asks, and my brows shoot up in surprise at his curt tone. If he's not careful, he's going to be eating a Marx fist soon.

"Probably not, since you're still so young, and the Marx family are new to this area," Amanda answers Jared. "They are very well known in the city and the northern and western sides of the state."

"We are a powerful family, Jared. It's better to be aligned with us than against us. Let's just put it that way." Conrad smirks, his demeanour relaxed as he slouches in his chair, the sleeves of his shirt rolled up as he brings a glass of amber liquid to his mouth.

"It's not like I was given a choice," Jared grumbles and Amanda nods.

"Yes, well, I'm not happy about that." She shoots a glare at Griffin, who shrugs, and she rolls her eyes before returning them to Jared. "Bec and I run Angel Org. We provide help and support to victims of heinous crimes and abuse, and the Marx family works with us to help maintain order across the state."

"Isn't that what cops are for?" Jared asks and Liam snickers.

"Even the police need policing."

"What Liam means," Oswald shoots his brother another glare, "is that crime is always going to happen and even police are corrupt, so there needs to be someone to govern over that."

"And that's you guys? Are you like, the mob or something?" Jared asks, sounding genuinely interested this time.

The Marx men all chuckle but don't answer Jared's question.

"And Hush," Bec takes over the conversation, "or Dee, as you know her, helps us with handling certain situations. Which brings me to why we're here." She turns her blue eyes to the other end of the table, honing in on Griffin. "Unfortunately, there seems to be some sort of confusion, because it's a well-known fact that all work for Hush goes through us, and the Dalton hit was definitely not run through us."

I sigh. Fucking hell. I was so close to getting out of this world. I just needed five damn weeks to convince Travis to run away with me and we would disappear.

"It aligns with the Vixen's Lodge case, which you are technically running, so in a way, she was also doing work for you, too." Griffin explains, looking smug, but a moment later it's wiped from his face as Bec slams her fist on the table.

"Work that we did not authorise! Hush is seventeen years old! She is still a child herself and yes, I know what she does to earn money, but we make sure to be very select with what we task her. Not to mention making sure there's decent time between jobs. We may not be able to stop her from doing what comes so naturally to her, but we can sure as shit control it so she doesn't fall in too fucking deep!"

A deafening silence settles in the air as Bec's words are absorbed. I've never seen her lose her temper like this before, and by the way each man at this table flinched as she spat her rage at them, I'd say they haven't seen this side of her either.

Amanda turns her attention to me. "Hush, you should have called us when these amateurs were trying to blackmail you. I would never have sent them if I knew they had an ulterior motive."

I do what I do best. I don't speak.

"You have nothing to say?" Bec asks, frowning at me.

"I do." Jared's voice makes me stiffen and I slowly turn to look at him.

"By all means. Let's hear it." Bec mutters.

Jared's blue eyes dart to mine for the briefest of moments. There's no anger in them this time. Not like earlier.

"I don't know much about what the fuck is going on, but I do know these arseholes left Dee," he stops and shakes his head, his eyes darting to me again before returning to Bec and Amanda, "I mean Hush, no choice but to accept their offer to work for them. There's no way she could have said no without something bad happening to her or someone she loves."

I turn back in time to see Amanda's blue eyes darken, turning to slits as she shifts her glare to Griffin. "Let me get this straight. After *I* asked for *your* services, which *I* pay *you* for, *you* took it upon yourself to take advantage of *my* consultant for your own gain? A young seventeen-year-old consultant by threatening her? What was it? She accepts your proposal, or she dies. Is that it?"

"You failed to tell us that we were doing a clean-up job for our fucking competitor and enemy." Devon hisses, leaning forward in his chair and shooting his own dark-eyed glare at Amanda.

Bec's brows hitch. "What?"

Griffin shoots his smirk my way before answering Bec. "It turns out the mess Hush found herself in involves her brother, who is the foster son of Douglas and Bianca Kerr."

The Angels' faces drop, shock contorting their expressions as their eyes dart to me.

"Excuse me, what?" Amanda asks, and I tap out a response on my phone before holding it up.

'My brother's foster parents are irrelevant. I'm here to get him away from them.'

"And then what? They will hunt you both down and kill you," Amanda deadpans.

'We will disappear. They won't be able to find us.'

"So, you want to run off with him? That's why you've been taking extra jobs? You needed the money to get set up?" Amanda's blue eyes widen, looking bigger than they already do, and a slither of guilt hits me. I didn't mean to lie to them. I just couldn't take the risk of being honest with them.

I shrug in response and Bec speaks up this time.

"When were you going to tell us?"

I stay silent, and Amanda nods.

"You weren't going to. You were just going to disappear."

Again, my silence tells them what they need to know.

"Does it annoy anyone else that she doesn't speak?" Liam Marx butts in, and his brothers and cousin chuckle.

"Yes." Jared growls, and they all chuckle again.

Naturally, my response to them is to flip them off, which just amuses the idiots more.

Bec ignores the immature men and turns back to me. "What about your other work? There are so many people that need you."

My face heats, and I know it must be turning red as my emotions remind me that I still care about the good I do for others. I tap out a response and hold up my phone.

'I haven't figured that part out yet.'

"You should have come to us. We would have helped you." Amanda sighs, sounding disappointed in me. I had thought about asking them for help, but the fewer people that knew about my brother, the better. It's the only way I knew how to keep him safe. It's not uncommon for loved ones to be used as leverage in the world I live in.

'I don't need help.'

Bec's brows lift in surprise at my response. "It kind of seems like you do."

Amanda turns to Griffin, pointing her long sharp nail in his direction. "What are you holding over her?"

"She has until her birthday to convince her brother to leave with her," Griffin states vaguely.

"And if she can't convince him to leave?" Amanda asks, and this time Devon answers.

"Then her brother has to choose sides. His family, or us."

"And if he chooses his foster family?" Amanda glares at

Devon, clearly getting annoyed with the Marx men only giving brief explanations.

"Then he dies." Griffin answers, and Bec shoots me a concerned look before turning to Griffin.

"What happens to Hush if her brother doesn't leave?"

Griffin takes a moment, rolling his tongue in his mouth, knowing his answer is going to piss the Angel sisters off. "She will be ours."

"Like fuck she will!" Amanda stands abruptly, her chair tipping over behind her with force.

"A deal is a deal." Griffin relaxes back in his chair, resting his elbows on the arms and linking his fingers together.

"You have no right to make that deal, or threat! She is strictly off limits to everyone." Amanda reminds Griffin, but he shakes his head.

"She's off limits until she turns eighteen, and then she's fair game. That was always the deal."

Fucking hell, why are they talking like they own me? This is how this world works, though, isn't it? Power. Ownership. Control.

Devon sits forward in his chair. "The moment she involved her brother, she became *our* problem."

"And what about this kid?" Bec points to Jared, who shifts uncomfortably next to me.

"I'm not a kid."

They ignore him.

"He's part of the deal, as well. If Hush doesn't disappear with her brother or he doesn't choose our side, then we own Jared, too."

I furiously tap out a response and hold up my phone.

'He's fucking innocent. He's not from this world. Just let him go, please.'

Griffin, Conrad and Devon lean closer to the table to read my words and Devon chuckles.

"Jared is not innocent. He has blood on his hands too, Hush. You know that. The only way we can ensure he keeps quiet is to control the narrative."

"Let me guess, you've threatened his family as well?" Amanda hisses, still standing, her hand on her hip as she glares at Devon.

Jared growls.

Griffin sighs. "It's business."

A wave of rage rushes over me and I have no control over my response as I stand and slam my hands on the table before grabbing up Amanda's glass and hurling it at Griffin's head. He ducks just in time as it sails past his head and smashes against the wall behind him, while Liam and Oswald shoot up from their seats with their guns drawn.

"You might want to remember whose table you're sitting at, kid." Devon chuckles, but I ignore him, leaping onto the table in one swift move to land in a crouch.

Slowly, cautiously, Griffin stands as I keep my death glare on him.

"You might be fast enough to get to me and slice my throat, kid, but you're not fast enough to get to my brothers before they fill you with lead." Griffin holds his hands up in front of him as I ignore his threat and stalk across the top of the table, pulling Thana from her sheath.

Amanda snickers, her voice coming from behind me now. "You've done it now. Pissing Hush off is never a good idea, Griff."

"Shut up, Manda. You're not fucking helping." Griff complains before I fall to one knee in the centre of the table and slam Thana into the surface.

With my eyes locked on Griffin's, I point back towards Jared, silently telling Griff that I'm not happy about them involving Jared.

Griff shakes his head slowly. "I'm sorry, kid. We can't let him walk."

Fury ignites my skin with red rage as I stand and stalk towards Griffin, leaving Thana still embedded in the tabletop. Griffin's eyes widen as I approach, my eyes never wavering from his as I crouch down and lean in close to his face with a sneer.

24

JARED

oly shit! Dee has turned crazed. She's in Griffin's face, and I swear she must have whispered something to him by the way he blanches.

And fuck, my dick is hard.

What the fuck is wrong with me?

Yes, it was hot the way Dee lost her temper, leapt on the table with the fluidity of a tiger, and made a clear fucking statement by slamming that huge fucking blade into the table.

And where the hell did she pull that from? I didn't see it on her earlier. How the fuck did she conceal it?

My head is swimming with what I've just learnt here tonight. I realise now how fucking far over my head I am. These aren't just nobodies. These are bad somebodies, and I'm mixed up in it.

"I don't take threats lightly, kid." Griffin rumbles, still looking surprised at whatever it was that Dee did or said.

Shit, did she speak to him? With her voice.

Fucking lucky prick. I wanna hear her voice. I want to be the one she shares that with. Not this motherfucker.

Dee slowly stands and I lean to the side to get a better view, not missing how she curls her lip at him before giving him her back and walking back across the table. She pulls that massive fucking knife out of the table's surface as she passes it, sliding it into some kind of holder at the small of her back, and her eyes land on me as she casually strolls to the end of the table before leaping back down and retaking her seat.

Fucking hell, she looks like a dark angel sent from the pits of hell to murder everyone.

I now have no doubt that I've been trying to capture the attention of an assassin. Or a serial killer. I haven't quite figured out which it is yet.

"Is he your fella, Hush? Is that why you're so protective of him?" Devon smirks as he stirs Dee, his eyes gesturing to me.

Dee ignores his question, placing her hands on the table as her eyes remain glued to Griffin.

"Let's get back on track." The tall blonde woman with the high slicked ponytail suggests. I think her name is Amanda.

"Yes. Let's." The shorter blonde, with her hair down in straight perfection, agrees with her sister.

"I think we've told you everything you need to know." Devon turns his attention away from Dee, to Bec.

"Hmmm." Bec taps her lip like she is considering something before her face hardens and she directs a scary fucking glare at Devon. "The problem is Dev, that *you* don't have the *authority* to overrule Angel Org. You might govern the underworld in the state of Victoria, but we govern the whole nation. Australia is one of the safest countries because of us. Don't forget *who* you have sitting at your table."

Devon blanches, and fuck, I suck in my lips, trying to hold in a laugh.

Nothing about this situation is funny, but seeing these

women hand the Marx fellas their balls is fucking entertaining.

"What would you have us do?" Griffin hisses. "We can't be seen to be covering up a murder for our opposition and get nothing in return."

Amanda nods. "Agreed. Because of that situation, I will allow you to use the expertise of Hush until her eighteenth birthday, at which time she will *not* owe you anything else." Amanda turns to Hush. "I'm sorry. I can't do anything about your brother. He has to choose his path."

Dee nods but points to me.

Amanda and Bec look at each other before Bec's blue eyes land back on Dee.

"Jared needs to comply. Devon is right. They can't be sure he will keep quiet. Honestly, if it were anyone else, they would have killed him already. They are doing you a favour by bringing him in."

My gut drops, and Dee stands abruptly, her head jerking in a shake.

Amanda sighs, her face falling with something that looks like sympathy as she speaks to Dee. "You know the Marx brothers are the better of two evils, Hush. You know they do more good than bad. Maybe your friend didn't choose a life like this, but you know as time goes on, he will have more than a crew that he works for. He will have a family who will watch out for him, and his family, too. You know they look out for their own."

Amanda's words sink in, confirming my worst fears. I'm stuck with the Marx Crew whether I like it or not. For good.

I'm about to freak the fuck out when Dee slams her fist on the table again, and I see a tear pop from her eye and roll down her cheek.

Shit. Is that tear for me?

"I'm sorry, Hush. You know the alternative." Bec states, although her tone is also sympathetic.

Dee quickly swipes the tear off her cheek, her chest rising and falling quickly as she tries to get control of her emotions. She gives Bec and Amanda a nod before flipping the men off around the table.

Devon growls, but Griffin chuckles and Dee turns to me, jerking her head in a gesture for me to follow her. I slowly stand, eyeing the men, whose eyes dart between me and Dee.

"Oh, and we won't be calling you Jared anymore." Griffin addresses me. "From now on, you will be known as Crow. And once Hush's eighteenth birthday hits, and you have shown you can be loyal to us, we will start paying you."

I glare at Griff, not having a choice but to accept this fate, and follow Dee out the door. I pay little attention to the moaning coming from the rooms we pass, or the naked women dancing on the stage, my head preoccupied with a clusterfuck of epic proportions.

Hurrying to my car, we stay silent as I pull out of the Red Room's car park with so much force that my wheels spin and the rear end snakes out.

I'm fucking furious. I may have learnt more tonight, but I still don't know everything and even though I should be avoiding this chick beside me and all the crazy she brings to my life, I find myself not wanting to drop her back home just yet. Part of me hates her for getting me involved in this shit, but part of me feels like we both had no choice. It's almost like fate or something like that would have pulled us together by some means, anyway.

Instead of staying on the highway back to Fox Pines, I take the turn I did earlier with Garrett towards the Timber Valley Lookout. I sneak a glance at Dee, waiting for her to give me a questioning look, but she doesn't give me anything. She makes no attempt to communicate with me, and I realise her brow is furrowed showing me that she's stuck in her head right now. I also notice her right leg jigging up and down, which is new. She hasn't shown me her anxious side before. I've never seen her so jittery.

Arriving at the lookout, most cars are gone now, given it's nearly 2:30am. There are a few along the tree lined cliff, so I drive up further to the end to make sure we are as alone as possible.

As soon as I pull my car to a stop, Dee leaps out, leaving the door open as she runs to the tree line and drops to her knees.

At first, I think she must need to throw up or something, but as I round the car, I find her wielding her knife, as she stabs the earth with it, over and over in a furious rage.

"Dee?"

At hearing my voice, she leaps up facing me, her dark hair whipping out with the force. Her chest is rising and falling, her dark eyes wide with rage as she lets it consume her.

"Hey, don't fucking turn your death glare on me. You dragged me into this, not the other way around."

With a silent snarl, Dee leaps forward, shoving me back hard, and I grab her wrists as I stumble, bringing her with me and swing her around, before shoving her back against the side of my car.

"I'll fight you if you want a fight, Dee. I don't care if you're a girl."

I mean, I do, but I'm pretty sure she could kill me before I even blink if she really wanted to.

I cage her in, and she bares her teeth in a hiss, and fuck it, I like that she made a noise.

Wait. No, I don't. I don't fucking like her.

"Instead of snarling at me like a fucking animal, why don't you talk to me?" I growl and she just continues to glare, her chest heaving in rage.

"I fucking know you can talk. You whispered something to Griffin earlier, didn't you?"

Slowly, she starts to relax, and a sinister smirk crosses her features.

I realise I should be really fucking scared of this fiery creature. Even the big, bad Marx brothers seem skittish around her. She could probably slit my throat and bleed me dry before I even realise what's happening. But there's a part of me that thinks she won't hurt me. Hell, she was fighting for me in that room before.

Still, she remains quiet, which does nothing but fill me with rage, and I lose my temper.

"Fucking talk to me!"

She regards me this time, her head tilting slightly as she takes me in, but still not a word falls from her mouth. It pisses me off beyond belief, and before I can second guess myself, my hand whips out and wraps around her throat.

Instead of looking scared, Dee juts up her chin in challenge.

"Tell me to stop." I hiss, and when she makes no attempt to move or speak, I palm her breast, not so gently.

Her response is to keep her chin held high.

Fuck.

"Tell me you don't want me to touch you." I lean in closer, dragging my hand down her body, coming to the top of her jeans while the hand around her throat gives a little squeeze. I flick the button open, and still, she makes no attempt to stop me.

"Do you want me to touch you under your clothes tonight, Dee? Or should I say, Hush?" I draw out the name Hush, seeing a little flicker of something in her eyes. With a need to push her further, I ease the zipper down on her black denim shorts, keeping my eyes locked on hers.

Again, she makes no attempt to stop me.

"Or should I call you, Ell?"

She frowns.

Yes. Finally, a reaction.

"No? Not Ell." I tilt my head to the side, studying her. "Why does your brother call you Ell? What the fuck is your real name?"

I release her neck and hook my fingers in her shorts, raising my brow at her in question. Still, she doesn't speak, so I lean in closer, feeling her breath fan across my lips.

"Tell me to stop." I push her shorts down, panties and all.

I hear the breathy intake of air she sucks into her lungs, and fuck my dick weeps at knowing I'm getting a reaction from her.

Fucking traitorous dick. Of course, it wants to walk on the wild side and sink into a fucking assassin's cunt.

I lower to my knees as I push her shorts all the way down before I lift her foot and drag off her Converse shoe before doing the same with the other. My eyes come face to face with her pussy and the small patch of dark hair sitting above it, and my dick jerks again with an untamed hunger.

My gaze flicks up to her face, latching onto her big dark pools that watch me as I pull her shorts completely free of her body.

"How many guys have you spread these pretty thighs for?" I ask, licking my lips as I run my hand up her bare, smooth calf. "Do you like to be eaten, Dee? Do you like feeling the sweep of a tongue over your sensitive little clit?"

Her nostrils flare as her breathing increases, and I part her legs further, almost expecting her to fight me, but she lets me spread her wider, her eyes wild with what I think could be excitement. It's hard to tell in the dull light.

Slowly, I drag my finger up the front of her bare leg and over her hip, before spreading my hands out to palm the round globes of her arse.

Her breath hitches, so I give a little squeeze, not able to hide my smirk before changing direction back over the curve of her hips.

"Tell me to stop." My voice is deep and quieter, not as menacing as it was a minute ago, and I move my sights back to the place of heaven I most want to touch.

Slowly, gently, I brush my finger over her skin, feeling it pebble with goosebumps as I draw closer to her needy flesh. My dick jerks again as I slowly drag my finger over the top of her folds before sinking in between them a little to find her hot and wet.

Her breath hitches again, and I glance up to see her biting her lip as she watches me.

"Tell me to stop."

She doesn't.

With two fingers, I circle her clit, and a whimper escapes her before she slaps her hand over her mouth.

I chuckle, and my dick weeps.

"Just give in, Dee. Talk to me. Scream at me. Moan for me. I know you want to."

She gives me nothing else, so I pull my fingers back, holding them up so she can see them glistening.

"Look how wet you are for me." I give them a little wiggle before sliding them in my mouth and moan. "Mmm, you taste like heaven."

She drops her hand from her mouth, her lips parted as she silently pants, her eyes wide with what I think is curiosity mixed with lust. She can stay silent, but her body doesn't lie. It's telling me everything I need to know. So, I lean forward and press my lips to her clit.

I don't hold back, gripping her bare arse as I hitch one of her legs over my shoulder to open her up and bury my face in her cunt.

My tongue lashes at her, licking a path from back to front and around her sensitive nub.

A husky moan falls from her lips, and fuck, my dick jerks at the sound, and that's all I need to know before I let myself go completely and drown in her. With my lips and tongue devouring her, I bring one hand back around and slip my middle digit into her heat, and fuuuck she's tight.

Dee jerks a little at my intrusion, another husky noise escaping her which just turns me into a crazed beast, devouring my prey. I eat and lick and suck as my finger fucks her, my tempo increasing as her body responds and takes what it needs. Her pleasure rises quickly, either because she was already turned on and halfway there before I made contact, or perhaps she's not used to being touched like this.

But that can't be it. You can't tell me someone with the skills to assassinate who lives in the world of criminals, and looks as naturally beautiful as she does, doesn't get regular action.

I could put more thought into that, but the squeeze of her inner walls around my digit gains my focus and before I know it, her walls start spasming as she explodes, a husky cry floating up into the night sky.

My dick is throbbing with need as she comes down from her high, and I ease back from her heat, slipping my finger free. I glance from her pussy and up to her big dark eyes, shooting her a shit-eating grin as her chest heaves.

"Happy Valentine's, Dee."

DEE

The first time I let a guy between my legs, and it's mostly with his tongue. I never knew it would feel like that. It was... I can't even think of a word that can describe how amazing it felt.

I've touched myself, and inserted a finger a few times before, but Jared's finger is thicker than mine. Longer too, and it did this curly thing pressing into me and fuck, it felt... epic. Jesus, is the word epic even enough to describe what I just felt?

I know I was more vocal this time. I couldn't find it in me to care. Fuck, if he had asked me one more time to speak, I think I would have given in.

Heat warms my cheeks as Jared grins up at me, his chin glistening under the moonlight from having his mouth between my legs.

How can I sever dicks, slice throats and gut other humans, yet feel fucking embarrassed about what he just did to me?

And hell, I forgot it was Valentine's Day. I mean, I knew it was earlier because of Rhys and her fellas, but that's about as close to celebrating Valentine's as I've ever come.

Slowly, Jared stands, his eyes remaining locked with mine as he hovers over me, caging me in against his car again, and I have to crane my neck back to look up into his eyes.

"How many have you let eat you, Dee?"

I'm not sure if he genuinely wants to know, or if he's just trying to shock me into speaking. I feel like it's the latter, so I keep my mouth clamped shut.

He takes my hand and moves it between us, pressing my palm to his straining dick still locked away under his jeans. Christ, it's big. And hard. And my pussy throbs like it's coming alive again.

"How many dicks have you ridden? How many have you sucked?"

Now would be a good time to tell him none, zero, zilch. But of course, I keep that to myself.

I let him slide my hand up and down over his jean clad length, nervousness picking up my heart rate.

Does he want to fuck me? Is that what's happening here? Will he get angry when I say no?

"Do you wanna suck mine?" He grips our hands around the outline of his dick, pushing into our palms to cause more friction. "Would you let me do that, Dee? Sink my dick into this pretty little mouth of yours?"

With his other hand, he runs his finger over my lower lip before sliding it inside my mouth.

"Suck my finger, Dee. Suck your juice off it."

I do as he says, not really needing to think twice about it. It's like a compulsion I can't control, my lids fluttering closed as I taste myself on his finger.

Hell, there's something really hot about that.

"Fuck. I should just bend you over my car and fuck you so hard you have no choice but to scream my name." He grits his teeth, watching where his finger disappears. "Because you will, Dee. When I finally fuck you, I need you to know I won't stop until I hear your voice. You fucking owe me that after what you and your brother have gotten me into."

My eyes widen and I jerk back, letting his finger pop free.

"I don't mean the fucking part." Jared shakes his head quickly. "I mean the screaming my name part. You owe me your voice."

I glare at him, but he ignores it, his blue eyes falling to my lips.

"I wanna fuck that mouth so bad."

Butterflies rush through me, and my core clenches at his words. A knowing flutter builds again between my legs and before I even realise, I find myself easing him back and falling to my knees.

"Fuck." Jared hisses, his eyes softening in surprise, almost as if he's about to change his mind. I get it. He's trying to push me, thinking I won't submit.

I've never done this before, and never really wanted to either, but right now, I want it so bad. I can't make sense of how I'm feeling. The thoughts of wanting to lick Jared's dick and taste it is foreign to me. Hell, I haven't even seen his dick yet. How can I want it so bad if I haven't even seen it or touched its flesh yet? Is that normal?

I peer up through my lashes as I set to work on his button and fly, and his eyes dart back and forth from my eyes to my hands as his excitement grows. He helps me with his jeans, tugging them and his jocks down, releasing his erection, which bobs before my face.

I flinch back away from it. Not just to avoid getting whacked in my face by it, but also because that thing is huge. Is it meant to be that big?

I mean, I know it is, but I've never been this close to one I actually want to do something sexual to, so I'm kind of freaking out, but at the same time, I'm so drawn to it.

"You think it will fit, Dee?"

My eyes flick up to his.

"Open your mouth and show me your tongue." His voice is husky, and I can only assume it's from arousal. I don't typically like being told what to do, but there's just something about this situation that I'm here for, so I do as he asks, dropping my jaw open and easing my tongue out.

His brows shoot high like he wasn't expecting me to obey so easily, and he moans, wrapping his hand around his shaft. He pumps it a few times, and my need to feel him becomes almost overwhelming, so I will my hand to stop trembling, and I wrap mine just above his.

He moans at my touch, his eyes falling shut briefly before he drops his hand away, and I continue to pump his cock. Even though his dick is hard, his skin is soft and tight, and the urge to lick him takes me by surprise.

When Jared opens his eyes again, they latch onto mine, watching me.

"I've dreamed of seeing you down there on your knees for me. Fuuuck, if you only knew the things I've dreamed of doing to you." Pushing his hips forward, his dick hovers just before my lips, and I take him by surprise when I flick my tongue over his tip. His dick jerks and he thrusts forward involuntarily, leaving me with a split second to react, so I open my mouth wide and let him sink in a little.

Oh wow. It really is big.

"Fuck, Dee," he pants, darting his hands out to hold himself up against his car while keeping me caged in.

I don't really know what I'm doing, so I do what feels right, and I take cues from the way he moves and the sounds he makes. I swirl my tongue around the rim of his head and give it a suck before letting him sink in deeper.

One of his hands fists into my hair, pulling tight, and shit, that has the opposite effect I thought it would, setting me alight. With a building fever deep inside me, I let him sink further as he thrusts into my hand and mouth.

"Eyes on me, Deranged."

I shoot him a dagger, and he grins.

"Thatta girl."

Shit. Why is that so hot? And why do I secretly love the way he calls me Deranged? It probably makes me a weirdo or something for liking that, and the way he is rough and almost unhinged. Hell, it seems to speak to my soul, and I find I don't need any more guidance to devour his dick. I just do it. Like it's second nature to know how to do this.

Jared sucks in a breath, shifting his stance wider as he presses me against his car. My bare arse is practically sitting in the gravel, and stones are digging into my knees, but this is so worth it. Even though he has me trapped, I feel so powerful knowing I can make him lose his inhibitions like this.

His thrusts come harder, and I squeeze his dick tighter as he starts to push too deep. I'm going to gag. I don't want to. How fucking embarrassing, but I can feel it.

"Dee." He growls, and I open my eyes, not realising I shut them. "Can I cum in your mouth, or do you want me to pull out?"

My eyes widen, because I have no idea. Also, even if I could talk, my mouth is kind of too busy right now to answer him. It also surprises me that he asked. He acts all tough and almost overpowering, yet he has the courtesy to ask.

Jesus, am I swooning?

"Fuck." Jared hisses as he thrusts faster. "Blink once for yes and twice for no. Do you wanna taste my cum on your tongue?"

I blink.

Once.

That's all he needs before his face contorts like he's in pain and it almost feels like his dick thickens even more before something hot spurts into my mouth. I gag because he's so deep, but he pulls back, leaving his tip just inside my mouth as more hot fluid fills my mouth.

I swallow, because I don't know what else to do. It would be rude to spit it out, right? Not that I hate it. I don't mind its salty taste, and I find myself squeezing his dick to try and get more.

He chuckles, jerking back. "Fuck, stop. It's sensitive." He pulls free slowly, and I try not to grin, but I can't help it because I really liked that. All of what we just did here tonight.

"Fuck, Dee. Your smile. It's beautiful."

My face heats with embarrassment and I shove him back, trying not to look at how manly he is compared to my little frame. I mean, I have curves, my hips womanly enough, and my boobs are like an overflowing handful for my little hand. They probably aren't enough for his large masculine hands, though.

I feel like an inexperienced child right now for some reason. A child that can kill easier than I can run, but my experience of the sexual nature is nothing compared to his obvious experience.

Suddenly, I feel inadequate.

I don't know why. We were having fun only moments ago. More fun than I can remember having. Ever. But maybe that's the problem. Maybe fun with Jared is a big no no since I'm leaving in a few weeks.

In fact, that's exactly what's happening. I like him. I like Jared Crowley as more than a friend, and it fucking scares me, and already the thought of leaving him is twisting my gut.

I get up quickly, rushing to find my shorts and panties while he pulls his pants back up.

"Seriously, a compliment and you're back to giving me the cold shoulder?"

I keep my focus on covering up my bare flesh, rushing to do the zip and button up on my shorts.

"Fuck! I don't even know why I try talking to you." Jared hisses and my chest hurts.

As he spins to give me his back, I reach out to grab him, not knowing why exactly, only that I want him to know that I care. He's too fast though, his anger pushing him forward in a hurry to round the car.

Tears heat my eyes as I scurry to redress myself, picking up my shoes and socks before looking for Thana, still embedded in the dirt.

The car starts up as I sheath my blade, and I dash to the car, almost certain Jared will leave me here if I take too long. I'm not sure how I'd explain that to my foster parents.

I risk a glance at Jared as I buckle up, and I almost wish I didn't.

His face is contorted in anger, his nostrils flaring as he shakes his head at himself.

He flies out of the lookout area as fast and angry as he left the lot of the Red Room earlier.

The drive back to Fox Pines is long enough that by the time he pulls up at the end of my street, he no longer looks like he wants to kill.

He shuts the engine off, sneaking a glance at me before directing his gaze out the windshield.

"Do you ever get nightmares about what you do?" His voice is low and quiet as it meets my ears in the confined space of his car.

I want to tell him yes. Not to make him feel better, but to

give him my honesty. I stay silent though, and he turns his eyes to me.

"I've had nightmares ever since I can remember. Well, they probably started when I was twelve when I was in the car accident with my brother Tim. He died." Jared glances away for a moment, shaking his head as he gets lost in his memory. "I can still hear the screech of the tyres, you know. The sound of metal twisting and crunching." He glances back at me. "My nightmares changed last year when Lexi's brother beat me to within an inch of my life. His face has been in my nightmares on the daily until last week when that thing with Pike happened. Now the three things just blend together." His jaw ticks as he studies me. "Does that happen to you?"

I stay silent.

"You communicated with me earlier by blinking your eyes. You only seem to communicate when you absolutely have to, but... don't you want to? Don't you just want to scream at me or tell me to fuck off, or, fuck, just laugh with me? What would be so bad about doing that?"

I remain silent, clenching my jaw tight as heat pricks the backs of my eyes.

"I know I've been a prick at times, but you have to admit, there have been times you've had fun with me. What do I have to do for you to trust me?" The plea in his tone just about breaks me, but instead I glance down at my phone and start tapping out a response. Jared huffs, throwing his arms up in the air.

"Get out."

My eyes dart up to see if he's serious. He's not even looking at me anymore, his angry glare directed out the front window.

"Just get out, Dee."

Tears fill my eyes as his dismissal slices straight through my heart.

Just tell him, Dee. Give him what he wants. Talk to him.

I open my mouth, the words right on the tip of my tongue.

I'm scared if I open up to you, it will make it harder to leave.

But instead of telling him my truth, I snap my mouth shut and get out of the car.

26

JARED

Not being able to sleep is becoming a little bit too fucking common, if you ask me. It was nearly four in the morning when I tiptoed back into my house. My olds were snoring as I passed by their room and headed to the back of the house where the other two bedrooms are. My brother's and mine. I fucking hate that his room is still set up just the same as the last day he was alive six years ago. It's like a fucking shrine now. It's creepy.

I wish my brother was around. I could really use his advice. On this Marx Crew shit. On Dee. Especially about Dee. With the Marx Crew thing, I basically know where I stand. With Dee, I can't tell if I'm actually wanted or not.

I know I shouldn't push her the way I do to try to get her to talk to me, but something deep inside me is telling me she wants to talk to me. She's just too scared. Or doesn't trust me, which is probably one and the same, but it just pisses me off.

I call in sick to work, not up to driving around town delivering pizzas when I'm this dog tired. I spend most of my Saturday in bed, telling mum I'm not feeling well so she stays off my case, and she brings me cereal for breaky and soup for lunch before I decide to drag my sorry arse out of bed to shower in the late afternoon.

The guys have been blowing up my phone with messages. They wanna have a boys' night. No girls allowed. I say no like ten times, not wanting to give them the time of day since they so easily ditched me of late, but they don't stop insisting and in the end, my loneliness wins and I say yes.

It must be Garrett's doing after the chat we had last night. I didn't mean to be so fucking insulting about his girl, and I didn't mean to sound like a whiny bitch. He wanted to know what was wrong with me, and I told him everything I could tell him.

The problem is there's just so much I can't divulge.

I feel alone in this mess with the Marx Crew. I can't get Dee to open up to me and fuck, I really thought for a moment there last night things had changed between us. I felt it. I know I did. We have a connection. It's why I can't get her out of my head. It's why I'm so drawn to her. And it's why I have this pain in the centre of my chest that just won't fucking go away.

I give my mum a kiss on her forehead on my way out, not missing how hazy her eyes already are from the half empty bottle of wine on the table. I feel like she's getting worse. Ever since I got put in hospital by Lexi's brother, my mum has been upping her red wine self-medication.

I don't know why my dad doesn't put a stop to it, instead he brings more bottles home every fucking day. Maybe it's just easier for them both that way.

What the fuck do I know?

I grab a slab of beer and drive out of town to Bossi's place. His family owns a small vineyard on the outskirts of Fox Pines, and they have a building for staff to live in, but the only person to occupy it is Simon. My clown of a mate.

He's been staying there since his parents split and moved away because there was no way Simon was leaving his mates, or his girl. The girl they all share.

Weird fucking arrangement, if you ask me. There's no way I could share a girl with anyone. Or at least, a girl I actually care about. But hey, that's just me. To each their own and all that shit.

As soon as I pull up, my car is doused in water as Simon comes running from the part of the building they call the man cave, shooting my car with an oversized water gun.

"Hahaaa! You're trapped now, Crowley. Get out of the car and face your punishment."

I arch a brow at Simon, his hazel eyes wide with excitement and his longish blonde hair a dripping mess. Clearly, he's already been hammered by water from someone else.

Sighing, I contemplate starting my car back up and leaving. Not because I don't like my mates, but because I seem to have lost the ability to know how to have fun. Hell, the only thing that has made me smile lately is Dee, and that is rare. Mostly I'm a fucking sour arsehole.

No wonder she won't open up to me.

A tapping noise sounds next to me, and I turn to look out the passenger window, where Shaun Bossier, AKA Casanova, stands, holding another huge water gun pointed at my window.

"You're surrounded, dude. Surrender or die." Bossi yells from the other side of the glass, and I shrug.

"I choose, die." I yell back, and Shaun grins.

"As you wish." He steps forward, pulling open the passenger door and starts spraying me with water.

"Motherfucker!" I yell, opening my door to leap out, only to be doused with water by Simon. Cursing again, I run towards the man cave and round the corner, hoping they won't bring the water fight inside, but as I round the corner, my eyes widen at Garrett and Marcus standing ready with water guns of their own.

I skid to a stop, holding up my hands, and they both grin right before they drown me too.

I can't help it. I laugh, the foreign noise leaping from my throat as I lunge for Marcus, knowing I'll have a better chance at overpowering him since Garrett is a beast of a guy, and I don't stand a chance against him.

I leap at Marcus, and we crash to the grass before another body crashes onto me.

"Stacks on!" Simon calls and I brace myself as the weight of two more bodies leap onto the pile.

We are a tangle of limbs, laughing and soaked through. It's fucking amazing to feel this light, compared to the darkness I've been living in lately.

With the hot Aussie weather and long daylight hours, we spend most of it outside, playing pranks on each other and helping Shaun cook up some snags for dinner. The guys have deliberately been avoiding talking about Rhys. I haven't said anything about it, but once night falls and we are inside setting up the pool table, I can't take it anymore.

"You know it's alright if you talk about your girlfriend, right?" Four sets of eyes turn to me, and I shrug. "I know you're trying to avoid talking about Rhys, because obviously Gaz told you how I'm feeling, but I don't want that. Just because I miss you guys and am a little jealous that Rhys gets more of your time than me, doesn't mean you can't talk about her. I know how much you all care about her. I'm fucking happy you have found someone to love."

The guys stay quiet as they look at me, but it doesn't last, Simon bounding up to me like a Labrador and throwing his arms around me.

"I love you, man." He says into my neck, and I grin, awkwardly patting his back.

"Love you too, Sy."

He pulls back, holding me at arm's length. "If I were a chick, I'd kiss you."

I flinch back as the others burst out laughing.

"Well, since you are definitely a dude, I'd appreciate some space."

Simon grins at my comment and slaps my shoulder before turning back to the pool table.

"We just didn't want to make you uncomfortable." Marcus approaches, handing me a beer.

We take a seat on the bar stools as Simon starts up a game of pool with Garrett.

"I wanna hear about your relationship. Well." I take a swig of my beer, "If your group sex involves guy on guy, then I don't want to hear about that."

Marcus and Shaun chuckle, Shaun taking a seat on my other side.

"Only a little bit is guy on guy." Shaun mutters and my eyes widen, and I look at him in shock.

"What?"

He shrugs before guzzling down his drink, and I look to Grady to confirm Bossi is messing with me.

Marcus just shrugs, too.

"Fucking hell. What has that chick got you all into?" I ask, and Marcus grins.

"All of us went to a sex party once. That's where we finally met her other boyfriend."

"What? A sex party?" I nearly choke on my beer.

"To be fair, we ended up locked in a bedroom with just our group, so we didn't really participate." Marcus explains, and my eyes nearly bug out of my fucking head.

"Ooooh, she likes food play, and foot play." I turn to see

Simon nodding at his words as he chalks his cue, pleased with himself. "And she likes blood play with Gaz."

I dart my gaze to my big brooding mate at the pool table, and he grins and shrugs like it's no big fucking deal.

"She also likes Garrett's monster dick." Simon keeps talking. "She even likes it when he chokes her on it. Like he actually shoves it so far down her throat that she can't breathe and she nearly voms."

"You know what?" I hold my hand up to stop Simon. "I don't need the details of what you guys do in the bedroom with your girlfriend."

"Oh, we don't just do it in the bedroom." Simon's eyes move over to the pool table. "Last night, we had her tied to the pool table. We made her come so many times that, in the end, she was spraying us."

"Fucking hell, Hastings. Jared doesn't need to hear about Kitten squirting." Bossi scolds from next to me, and my brows nearly fly off my fucking head.

"I retract my statement. I don't want to talk about your girlfriend. Ever."

They all chuckle.

"Tell us about Dee, then." Marcus asks.

Shit. Dee. I don't want to tell them or anyone else about Dee.

"You obviously like her, man. Something is definitely going on with the two of you. She asked Rhys to find out why you weren't at school yesterday." Marcus explains, and my brows furrow.

"She asked Rhys?"

"Well, I mean, she didn't speak, but she used her phone to ask her."

Relief washes through me at hearing that. If she was talking to other people and not me, then I think I'd lose my shit to the max.

"Are you two a thing?" Shaun asks this time, and I sigh, my shoulders slumping as I realise I really *do* want to talk to them about her. I just don't know how to do that and *not* bring up the trouble we've found ourselves in. "You know this is a safe place, right? We would never tell anyone what you tell us. Hell, if you want us to keep our mouths shut, we won't even tell Rhys."

"I can't commit to the Rhys part." Simon holds up his hands. "She totally uses sex to get me to talk. One blow job and I'd tell her everything."

My face falls. Simon's a funny fucker, but his comment does nothing but piss me off.

"It's nice to know a blow job means more to you than our friendship." I snap and Simon's eyes widen as worry contorts his face.

"Nah, man. I didn't mean it like that."

"How the fuck did you mean it, then?" I hiss and Simon opens and closes his mouth before looking to Marcus for help. "Don't fucking look at Grady. I'm talking to you!"

"He was just joking." Shaun jumps in to save his mate. "Weren't you Hastings?"

"No, he fucking wasn't!" I turn my glare to Bossi, the Spanish Casanova of FP Catholic. "All of you have done nothing but fucking ditch me to get your dicks wet. You haven't even thought fucking twice about what might be going on with me!" I turn my glare to the four of them. "I tried to give you all the benefit of the doubt. I tried to convince myself that it's just a phase, but it's been over three months, and if anything, you're even more immersed in Rhys' pussy than you were in the beginning. Fucking hell, this shit with Rhys and Bossi started only a few weeks after Mike West put me in hospital. I couldn't play in the footy Grand Final. I've had to get dental work done to repair the teeth that were broken. My mum's been an even bigger fucking mess than usual. Both her and my dad have escalated into some sort of fucking alcohol induced ritual over Tim, who died six fucking years ago. And where the fuck are you guys? Too busy eating snatch to know I've been hanging out with Travis Watson and trying to numb my existence with weed!"

"I know you're angry, man, but you gotta stop saying that shit about my girl." Garrett growls low, his icy blue eyes turning to slits.

"Or what? You gonna hit me? You gonna stop hanging around me?" I scoff at Garrett. "In case you haven't noticed, you've already been ditching me, so punch me already. Feed me your fist, Cole. Let's put a fucking end to things right fucking now."

Garrett takes a step towards me, but Marcus jumps between us.

"Stop!" He holds his hands out, one in my direction, and one in Garrett's. "Jared is right. We've been bad fucking mates."

"It doesn't mean he can talk shit about our girl!" Garrett snaps.

"Fucking hell, Cole. I don't want to say shit about her! I'm fucking happy you have found someone to love. Hell, I fucking like that crazy chick." My emotions get the better of me and it takes two tries to swallow the lump in my throat. "I just miss my mates." I drag my hands into my hair, tugging at the roots as I turn away, hoping they don't see me turning into a fucking cry baby.

It's quiet behind me. They are probably gearing up to walk away. Who'd want an angry fucker like me as a mate, anyway?

"Jar." Marcus' voice is quiet as he steps around me to take in my face. "You're my best mate, you know that. We grew up together. Been through so much shit together. I'm so fucking sorry I didn't see what was happening with you. I'm a shit friend, and I know I don't deserve a second chance to make things right, but I'm asking for it. Please."

A tear, an actual fucking tear, rolls from my eye.

"I'm sorry, man." Marcus says again, taking a step towards me, and the moment my shoulders drop in defeat, he lunges forward and wraps his arms around me.

I practically chew the inside of my cheek raw, trying to fight back stupid tears, and it works for the most part as I hug my best mate back, slapping him on the back. A moment later, we are nearly bowled over by Simon as he throws his arms around us, apology after apology flying from his lips. Shaun joins us too, and after a minute or so, we break apart, and I turn to face Garrett.

"I'm sorry too, man." His voice is low before a smile tugs at his lips. "But I'm not sorry for pushing you until you opened up to us. So now, tell us the rest of what's going on."

I shake my head. "I can't."

"You can't because you don't want Rhys to know?" Garrett asks, frowning.

"Look, I can tell you some stuff, but not everything."

The four of them frown at each other, and I still can't help but feel like the outsider here.

"Let's start with what you can tell us, then." Garrett lifts his brows, gesturing for me to divulge.

For a few long tense moments, I feel uncomfortable under their scrutiny. But I know I need to talk about it, so I let down my walls and open up to my mates.

"Me and Dee have something… and nothing." I shake my head. "We have some sort of weird connection, but I can't get her to open up to me enough for it to be more."

"Tell us about the something." Marcus urges, and I nod.

"We've had a couple of private moments of the sexual kind."

"You've had sex with Dee?" Simon asks, and I shake my head.

"No. Just some other stuff."

"What are the chances of you giving us the details?" Shaun asks and I frown at him.

"Slim."

"Has she spoken to you?" Garrett asks and I shake my head.

"Nope. It's pissing me off."

"But she's mute, right? Why is it pissing you off if she can't speak?" Shaun asks and I sigh.

"It's not that she can't speak, it's that she chooses not to speak. If she really wanted to, she could speak to me."

"Why does she choose not to speak?" Simon asks and my lips thin.

"I don't know exactly, but I'm pretty sure it has to do with her brother, Travis, and why they went into foster care in the first place."

"Does it blow anyone else's mind that Travis Watson is Dee's brother?" Shaun asks and we all nod.

"Yeah. I was pretty fucking shocked when I found out." I rake my hand through my hair as I remember that night in Pike's shed. "Travis calls her Ell, so I don't even know her real name."

"Really? Ell?" Garrett asks and I nod.

"So, how do you communicate with her? Does she use her phone like she does with Rhys?" Marcus asks, and I shrug.

"Kinda. Mostly, I just harass her, trying to get a reaction from her. I had a breakthrough last week. I got her to play hangman with me, and she took the bait, but every time I feel like I'm getting somewhere, something happens, and she becomes even harder to communicate with."

"What do you mean by harass her?" Garrett asks, frowning, and I cringe.

"I'm an arsehole to her, basically. Fucking hell, I even used foreplay to try to get her to tell me to stop."

All four sets of brows hit their hairlines, and I realise that must sound like I'm forcing myself on her.

"Trust me, when she wants me to stop, she finds a way to tell me."

"By knocking you on your arse?" Garrett chuckles and I grin.

"Yeah. Sometimes."

"So, what else is going on? That stuff with Dee isn't what's turned you into the incredible hulk lately."

Fucking Marcus. He always knows how to read me. He's been able to since we were kids.

"That's the part I can't tell you. Trust me, If I could, I would."

They all frown again, and Marcus nudges me with his shoulder.

"Well, we are here, no matter what. And when you're ready to tell us, we will be ready to listen."

I smile at my mate, feeling a pang in my chest at the knowledge that I'll never be able to tell them the truth. It's the only way to keep them and my family safe.

27

DEE

Rhys has called a sleepover with her friends, Lexi, Tillie, and Bell, and insists I join them. I'm sure Cynthia had a hand in it, but either way, Rhys isn't letting me bow out.

Since the twins are home tonight, Rhys has been busy dragging mattresses into the theatre room for us to sleep on, which fills me with dread. I don't do slumber parties, and I know I'll end up back in my own room at some point, even if I have to wait for them all to go to sleep.

Bell, Rhys' Wednesday Addams lookalike friend, sneaks in some alcohol and a couple of joints, while Tillie, who looks like an auburn-haired pixie, hides a plate of brownies at the back of the room, so my foster parents don't accidentally eat some and get themselves unknowingly baked. Lexi brings a heap of junk food, which I'm partial to, and Rhys assures us that if we want to watch porn later, she has us covered.

Jesus. If she brings porn out, I'm gone.

I've never considered myself a prude, but maybe I am. Am I meant to want to watch porn with a group of friends? Is that normal? I've watched porn, and all it does is make me horny. Why would I want to get myself that way with a bunch of friends?

Unless these girls share something else I'm not yet privy to?

Shit. I'm definitely bailing later. I know for a fact that I like dick, and these girls don't have that.

Plus, they aren't Jared.

Shit. Jared.

I spent most of the day thinking about our time up at the lookout. About how fun it was until I ruined it. Why can't I just go with the flow? Surely, I can let myself live a little before I move away?

"Come sit with us." Rhys calls to me, patting the floor next to her where she and her friends are sitting cross-legged in a circle.

With reluctance, I move over to them, taking the spot next to Rhys while coming face to face with four sets of eyes studying me.

I'm ready to leave now.

"Don't you ever want to yell at people that piss you off?" Bell asks, tilting her head at me, her dark eyes thick with black makeup giving her a very goth look.

Usually, I don't even respond to people. I don't nod or use my phone. I just stay silent, and people tend to get uncomfortable and leave me alone.

I could do that now, but I kind of don't want to disappoint Rhys, which is new for me, so I nod.

"Can you speak?" Tillie asks this time. "You know, if you wanted to. Can you?"

I nod and she nods back.

"So you choose not to talk on purpose?"

Again, I nod.

Tille laughs, her face lighting up in glee. "That must really piss a lot of people off."

I give her a small smirk and nod.

"Do you make sex sounds?" Rhys asks, and I cringe as I look at her. "What? It's a legitimate question."

"Stop it, Rhys." Lexi laughs. "Other people's sex lives are none of your business."

"Well, it should be. I love sex." Rhys beams.

"Yes, Rhys. We know you love to fuck." Tillie giggles and Bell cringes.

"Yes, and you love to tell us the details, even if we didn't ask. That's not going to be what tonight's about, is it? Because if it is, I'm going home now."

"Fine, but can I tell you one thing? Pleeease?" Rhys begs, and I'm about ready to flee now.

Sighing, Bell nods her head. "One thing, and then I don't want to hear about your sexcapades for the rest of the weekend."

"Boo, fine." Rhys pokes her tongue out at Bell, who just rolls her eyes. "Let me see…" Rhys taps her purple polished nail to her chin as she thinks, "Oooh, I got it. The other week, I had every hole filled with cum by four guys. At the same time."

My mouth drops open.

Lexi bursts out laughing as Tillie frowns, tilting her head from side to side.

"How did that work logistically?"

Rhys wags her dark brows. "Well, Gaz had his big cockzilla in my Kitty, while Marcus plugged my arse up good, and Sy and Shaun double penetrated my mouth, rubbing their dicks together until they nearly drowned me in their cum."

Oh. My. God. She did not just say that.

My cheeks flare with burning heat as I get uncontrollable flutters between my legs. I nearly make a fool of myself and get up and bolt from the room, but then I take in Lexi's flaming cheeks and Tillie's cringe, and I don't feel so alone.

Bell, on the other hand, looks almost sinister. "Did they hold your nose so you couldn't breathe?"

"Bell!" Tillie cries as Lexi gasps and Rhys smirks.

"No, but thanks for the idea. I'll totally get them to do that next time."

"Fucking hell, Rhys. You need to be careful." Lexi tells her with concern, and Rhys shrugs.

"Gotta live on the edge a little, otherwise what's the point of living?"

"Ummm, living!" Tillie balks.

Rhys giggles. "You know my guys treat me like a queen. They will never let anything happen to me."

A pang of jealousy hits me then. What would it be like to have someone to love and protect you as much as Rhys' boyfriends do? It must be nice to not have your guard up the whole time. To know you have someone watching your back, no matter what.

"Yes, we know they worship you. Now that's enough of them. I'd like to hear about other dicks besides those four for once." Bell turns her eyes to Lexi. "So, is Ayden railing you hard these days?"

Lexi nearly spits out the mouthful of drink she just guzzled, her cheeks flaming red again, before she smirks.

"If you must know, Bell. Ayden rails me *real* good."

They all laugh, and I bite the inside of my cheek to stop myself from making a sound, only letting a brief smile appear.

"What about you, Tillie?" Bell turns her sights onto her pixie haired friend. "You been riding Travis like a cowgirl again?"

My eyes widen, and I shoot my gaze to Tillie. Surely Bell isn't talking about the same Travis? It's when Tillie's eyes widen and connect with mine that I realise Bell is most definitely talking about my brother.

"Ahhh… ummm… It was only a few times." Tillie stutters her way through her sentence and Bell frowns at her.

"A few? Girl, you've been boning him the better side of a year."

"Bell!" Rhys hisses, shooting her friend a pointed look.

"What?" she asks, sounding annoyed.

"Travis is *Dee's brother*." Rhys says through clenched teeth, and Bell shoots her dark eyes to me and shrugs.

"What's the big deal? I didn't go into detail. She's not going to be scarred for life from finding out that her brother's favourite position is a sixty niner."

My eyes almost fall out of my head at Bell's words, and Tillie whacks Bell's arm.

"Shut the fuck up. I told you that in secret, Bell."

And, on that note, I'm outta here.

I stand, beelining for the door as the other girls all tell Bell off.

This is why I don't have friends.

Firstly, they are exhausting.

Secondly, they can't keep secrets.

And third, they don't understand the concept of too much information.

I shut myself in my room, glad to finally be alone. I pace and pace, trying not to think of my brother in any kind of sexual scenario, while wanting to go back and ask Tillie a thousand questions.

Like, does Travis seem happy?

Has he had a good life so far despite his family?

Does he ever talk about his future and what he wants to do?

Has he ever mentioned that he has a biological sister?

Has he said anything about me since I came here?

If she's been seeing him for over a year, surely she knows some personal stuff about him.

A knock at my door has me freezing. I take a moment to look at my window and wonder if it might just be easier to flee at this point.

"Dee? It's Lexi. Can I come in?"

Shit. Lexi. I'm not sure how I feel about this girl yet. She seems nice, but is she trustworthy? Did she overhear Travis at community service yesterday? And if she did, did she tell anyone about what she heard?

"Please, Dee. I just want to talk to you for a minute, and then I'll leave you alone."

Sighing, I turn my back to my window and open my door, leaving it ajar for Lexi to come in.

"Try to ignore the shit that comes out of Bell's mouth. She can be a bit of a troublemaker sometimes." Lexi looks around my space for a moment before turning her blue eyes to me. "So, I was hoping we could have a conversation about Jared."

I stay silent, sitting on the side of my bed as my eyes remain locked with hers.

"Would you rather I text you? I know you use your notes app to communicate sometimes."

Still, I stay quiet.

"This is the part that pisses people off, isn't it? They want to talk, you don't. They get frustrated and eventually give up. Am I right?"

I smirk.

She nods. "Right, well, I'd really like to know what's going on with you and Jared."

My eyes narrow. Does she now? How interesting.

I can't help myself. I pull my phone out and tap out a response.

'Why?'

"Because Jared is my friend, and something isn't right with him. I'm worried."

'Were you worried when he was pining for you?'

Lexi's brows hitch. "Of course, I worried then. We have been friends since we were kids. I care about him. And he's not pining for me anymore, so that's irrelevant."

'How does that make you feel? Are you jealous?'

I don't know why I'm being such a bitch.

Actually, I do know why. The jealous one is me, it seems. I realise I hate the fact that Jared was so wrapped up in Lexi, pining for her, hoping her relationship with Ayden would fail.

Lexi laughs and shakes her head. "I'm not jealous, Dee. But I am protective of people I care about, and since I don't know you, I'm wary. Are you the reason he's been so angry lately?"

'Maybe.'

"Why?" she asks, propping her hand on her hip.

'None of your business.'

"Rhys told me you're leaving soon. Do you plan on taking what you can from Jared and then breaking his heart?"

My heart sinks. She's so close to the truth, only I'm trying to stay away from him to avoid breaking his heart.

'I don't need to break his heart. You already did that.'

Lexi hisses. "I can't help it if I don't feel the same way about him!"

'And I can't help it if I have to leave soon.'

"But you can, can't you? You don't *have to* leave. You can choose to stay here. Travis has built a life here. How can you expect him to leave it?"

She's right, of course. Travis has built a life here. A bigger one than I realise, but it doesn't change the way he is living it.

'He's built a criminal life. He can leave it easily.'

"You can't know that, Dee."

'You'd be surprised.'

Lexi sighs, running her hand through her blonde waves. "Look, I'm not trying to be nosey, but I will fight for my friends. That includes Jared *and* Travis."

I can see her honesty and hear it in her tone. She would fight for those she cares about. I think I can see what Jared saw in her.

'He has nightmares, you know? Of what your brother did to him.'

She flinches.

'I'm not trying to make you feel bad, but maybe you and his so-called mates can get your heads out of your arses and see that he is really struggling. He was like that before I came along.'

Lexi's eyes glass over, and she bites her lip as she nods.

"The guys are with him tonight. Hopefully they will talk, and it will help."

Shit. I hope he talks to his mates, but not too much. Not about the whole Pike thing and the Marx Crew.

'Good.'

"He really has nightmares about my brother?" Lexi asks, shaking her head. "Of course he does. Mike nearly killed him. Why didn't I consider that?"

It's a rhetorical question, and I watch as Lexi's face falls before she turns and leaves my room.

Shit. Now I feel like a bitch.

28

JARED

For the second time this weekend, I'm walking through a fucking strip club, something I didn't envision doing with my Sunday afternoon. Griffin sent me another message, but this time it was more casual.

Griffin Marx
Crow. Pick up Hush and bring her to the Red Room, please.

Jared Crowley
Then what?

Griffin Marx
I don't know. Hang around and wait for Hush to be done, and then drop her home.

Jared Crowley
Fine. I'll pick her up in ten.

His texts lacked the formality they have previously. Either that's because he thinks of me as one of his crew now, or we aren't going to the Red Room for a job. He also didn't ask me to use the Audi, so I take my own car.

Dee is waiting on the path outside her house when I pull up. Once again, she has that damn backpack that I'm itching to get my hands on and look at what she carries around. I caught her getting out of my car the other night, and if it wasn't for the fact that I'm extremely fucking curious as to what she was doing in there in the first place, I probably would have lost it.

Today she's wearing blue frayed denim shorts and a white long sleeve top that clings to her like a second skin. It's cropped, and has big slashes in the front and back, her dusty blue crop top peeking through. She tends to wear darker or more bold colours, so this is a different look for her. It's an odd outfit for her to wear if she's about to do a job, which is why I think our visit to the Red Room is for a different reason.

I don't look at her when she gets in the car, instead forcing my eyes to remain on the road as she gets settled. I do the same as we drive the twenty-five minutes to Redfield, my eyes darting to the soft creamy skin of her thighs every now and then, remembering how it felt to have them wrapped around my face a couple of nights ago.

Fuck.

Thinking of that is a bad fucking idea, because my dick wakes the fuck up and I have to fight the urge to rearrange my junk. Letting her know what she does to me isn't on my agenda. Although maybe I should let her know. Maybe it would piss her off and she might react and finally use her voice to tell me what she thinks. Unfortunately, it's more likely that she'll pull that ninja shit on me again and hand me my arse, so I think better of baiting her. For now.

When we arrive at the Red Room, I park in the same spot

I did on Friday night, and we both get out of the car before making our way through the entrance.

The bouncers are on the inside today. Probably because it's not as busy, and also because of the heat. I'm still surprised when they simply give us a nod, and don't ask for ID or anything. Either they know who we are, or they don't care if under-agers go in. Not that I'm underage, but Dee is. For a little longer, anyway.

I follow behind Dee as we move through the strip club, trying to focus on my surroundings, yet finding my eyes drawn to watch her small frame move gracefully in front of me. I note that she isn't wearing that big fucking knife today. I also note how good her arse looks in those shorts. I have to stop myself from reaching out to give her cheeks a little squeeze, and my mind instantly goes back to the other night when I had those cheeks in my hands.

And there's my dick again.

Fucking hell.

Griffin spots us, finishing up his conversation with a waitress by the bar as he gestures his head for us to follow him. He leads us through the same doors as last time before turning back to us, holding up a key.

"Here, kid. Room eight is all yours."

Dee gives Griffin a nod, accepting the key. Her brown eyes dart to mine briefly, making it the first time we have made eye contact today. She looks tired. As tired as me, but she quickly dashes down the passage as Griffin steps in my line of sight, blocking my view.

"Come to my office." He holds his hand out for me to take the side passage, and I frown, concerned with leaving Dee alone in a fucking strip club. Griffin raises a brow at me, looking impatient, so I huff out a frustrated breath and move my feet in the direction he wants me to go.

We step into an office that has a viewing window into the

strip club. I realise it's not unlike the one at Dee's dance studio, which just seems fucking wrong now.

Taking his seat behind a big, but well used black desk, Griffin rolls up the sleeves of his white shirt to reveal ink covered arms.

"So, Jared Edward Crowley of nineteen Willow Lane, Fox Pines. What do you want to be when you grow up?"

My brows hitch as I take in Griffin and his shit-eating grin before I flop down on one of the chairs.

"What does it matter now? I'll either end up dead or one of *your* lackeys."

Griff chuckles. "Let's pretend you didn't get tangled up with this shit. What were you planning to do with your future?"

I shrug. "I dunno. I was planning on taking a gap year after school and doing some travelling. I kinda hoped I'd figure out what I wanted to do with my future then."

"Travelling is good for the soul." Griff nods. "Where did you want to go?"

"Europe. Maybe Alaska." I shrug, knowing it probably wouldn't have happened, anyway. Who the fuck was I going to travel with? My mates will never leave Rhys, and my brother is dead. Do they have travel groups for people like me? Lonely fuckers.

"I highly recommend Alaska." Griff grins. "Tell me more about your parents. Gregory and Janie."

I arch a brow. "Why don't you tell me? I feel like you've done your homework on me. So, what did you find out?"

"See. I told my brothers you'd fit right in." Griff grins, nodding his head. "Janie works three days a week at Orchid Street Primary School. Gregory is a supervisor out in the mines. They both used to be highly involved in community programs, but that all stopped when your brother Tim died."

Hearing him say my brother's name sends bubbles of

anger to the surface, and I clench my fists, trying to calm the fury.

"You look pissed all of a sudden." Griffin narrows his eyes and I nod.

"I'd prefer it if you don't speak of my brother. Actually, I'd prefer if you don't speak of *any* of my family."

Griff studies me for a long, tense beat before giving me a curt nod. "Fair enough. Let's talk about something else."

"Fine." I grumble, pinning him with my glare. "Dee's a killer, isn't she?"

"Something like that." Griff nods.

"An assassin?" I ask, watching his face for the slightest change. Then he grins.

"You found it hard to say that word."

"It's a hard pill to swallow. She's only seventeen. She must have been doing it for a while to become so good at it. And I know *you're* scared of her."

Griff chuckles. "You should be scared of her, too."

I know I should be scared of her, but I'm just not. What I'm scared of is something happening to her. Of her vanishing and never seeing her again.

"How did she get into it?"

Griffin stays silent for a few beats, his gaze studying me carefully. "Shouldn't you ask her?"

"In case you haven't noticed, she's not very talkative."

Griff laughs. "She can talk when she wants to."

I narrow my eyes.

Interesting.

"What did she whisper to you on Friday night?"

Surprise washes over Griffin's face before a sinister smirk contorts his face. "She told me if I hurt you or your family that she will string me up by my balls and peel my skin from my body before setting me on fire and only once I stop screaming will she slice my throat to deliver me to the pits of hell."

I balk. "Fucking hell. She did not say that."

"She sure fucking did." Griffin chuckles. "I'm a fucking saint compared to her."

It's hard to imagine the sweet face of Dee Porter killing a fly, let alone a person. But maybe that's what makes it easier for her. Maybe people assume she's innocent, and then get trapped.

My heart sinks at that thought.

"Is she… A honey trap?"

Griff's brows shoot up this time. "Hell fucking no. We would never ask that of a child. That goes against everything we are trying to achieve."

"But you'll ask her to kill for you? Just not spread her legs?"

Griffin's lip curls. "You're walking a very fine fucking line, Crow. Remember who you're talking to."

I roll my eyes this time. Mostly to piss him off, because that shit is satisfying.

"Are you gonna ask me to kill anyone?" I ask, and he scoffs.

"Not yet."

My glare returns. "But maybe one day?"

Griff shrugs. "Maybe one day you'll want to."

I huff at his response, feeling like I'd happily kill him now.

"We aren't that bad, you know." Griffin links his hands in front of him and places them on the desk. "We are trying to clean up the drugs in the area by making sure the stuff that gets dealt is clean. The Kerr family don't care what they lace theirs with, as long as it gets a huge high and has people coming back addicted. They are poisoning people. Too many are dying from their shit, and they have a cop in their pocket who works to keep them from getting raided. We are going to find out who this cop is and stop him. And in turn, stop them."

"But you'll take over the drug trade in the area?"

"We will." Griff nods. "You can't avoid it. Users will get it from somewhere. It's our goal to make sure what they are getting isn't going to kill them."

"Unless they take too much."

Griffin sighs. "We can't stop everyone from their self-inflicted ending. But we can try."

I guess he has a point. That's if he's even telling the truth. I don't fucking know this guy. For all I know, he's telling me a line of bullshit to appease me.

"Who was that guy that Dee killed the other night?" I know I'm not meant to be asking questions about that, but for some reason, I feel like Griffin will divulge.

"A sick fucker that paid top dollar for kiddie porn and live shows." Griffin deadpans and my brows hitch.

"And it's linked to that sex club that burnt down?"

"Yes." Griffin nods. "Vixen's Lodge Feasts. The Angel sisters have agreed to let us handle the punishment to any locals that were caught up in it. Just when we think we are nearly through the list, someone else pops up. I don't know how Timber Valley has flown under the radar for so long. The more digging we do, the more years of sick and malicious behaviour we find. While we have Hush at our disposal, we are going to eliminate as many of those sick fuckers as we can."

Shit. I kind of agree. Not about using Dee, because she's still a kid and I hate the thought of her getting involved, but eliminating the vile fuckers is a good fucking idea.

"So you think you can lose the arsehole act and get on board now?" Griff asks and I shrug.

"Maybe. Are you gonna hurt Dee?"

"You need to start referring to her as Hush when you're

here. For her protection." Griffin frowns and shakes his head. "And to answer your question, no. Despite us arseholes manipulating the situation we came across last week, we all have a soft spot for the kid. I would never hurt her, and you can be sure that if anyone else even tries, they will have me to deal with."

I nod, feeling some relief about that. As fucked up as this situation is, I don't actually think they will hurt her. Not physically, anyway. I guess emotional pain doesn't count though, because if they kill her brother, it will destroy her.

"Do you know why she doesn't speak?" I ask Griffin, knowing he has a past with her, and potentially an answer to this one question that I can't figure out.

"Not exactly," Griff shakes his head, "and even if I did, I wouldn't tell you. If she wants you to know, she'll tell you."

I glare at Griffin and he chuckles.

"You like her, huh?"

Still pouting like a sour bitch, I shrug and turn my gaze out the viewing window. "It's complicated."

"Women always are." He sighs knowingly.

"You ever sit out there and watch the dancers?" I nod my head towards the viewing window before turning back to Griffin. His face looks almost disgusted as he shakes his head.

"Yeah-nah. Doesn't interest me. The only woman I want to watch dancing is the one I sleep next to every night." His face lightens at the mention of his woman. "You can go out and watch them if you like."

"Nah. All g." I shake my head, also having no interest in watching the strippers dance. "You don't ask Dee... I mean Hush, to do that, do you?"

Griffin balks. "Hell no. Haven't you heard anything I said? We are killing paedophiles in the area. No way am I or anyone else in my crew contributing to those fucking monsters."

It's a good fucking answer. I needed to make sure. If I'm going to be wrapped up in this shit, then it better be for a good fucking cause.

I think back to the sex club, and how my mates' girl, Rhys, was involved in it. She was, and still is, only seventeen. The members of the club did unthinkable things to her, and in the end, she had a hand at burning it to the ground.

"The leader or master or whatever the fuck you call it, from the Vixen's Lodge sex club, was murdered in his hospital room in the city. Was that you? Did you kill him?"

Griff grins. "That wasn't the Marx Crew, but Hush could probably fill you in on who did that."

My gut drops, and my eyes bulge as I piece his words together in my head. "*She* did it?"

"I didn't say that. Just said she could fill you in." Griffin shrugs, and I stare at him for a long minute, wishing I was privy to all the details in his head about my girl.

Wait.

I mean, Dee.

Not my girl.

Fuck.

"Why is she here today?" I ask, trying to deny my inner dialogue. "Is she killing someone in your club?"

"Hell no. We gotta keep the cops away from here. We try to keep the killings to people's homes or places of work. Or in the middle of nowhere." Griffin doesn't sound like he's talking about ending people's lives. He sounds more like he's discussing a fucking dinner recipe or something.

"Then why is she here?"

Griffin shrugs. "Not sure exactly. She asked for help. Said she needed a room and privacy."

"What for?"

Griff shrugs again.

I try to think up a reason why Dee would want to come to a fucking strip club to have privacy in a room.

"She... She isn't here with a guy, is she? Or a girl?"

Griff shrugs again, his face shifting into a smirk. "Fucked if I know. She asked me not to ask any questions. So I didn't ask any damn questions."

Before I even know what I'm doing, I'm on my feet and out the door, running up the passage back towards the private rooms. In my haste, I nearly knock into a burly biker looking dude and a bony stripper that looks like she could use a good feed. Mumbling an apology, I turn down the passage, looking for the room numbers.

Earlier, Griffin had handed Dee the keys to room eight, so I glance at each door until I find the one I'm looking for. I try the handle, hoping for a quick entrance, but it's locked.

"Dee!" I yell, banging my fist on the door. "Dee!"

The door suddenly flies open, and I stumble into Dee, who is wide eyed. I ignore her, though, my eyes darting around the dull light of the small red room to find it empty.

Spinning back to her, she raises a single dark brow at me, her hand on her hip as she waits for me to explain myself.

"Who was in here with you?" I snap, taking an angry step towards her, but she steps back, dropping her hand from her hip, and she frowns and shakes her head at me in confusion.

I glance around the room again, noticing a laptop and some sort of device.

"What's that stuff for?" I point to the items, and she glances at them before glancing back at me. "Are you... like camming or something? Is that why you're dressed like that today?"

Slowly, Dee's face frowns harder, before a smile spreads her lips wide.

"Am I right? Are you like sexing it up for some sick fuckers on camera?"

A weird choking sound comes from Dee as she slaps a hand over her mouth, her eyes glassy with amused tears.

"Are you fucking laughing at me?"

She drops her hand and sucks in her lips, an obvious attempt at holding back her reaction. I almost forget what I burst into the room for, her responsiveness to me softening the barbed wire around my heart.

Shit.

I like playful Dee.

"Dee?" I ask quietly, and her amusement falls. "Just tell me I'm wrong."

I'm not prepared for the hard glare she shoots me, or the shoulder into the ribs I get as she passes me by before packing up her things and putting them back in her fucking backpack.

I'm also not prepared for her eyes to look so coldly at me as she walks out of the room and drops the keys into Griff's open hand before hurrying to leave.

"Real smooth, Crow." Griffin chuckles as I shoulder past him.

"Shut the fuck up."

29

DEE

There's really no point in bothering with school at this point. I'll be out of here in a few weeks, yet I still get dressed and go through the motions. I'm not sure if it's to appease Cynthia, or to feed this ridiculous need I have to see Jared, but I decide not to analyse it too much, because I probably won't be happy with the answers.

Even though I turn up to school, I don't bother doing the work. I use my time to read a book on my phone, hoping people can't see the blush creep over my cheeks every time I get to a sex scene.

I don't usually read romance books, instead sticking to true crime stories about serial killers and assassins, but I've stumbled across a romance genre that is jam-packed with some dark stuff that also includes serial killers and assassins, just with more sex.

I realised after Rhys' slumber party the other night that I am waaaay behind than most girls. Yes, Rhys is an exception, and hell, maybe even her creepy friend Bell is too, but Lexi and Ayden are relatively normal people, and hell, even my brother who is younger than me sounds like he has more experience if the stuff between him and Tillie is true.

Clearly, when it comes to sex, I've been living under a rock.

I'm still a little confused by Jared's reaction at the Red Room yesterday. At first, he thought I had someone in the room with me, and then he thought I was performing on camera. I wish he knew me better, because if he did, he'd know I wouldn't do something like that. Sure, I kill to earn money, but I do have some morals. Of course, Jared wouldn't have a clue about them, because I haven't let him in. I've kept him at arm's length, so I can't blame him for jumping to conclusions. I just wish he knew I'd never do those things.

I nearly told him too. With my actual words. My lips nearly parted to tell him I'd never do that, but instead, I opted for my typical reaction, which is to freeze him and everyone else out.

The only problem is that it's getting harder and harder to do that. My brain is telling me to push him away, but my heart is yearning to pull him closer. I don't know how I got myself in this situation, and I'm even questioning if I want to get myself out of it. Which is ridiculous because I don't do peopling, let alone relationships.

Jared still looks tired today, and it annoys me that I'm worrying about him instead of keeping my focus on Travis and how to change his mind. I'm not worried about the Marx Crew killing him if he refuses to leave with me. They won't get a chance to because I'll have no choice but to go after them first.

I know that, and they know that, which is why they'll already have a plan in place. They will have one of their lackeys on standby, ready to take the call and complete the hit. Griffin, or his brothers or cousins, won't get blood on their hands. Yet still, if they make that call, it will mean their death sentences. By the time I'm done, I'll have turned Timber Valley into a bloodbath.

It won't end well for anyone.

I sit on the sidelines in PE, pretending not to watch Jared's exhausted body trying to keep up with his mates, or watch how his mates' concerned gazes fall to him frequently. He tries to avoid looking anyone in the eye for long, and pretty much avoids me altogether.

Because I opt not to do any work at school, it makes my Monday extremely long and drawn out. During recess, I hide in the toilets and scroll TikTok, then in English I sit next to Jared, watching him sleep with his head in his arms on the desktop while he takes a power nap. When Miss Dice approaches to wake him up, I quickly dart my hand out, indicating for her to stop, and her eyes widen as she watches me communicate with her, shaking my head. She listens to my body language and walks away, leaving Jared to sleep.

During lunch, I hide in the shade of the tree line pretending like I'm not hoping Jared will come and find me, which he doesn't, and then I pretend like I'm not bummed about that.

In fifth period, I cave and do some work in textiles, sketching a design of a dance costume I would love to make myself if I were actually going to be staying here long enough to do it.

After school, I hover around waiting for Travis to start his community service, and when he sees me, he does an eye roll so big that it must strain his eyes.

"You don't know how to take a hint, do you?" he snaps, and I use my phone to communicate.

What do your foster parents do with all the money you guys make them?'

He frowns at my question. "I don't know, ok."

'Are you looking into it?'

Huffing, Travis steps closer and lowers his voice. "I'm trying, but Bianca can be an old bat when she wants to be. She's hard to get close to and is suspicious of any questions I ask."

His admission takes me by surprise. Am I finally getting through to him? Is he considering my offer to leave with me?

'Do they know I'm in town?'

"Not that I know of." He shrugs, and I nod.

'Good. Keep that quiet.'

Travis nods at me, his eyes softening as he shuffles awkwardly on his feet. "What did you mean the other day when you said mum used to hurt me all the time?"

Damn. He really mustn't remember. Definitely has to be a repressed memory type of thing. I don't really want to have this conversation here before he prepares to do his community service, but he's finally opening up to the idea of questioning his foster family, and I may not get another chance to talk to him about this before shit hits the fan.

'I meant that she used to hurt you all the time. The same way she would hurt me and dad.'

"I don't remember that." Travis frowns and I nod.

'You were young.'

"Only a year younger than you. Nine years old isn't so young that you forget."

I shrug. *'Maybe you repressed the memories.'*

Travis scoffs. "What are you? A shrink?"

I grin and shake my head before tapping out a response.

'Maybe we can get together sometime and talk about this stuff.'

Travis reads over my words and shrugs, which isn't a no, so I'm taking that as a win.

Tapping out another note, I hold my phone out to him.

'So, you and Tillie, hey?'

Slowly, his face morphs into a smirk.

"She been talking about me? About how good I make her feel?"

Frantically, I shake my head, not wanting to hear those words fall from my brother's lips ever again.

Travis chuckles, and our conversation ends with the arrival of Lexi. We both stand awkwardly, almost like we both want to say goodbye. See you soon, but we just aren't there yet, so I offer an awkward wave and rush off, feeling my cheeks heat as I charge from the school grounds.

I head in the direction of town, knowing I'll probably walk into my dance class late, but before I even make it to the school crossing, a familiar car pulls up to the curb.

Don't look, Dee. Keep walking.

Internally flipping my own inner voice off, I glance over to see Jared looking at me expectantly. Waiting. The small gesture of his head for me to get in has me moving, even though I know I shouldn't. I'm just making it harder by letting myself be near him. I'm honestly finding it harder and harder to stay away. I'm so incredibly drawn to him, and I know I should do us both a favour and back off, yet still, I open the passenger door and climb in.

His piercing blue eyes haven't left mine yet, and it makes me squirm a little, my cheeks heating as I shut myself in with him.

"Hey."

Hey, I think in my head.

Say the words, Dee. Tell him, hey.

Instead, I give him a small nod.

A slither of a grin tugs up the corner of his lip and immediately I react, biting my lower lip as he studies me.

"You got dance class?"

I nod again, and his grin grows a little bigger. He still looks tired, but the nap in English class seems to have boosted him up. I'm glad. He deserves some sort of peace.

"Let's get you to your dance class, then." He shoots me a wink, and I nod fast, my cheeks flaring to life even more.

What the hell is happening right now?

Why am I reacting like this?

And why is he grinning like he's winning a spelling bee?

Wait. Maybe he's grinning because I'm reacting.

I shift my gaze out the windscreen quickly, needing to break our eye lock, and the smartarse chuckles.

Shit. I'm reacting too much.

Sometime between yesterday and today, I've forgotten to keep my walls up and I've lost control of the narrative.

This wouldn't be a problem if I was planning on staying in Fox Pines. I almost wish I could, just so I could have the chance to see where this thing between us goes. What if we had a connection as tight as Rhys and her boyfriends, or Lexi and Ayden? What if I could finally let down my walls and just fucking breathe?

I want that so bad, but I owe it to Travis to try and turn his life around. He got put in foster care because of my actions. His path was forever changed that day, and instead of growing up with his dad and sister, he got put into the care of the Kerr family.

Heat pricks the backs of my eyes at remembering our dad. He was a good man, just had really bad taste in women. Both my mum and Travis' mum were bad eggs. Both loved drugs and alcohol more than their own children, but it never worried me too much, because Dad was always there.

Even when he took me from my mum's dead overdosed arms when I was five, Dad was a constant, taking care of me and moving me in with Travis and my step mum. He tried to protect me and Travis from Catherine, but she was another level of crazy. In the end, my dad couldn't fight her off. He tried, though. He tried so hard.

The car pulls into a parking spot just down from my

dance studio, and I need to shake myself out of my thoughts. I can't even remember driving here because I got so lost in them.

"Dee?" Jared's voice draws my attention, and I swallow the lump in my throat before turning to him. He shifts closer, stretching one arm out to rest on the back of my seat, and his other hand presses against the dash, caging me in a little. "I need you to hear this. Like *really* hear this, because it's important."

Parting my lips just a fraction, I suck in a breath before giving him a nod.

"I'm sorry for asking those questions yesterday. I don't think you are someone that goes on camera for sex or money." His gaze is so intense as it locks hold of mine. "If you haven't already realised, when it comes to you, I go a little crazy. I want to know everything about you, but I understand that things aren't so simple. This shit with the Marx Crew, and Pike, and the Angel sisters is adding to my crazy right now."

With the hand he has resting on the seat beside my head, he picks up some strands of my hair, running them gently through his fingers.

"And through all the shit we are dealing with, you're all I can think about." His fingers graze over my cheek this time. "So, I'm sorry for being a fucking prick. I'm sorry for jumping to conclusions. And I'm sorry, but I can't leave you alone."

My eyes widen, and he bites back a grin.

"So, get your arse out of my car and into that dance studio, because I'm watching tonight, and you're gonna dance like you don't know I'm there."

I study him for a moment, sitting so close to me that if I lean forward, I could easily press my lips to his. Instead, I nod, turn, and open the passenger door.

I hurry inside the studio with my bag, not looking back to see if Jared is following, and I dash into the change rooms to get out of my school uniform and slip into my black high waisted dance briefs and my electric blue long sleeve crop. By the time I've wrapped my hair up in a messy bun and I step out of the change rooms, my class is about to start, so I dart upstairs.

My eyes land on Jared, grinning and chatting away to Ruby's boyfriend, Caleb, as they stand out in the passage in front of the viewing window. When Jared notices me approaching, he shoots me a wink, crossing his arms over his chest as he turns back to Caleb, showing me that he isn't going anywhere.

The flutter of butterfly wings tickles my tummy at the thought of Jared staying to watch. I don't know what the hell is wrong with me. I don't like people watching. I don't like an audience. I dance for myself, to let my feelings out through movement since I keep them locked up the rest of the time. Yet here I am, walking into the studio, knowing his eyes will be on me every moment I dance.

I mark my name off the sheet and try to ignore the blue eyes I can't see watching through the mirrored glass as I claim the back corner. Miss Adele instructs that we are learning a routine today, focused on emotion, and she will choreograph the first part, while we have to improvise the second half.

Relief washes over me at hearing that, because it's exactly what I need to let these feelings free. I'm also good at improvisation, so I wait and listen as she plays the song for us. Lewis Capaldi's 'Bruises' comes to life through the speakers, and immediately my heart opens to let the raw lyrics ooze in and engulf me.

I forget that Jared is on the other side of the glass,

watching. My eyes, ears and heart locked onto Miss Adele as she goes through simple yet impactful choreography.

My limbs, the blood in my veins, my heart, they all come alive with purpose as I move, turn, roll, kick, and bend my small frame in ways that most people can't.

As emotional as the song is, it does nothing but make me feel light and free, and I realise that when the class finishes and Miss Adele is singing her praises for our commitment to today's class, I can't seem to wipe the smile from my face.

30

JARED

Tuesday and Wednesday are quiet. Even though I apologised to Dee on Monday after school, basically admitting to how I feel about her, she probably thinks I have ten thousand fucking personalities with how hot and cold I am.

I hadn't intended on telling her. I'd only wanted to apologise, but as soon as I looked into her deep brown eyes, I started drowning in them, helpless to hold back.

The problem is, I wanted to stay mad at her. For getting me involved with the Marx Crew. For killing a man while I sat in the car. For coming here in the first place and turning my life upside down.

Mostly I'm mad that she's going to leave soon because I know once she does, I'll never see her again.

I'm so fucking confused.

So, instead of giving her the cold shoulder I had wanted to give her this week, I sit next to her at school when we have classes together. I push her boundaries in PE, making sure to challenge her because she's a competitive little pocket rocket. And, then after school, I drive her to dance class.

Let's not fucking forget how I stand outside that viewing window like her boyfriend and watch her.

She's coming out of her shell in her dance class, using her body language and gestures more to communicate with the other dancers, and fuck, that smile. It's perhaps the most beautiful thing I have ever seen.

I realise at this point I am royally screwed. There's no way I'm ever going to get over this girl when she does leave. I've just gotta figure out how I'm going to handle it, because of late, I've handled things in the worst possible way.

Today is Thursday, and probably the cruisiest day I've had at school yet this year. With the day starting off with a double study, I stayed in bed, and then took a long hot shower, wrapping my hand around my cock to thoughts of Dee at the lookout the other night.

When I eventually turned up at school, the double PE class was spent playing basketball, which is my favourite sport, and I deliberately swapped teams with Hastings so I could go up against Dee.

She fucking grinned at that. And of course, I fucking liked it.

Then my last class was Maths, something else I'm good at, so all in all, an ok day as far as school goes.

Today is Ayden's nineteenth birthday, and Lexi is throwing him a small party at her house tonight. If Ayden's birthday had been a month ago, I probably would have lost my shit over the way Lexi fawns over him because I was jealous. Now that the jealousy veil has lifted, I can see how much they are right for each other.

It's a fucking relief, to say the least. My obsession with her is officially gone, and I can finally feel normal around her and Ayden. If anything, I feel stupid. Looking at Lexi, I only see my friend now, and I have to wonder if perhaps my obsession was with the idea of what her and Ayden have, more than wanting Lexi to be mine.

It could explain my hateful feelings about my mates' relationship with Rhys.

Am I just a big fat jealous motherfucker?

Probably.

I guess I'm not a very decent person. I should have been happy for Lexi. Happy for my mates. Not hating on them all for finding their true loves.

So yeah. It's nice to not want to strangle Ayden, especially on his birthday. He's actually a decent bloke, and he loves Lexi fiercely. He's perfect for her.

When I arrive at Lexi's, I'm surprised to see Dee here, hovering in the corner. I watch her for a bit as Marcus tells me that pre-season footy is starting up again. I'm actually considering not playing this year, but I decide not to bring that up tonight. I still have time to think about it.

Originally, I was on the fence about footy because of the high possibility of getting hit in the head. It's a high contact sport, and concussions are sometimes inevitable. After nearly having my head caved in by Mike and the length of time I was out because of how brutally my head had been bashed, I'm reluctant to put myself in a high-risk position again. A couple more blows and I might have been needing to learn how to speak again. I'm also fairly certain my lack of control of my anger may be related to having my brain shaken up like it was.

Now I'm on the fence about footy because I may not get time if I'm in a fucking gang, for fuck's sake.

Lexi approaches Dee, offering her a warm smile, and a pineapple cruiser. I haven't seen Dee drink before, so it doesn't surprise me that she accepts it to be polite but doesn't take a sip. Lexi's mouth is moving, and I wish I could hear what she is saying to her, but then I watch Dee place her drink on the ground under her chair and take out her phone before having a voice and note conversation with Lexi.

They go back and forth, both smiling at times, and Lexi laughs before Bell and Tillie join them, and just like that, Dee is one of them.

Her lack of voice is no longer a barrier between the girls, and I realise they must have overcome that hurdle at the slumber party Rhys had while I was with her fellas for a boys' night.

The whole sight warms my chest and fills me with hope that if Dee makes friends, she might choose to stay. But then, the self-hating demon that lives inside my head reminds me that Dee is here to save her brother, and at the first chance she gets, she will leave.

The thought puts my always lingering scowl back on my face.

Fucking hell, Jared. Stop being a fucking downer all the bloody time.

When Lexi and her friends leave Dee's side, I find my feet moving in her direction, and I don't even hate myself for it.

"Hey there, Deranged." I smirk, gaining her attention, and her big browns flare with her pissed off anger at the name I call her.

I'm ready for the fight, but it doesn't come. Instead, she rolls her eyes at me.

Cute.

"You don't drink alcohol, do you?" I ask her, gesturing down to the untouched cruiser, and after a brief study of my face, she shakes her head.

"Why?" I ask, being a nosey prick, but she doesn't seem bothered, using her phone to tap out her response.

'I never know when I'll need to bring out my a-game. In my line of work, I always have to be prepared.'

My brows shoot up, not expecting that answer, and then

my eyes fall to the barely touched beer in my hand and realise she's right, so I place it down.

"Is that the only reason?" I ask, and she shrugs.

'Growing up with alcoholics and drug addicts also tends to ruin the appeal.'

Fuck. Not only is that a sad fucking response, but holy shit, she's actually answering my questions and opening up to me.

"Is that why you and Travis ended up in foster care?"

She shrugs and holds up her phone with her response. *'Kind of.'*

I study her for a moment, shifting a little closer because I can't help myself. My need to be near her is almost overwhelming.

"Why were you separated?"

The long stretch of silence worries me that I've pushed too hard, too fast, but then she taps out her response.

'I was sent to a psychiatric facility for a while. That's why we were split up.'

Fuck. My brows shoot up at her admission. Something extremely personal.

"Were you sent there because you stopped speaking?"

Dee shakes her head but doesn't use her notes app to explain.

"What are the chances of you telling me why?" I ask, keeping my expression soft. I don't want to pressure her. I want to know these things about her, but only if she's happy to share them.

She holds up her phone. *'Slim.'*

I chuckle at her response, knowing I wasn't likely to get an answer.

Dee holds up her phone and my brows lift as I read her question.

'Why don't you look like you want to murder Ayden

tonight? Is it because it's his birthday? You giving him a night off having to watch his back?'

A laugh bubbles up, bursting free, and I shake my head, not able to hide my smile. "Yeah-nah. I'm just over it."

Her brows lift, and I realise we are actually having a conversation.

'So you're not in love with Lexi anymore?'

Suddenly, I wish I had my beer in hand. I could use its entire contents right now. But that's cowardly, right? Dutch courage and all that.

"Actually, I don't think I was ever in love with her. Honestly, I think I was in love with the idea of what they both have. Hell, even with what my mates have with your foster sister... just with less people. I'm not into the group thing."

Dee snickers quietly, bringing her hand up to cover her mouth, and my brows lift.

"Shit. Did you just laugh, Deranged?"

She rolls her eyes at me, and I have the overwhelming urge to cup her heart-shaped face and claim her lips.

Fuck, I have it bad, so I'm kinda relieved when Lexi's mum and Ayden's mum come out of the house with a cake, topped with nineteen candles. All eyes turn to the birthday boy, and we all move in close, singing Happy Birthday as Ayden hugs Lexi to his side, looking down into her eyes with undeniable love.

Yep. I'm definitely jealous of what they have. What I'd give to have that. With Dee.

As the night goes on and I get dragged into conversations with my mates, I watch Dee hover on the sidelines, interacting occasionally when someone approaches her, and fuck, I'm confused. She's never been this interactive before. Not with me, and not with everyone else. So why is she that way tonight?

I'm too scared to ask her, afraid that she will erect those metal walls again, and we'd be back to square one, so I keep my thoughts to myself and just watch her every move.

It's around 10pm when my phone vibrates with a message, so I take it out of my pocket.

Griffin Marx
Pick up the car at the train station. The same one as last time.
Collect the package at corner Dunmore and Bridle at 1am.
Hand the package the envelope under your seat.
Take the package to 1129 Old Emmerson Road, Fox Pines East.
Go dark on approach.
Stay in the vehicle until the package returns and then return to their desired location before returning the car.

My eyes dart up to find Dee's through the crowd. She's looking up from her phone, having just read whatever message Griffin sent her, and the relaxed persona she'd been wearing all night evaporates before my eyes.

Fuck. It looks like she's shedding more blood tonight. I'd previously thought it didn't bother her, which really bothered me, but now as I watch her walls slam back in place, I realise I was wrong.

This shit affects her alright. She just deals with it differently.

I find it hard to concentrate on any conversations after that, so I bow out early, about five minutes after Dee gets picked up by her foster dad, and I walk home.

As usual, my mum is asleep on the couch, empty bottle of wine leaving a red ring on the table, while my dad snores in his armchair with the footy channel humming in the background.

Fuck, I hope I don't end up like them when I'm older. How fucking sad.

I have a couple of hours before I need to pick up the black Audi from the train station, so I make myself some toast and drink down a heap of water before taking another shower. And you guessed it. I close my eyes as I remember the feel of Dee's pussy under my lips and tongue while I piston my dick in my hand. I'm horny as fuck lately, and I know it's all because of the dark haired, dark eyed, dancing assassin.

By the time I creep out of my house, my olds have somehow made their way to bed, the living room now dark and empty. As I drive to the train station and swap cars, I can't stop my leg from jittering with nervous energy. It doesn't stop when I pull up on the corner of Dunmore and Bridle and Dee, dressed all in black, slips into the passenger seat.

"Hey." I say because what the fuck else do I say when I'm about to deliver an assassin to her next kill?

Dee gives me a solemn smile, and I wonder how I missed it before. She doesn't exactly enjoy this. She just does what she has to do.

After handing her the envelope, I drive Dee to the outer east side of town, past Bossi's place, and the burnt rubble of where Vixen's Lodge used to stand. And I drive further again. It feels like this property should be classed as being in another town, it's so far out.

Dee reads through the contents of the envelope as we drive, and I open my mouth numerous times to ask what's inside, but I know she won't answer me with her voice, so I'm better off waiting to read it once she goes in to do her job.

As we approach the property, I turn the headlights off and turn in, driving slowly up the long gravel driveway. There's decent moonlight tonight, so it helps to navigate out here where there are no streetlights, until we reach a farmhouse.

I keep the car back a bit, turning it around so we can make a fast getaway, and then put it in park before turning to Dee.

"This place is giving me the heebie-jeebies."

Her brows shoot up, and she uses her phone to tap out a response.

The only thing anyone has to be scared of out here is me.'

I smirk. "I'm not scared of you, Deranged."

She bites back a smile, nodding before showing me her response. *'Good.'*

We stare at each other for a long moment, my lips wanting to release the words I'm holding in for fear of scaring her off, but then, she checks over her body, doing some sort of weapons check, before turning and quietly exiting the car.

Before she has a chance to blend in with the shadows, I get a glimpse at the blade she has strapped around her waist and hope like hell it does its job and protects her.

As Dee disappears, I take the envelope and start scanning the contents. There are two marks. A husband and wife.

Shit. Shouldn't there be two people going in there if there are two people to kill? What if they overpower her?

Fuck. What if, what if, what if!

It's quiet as hell out here. You could probably torture someone, and no one would hear. The thought sends a shiver up my spine.

I want to read more of Dee's job outline, but I can't stop checking my mirrors, wishing Dee would just come back already. That's when I notice it. A shadow moving.

Wait, not *a* shadow. Multiple shadows.

My heart nearly leaps out of my throat when the moon lights up a man holding a gun as he silently approaches the house.

Shit! Dee!

Snatching up my phone, I try to ring her, but she doesn't answer, so I shoot her a message.

Jared Crowley
Abort. Armed men approaching house.

Then I open my contacts and call Griff. It only rings once before it connects, and I speak before he has a chance to.

"We aren't alone. There are armed men approaching the house."

"Fuck! How many?" Griffin demands.

"Four. Maybe five that I could see in the dark."

"Is Hush still inside?" he asks, sounding panicked.

"Yes. Fuck, yes, she is. What do I do?"

"Calm down and reach under your seat. There's a case attached to the underside. Tug it free and take out the gun. It has a silencer and is loaded and ready to go. You need to get in there and protect Hush with your life."

"Fuck! Ok." I rake my hand through my hair before reaching under the seat. "I've never fired a gun before."

"Just point and shoot. Just don't get the kid. Oh, and turn the safety off."

He quickly walks me through that, and I slip quietly from the car, straining my ears for any sounds of a confrontation, but all I can hear is the sound of blood rushing past my ears.

This week's assassination is a husband and wife. Holice and Belinda Crawford. This sick couple are reported to be making their own videos and selling them through the same site used by the crispy fried skin guy I killed back in December. Terence Hill.

It's about 1:25am as I creep silently through their farmhouse. There are no pets I need to be concerned about, but as I pass through the house, I notice the walls filled with family photos. Not out of the ordinary, but the problem is I recognise one of the girls in most of the pictures.

It's Ruby from dance class. Her parents are my marks.

Taking out my phone, I shoot Griffin a message.

Dee Porter

Are you sure these are the right people?

Griffin Marx

Yes. 100%

My gut twists at that knowledge. There's no point in

discussing it further. If Ruby's parents are involved in paedophilia, then she's probably in danger. So too is the other little girl in the pictures, which must be her little sister.

Sucking in a breath of courage, I centre myself, turning my focus back to the task that has to be done before I creep upstairs to the master bedroom. I memorised the floor plans in the car, so it saves time having to hunt people down.

Their bedroom door is wide open, making it easier for me to remain unnoticed, because sometimes doors squeak. It's a hazard of the job which usually results in people waking, and then screaming, and then, I have to use my energy chasing them, and dodging things they throw at me, or get in a scuffle because they think they can take me.

Idiots.

Moving up to the side of the bed with the smaller sleeping form, I study what I can see of Ruby's mum's face for a moment, noting how similar they look. Then I slowly unsheathe Thana before covering Belinda's mouth with my hand. The moment her eyes shoot open, I slice Thana across her throat.

As she jerks and gurgles, I glance over at the larger snoring lump in the bed, and it pisses me off that he doesn't even stir.

Wake up, you useless excuse for a husband. Your wife is dying here!

As the last sparks of life leave Belinda Crawford, I move around to the other side of the bed, deciding this arsehole needs a stab to the gut before I end him. Since he's lying on his side more, I position Thana and, with a thrust, stab her hard into his flabby belly. His eyes fly open as he cries out, but I quickly send him to hell with his wife a moment later by severing the arteries in his neck as well.

Killing isn't necessarily fun, but it can be satisfying when it involves ending the life of someone that wasted their one life by violating others.

Given the fact that Holice made a little noise, I cautiously leave their bedroom, keeping Thana at the ready while listening to see if Ruby or her sister have woken up.

Fuck, I hope they didn't! I don't want to end them too if they see me.

A little further along the passage are two more doors, and I approach the first one, seeing a name plaque with Ruby's name on it, and a pair of pointe shoes next to her name.

Gripping the handle with my gloved hand, I try to open it, but it's locked from the inside. Thank fuck! Relief fills me.

Good girl, Ruby.

Moving to the second door, the name plaque has Angela on it with a unicorn next to her name. My blood turns to ice as I remember the name of the dark website, Carnal Unicorn. Fuck. Is this little girl the one they sell footage of? I feel sick at the thought, noticing her door slightly ajar.

Knowing I won't be happy unless the police have some hard evidence to find, I leave the sleeping girls and move back downstairs, looking through each room before moving down to the basement. Australian houses don't typically have basements. Some rich arseholes like to have wine cellars, but honestly, nothing good comes from a basement in an Aussie house.

At the back of what looks like an old wine cellar is another door, which I rush forward to, wanting to hurry up and get out of this house. The door has a lock on it, so I turn my phone torch on, and set to work picking it, relieved when the process is quick.

Inside, I find what I was looking for. There are monitors set up, displaying live feeds into two bedrooms. One is Ruby's, and one is Angela's. I move closer to the screen, and see my dance friend asleep in her bed, and then on the other screen, a little girl cuddling a fucking unicorn.

Jesus Christ, these people have ruined unicorns for me for good.

Below the monitors are stacks upon stacks of hard drives and DVDs, and I don't even need to bother checking them to be sure. Just the fact they have cameras in their daughters' bedrooms is violation enough.

Fucking sick arseholes. They deserved a more painful death than the one I delivered them.

I take a few pictures of the evidence and send it to Griff as I walk back towards the basement stairs. Suddenly, my phone vibrates with an incoming call from Jared, and I frown at the screen.

Why is he calling me?

Then, a message comes through.

Jared Crowley

Abort. Armed men approaching house.

Oh, fun. An ambush.

I consider briefly that this could have been a setup, but then dismiss it, knowing the Marx family doesn't roll that way. At least I'm pretty sure they don't. Time will tell, though.

This ambush could be in response to Jeremy Dalton's life ending in such a shameful way. Maybe the word is out that someone is here to hunt them all down, and perhaps they've hired protection.

If that's so, then they're too late. Mr and Mrs Crawford have already bled out silently in their bed. And me, I'm ready to paint this house red if I have to. I just hope Ruby and her little sister don't wake up.

Giving my wrist a twirl, Thana gripped tight, I let my

adrenaline take over as I become laser focused and slowly make my way up the stairs to the main level.

As soon as I reach the top, a shadow leaps out pointing a gun, but I duck and kick my foot out low, tripping the figure before leaping on him and slamming Thana into his oesophagus. He gurgles and jerks and I move off him as I draw Thana out, blood spraying before I pry his fingers from his gun and press it to his head. He's wearing a ski mask, but I don't miss the way his eyes widen as he watches me with fear, right before I press the gun to his temple and pull the trigger.

The click and whirl of air sound, but the bang doesn't come as the silencer on the gun does its thing. Brain matter sprays out to the side as I send intruder number one to hell.

Movement to my left has me ducking back in the doorway just as a bullet whizzes past my ear. I don't want to get trapped in the stairwell, so I take a calming breath and leap out, shooting at the glass windows to create a distraction as I bolt towards intruder number two.

My distraction works and he doesn't realise until it's too late when I'm on him, Thana piercing his heart with a crunch through his ribs. As he falls free of my blade, another figure catches my attention and I look up to see Jared, eyes wide, holding a gun of his own.

Shit. He just witnessed what I did.

More silent bullets fly through the air toward Jared, and he manages to leap out of the way while I crouch low and use the kitchen island as cover.

I glance at Jared, glad to see he's not hurt, and he holds up three fingers before pointing towards the other end of the room.

Three more arseholes are about to die.

Cool.

Nodding, I silently roll across the floor, keeping low to

peek out from the other end of the counter. The intruders are on the other side of the island, approaching Jared's position.

That's all the information I need before I spring from my hiding spot, leaping onto the counter as I shoot one douche right between the eyes before I leap on dickwad number four's back and deliver him to hell with Thana.

Another whirling sound of a silencer grabs my attention just in time for me to see intruder number five with eyes wide, pointing his gun at me.

I look down at myself.

Did I just get shot?

But then, the last lackey falls to his knees, blood spraying from his mouth as Jared's silhouette comes into view behind him, and the glint of the gun he just used to kill a man. To protect me.

There's a beat of absolute peace right before a piercing scream shatters the silence from upstairs.

Shit. It sounds like one of the girls has just found her parents dead.

32

JARED

What the fuck did I just witness? It's one thing to know Dee is a killer, but it's another fucking thing to see it. Much like the night at the Red Room when she leapt on the table with ease, Dee moved like a tiger with skill and precision, taking out man after man in a way that would ensure they can't be saved.

Even though it was dark in the house, there was enough moonlight for me to see her face as she killed. It was alight with something else I'm a little too afraid to analyse, because I get the feeling she fucking enjoyed what she just did.

She's only seventeen. How the fuck is she so good at this? Who trained her to be a killer? A child killer.

I was so fucking terrified that I'd be too late, and those arseholes would have already ended her, but what she said earlier was true.

She's the only thing out here people should be afraid of.

And fuck, for once, I think I am afraid of her.

Not that I think she will slice me up the same way she did to these men. That's not why I'm afraid of her.

I'm afraid because I think I fucking liked watching her

kill. There was a raw animalistic beauty to it. And doesn't that just make me a fucking freak?

Seriously. I need my head checked.

Dee tugs on my sleeve again, silently telling me to hurry the fuck up as we sprint from the house, leaving the chaos to those poor fucking girls screaming upstairs. I can only imagine what they found. I don't think Dee is subtle in her killings.

As light starts to fill the house behind us, my gut drops at knowing the girls are about to find five dead bodies in their kitchen and living area.

One that I killed.

Fuck.

A few weeks ago, I thought I may have played a part in killing Pike by accident. Then last week, I realised I was an accessory to murder when I sat outside that house while Dee killed that creeper. Now, there are no blurred lines. I am a killer.

The thought makes me feel sick, and I suck in air, needing to tamp down the urge to throw up as we get back into the car.

Dee taps furiously on her phone, messaging Griffin as I hightail it out of there, and instead of turning right to head back towards Fox Pines, I turn left.

The more distance I put between us and that farmhouse, the more my hands start to tremble on the steering wheel as a crazed anger builds inside me.

I'm a killer.

I'm a fucking killer.

Because of Dee.

That's a bad thing, right? That's a really fucking bad thing, yet I still feel fucking drawn to her, which just means I must be a sick fuck.

How can I still want her after this?

She's put me under some sort of spell. I would never have been put in this position if it wasn't for her and her brother.

"Fuck!" I yell, my voice booming in the small space of the car as I punch the steering wheel.

Beside me, Dee jumps with fright, and I know I'm truly fucked in the head when I'm pleased that I scared her.

What the fuck?

Seething with anger, I plant my foot harder on the accelerator, picking up speed as the last lights of Fox Pines disappear in the rear-view mirror. I'm hoping my anger will ease the further away we get, but images of the way that man jerked as the bullet from my gun pierced through his back, keep flashing through my head.

You're a killer. Just like her.

I didn't want this.

As we approach the turn for Ebony Falls, I ride the brake, snaking the car as we turn onto the dirt track. With less friction under the tyres, the car slides on all the bends, and I know if I'm not careful, I'll end up wrapping the car around a tree.

When the car park for Ebony Falls comes into view, I speed up on the last bit of straight road and slam on the brakes hard, skidding us to a jarring stop before I cut the engine and leap from the car.

There are no other cars here, so hopefully that means we are alone, and I finally release my seething rage in a bellowing scream up into the tall trees surrounding us. I fist my blonde hair, sucking in air as I spiral out of control, and without checking to see what Dee is doing, I run down the path towards the falls.

I trip a few times, my feet catching on sticks as I blindly navigate the path, but I get back up, charging on, needing to just fucking get this rage out of me. Somehow.

When the sounds of Ebony Falls meet my ears, I pick up

my pace, running forward across the clearing towards the waterhole. I don't stop when I leap down from the grass to the sandy bank. I keep running straight into the dark water until it engulfs me entirely, and I go under.

I scream under the surface, letting the water muffle my agony as I try to expel this fucking rage from my body.

Eventually, I can't breathe, and I push my feet to the stony mud bed and breach the surface with a gasp.

As I wipe the water from my eyes, a small framed shadowed figure comes into view, watching me from the bank. The urge to yell and scream at Dee is overwhelming, but fuck, what good will that do?

Slowly, she walks into the water, the moon lighting up her face as the shadows of the trees fall away. She's watching me warily, which is good. She should be fucking wary. I'm a fucking ticking time bomb right now.

As she moves in deeper, she starts to cup water in her hands and rub it over her clothes. It's not until she bends and splashes water onto her face that I realise she is washing the blood off her.

Fuck. The blood. There was so much.

I wash over myself, knowing I probably have bloody evidence on me somewhere too, and then I stomp out of the water and sit my arse on a boulder, drawing my knees up to support my elbows as I clutch hold of my head and watch the water droplets fall from my hair into my lap.

I don't look up, but I keep my ears focused on Dee's movements, hearing her in the water for a bit longer before the telltale signs of her walking out meets my ears. I hear her moving off to my left. She doesn't come too close, but I know she's nearby.

I close my eyes, trying to calm the rage in my heart, but it won't calm the fuck down. Flashes of Dee assassinating black clad masked men engulfing my mind.

Fuck. I need to get away from her. I'm fucking worried what I'll do if she tries to fucking touch me.

With a hiss, I leap up off the boulder, storming into the clearing towards the toilet block. I can hear her moving behind me, so I fucking sprint like a coward, trying to put distance between us.

My chest is heaving with an adrenaline rush that won't fucking leave, and I hide behind a huge tree, pressing my back to it as I try to calm myself down. But fuck, Dee's footsteps are nearby and if anything, my heart rate picks up.

When she steps past the tree, I leap from its shadow and grab her from behind, intending on pulling her against me to… what? I don't fucking know.

I don't get the chance.

Like the badass she is, Dee spins, grips my wrist and uses her whole body to flip me over and land me on my back. The wind whooshes from my lungs, and I cough, struggling to get air in as Dee's moonlit face comes into view.

I hiss at her, baring my teeth. "Who the fuck are you?"

She doesn't answer. No fucking surprise there.

She moves to step away, but this time she doesn't anticipate my move, and I grab her ankle, pulling her foot from under her and scramble up and over her as she crashes to the ground. Her chest is heaving this time, her face contorted in anger, and I press against her, letting her feel my heavy weight as I trap her below me.

"Stop me, Dee. I know you can. You could kill me in the blink of an eye, couldn't you?" I rear back, releasing my anger. "So why don't you just fucking do it?!" I scream, and fuck, I hate the way she flinches.

Don't let her fool you. She's a killer. This innocent act is just that. An act.

I shove off her, leaping up from the ground to put some space between us.

"What will it take to get you to show me your true colours?" I growl, stalking around her as she drags herself up off the ground. My foot crunches on a large stick, and I eye it before picking it up.

Dee's wide eyes watch my every move as she starts to step back, and a sinister fucking smirk turns up my mouth.

"Do I have to use a weapon on you? Will that make you fight back?" I stalk her, feeling like a prick, but needing her to give me something. We just fucking killed together tonight. I'm in the thick of this world of hers now.

When I'm a foot from Dee, I lift the stick and gently poke it against the centre of her chest, and instead of cowering, she juts up her chin. Then I pull the stick back and whip it against the side of the tree trunk right near her head. It breaks, splintering against the bark, but she doesn't even blink.

"Do I have to force myself on you, Dee? Is that what will push you to fight back?" I hate the words that fall from my mouth. I'm not that fucking person. Why am I acting like this?

Rage. It bubbles further and I stalk closer to her, but she keeps her chin held high and doesn't move. So, like the prick I am, I cup her pussy and snarl in her face.

"Is that some sort of kink you like? Dub-con? Is that what it's called? Is that why you don't stop me? You haven't let my dick sink inside you yet, though. Maybe I should just do it already. Would you stop me, Dee? Or would you keep your consent to yourself and then cry rape later?"

Fuck.

I hate myself.

Why would I say such a heinous thing?

My face heats with humiliation at how low I have sunk, and heat pricks my eyes before I scream in her face.

"Just fucking talk to me!"

I shove forcefully away from her, fisting my hands in my hair and bellow up to the sky, finally tipping over the edge.

"What the fuck did I do to deserve this, Tim?!" I demand of my dead brother, the one person I talk to in my head. "What the hell did I do that was so bad that I'm never anyone's fucking number one?!"

Hot tears fall from my eyes as I drop my gaze back down to Dee.

"What do you think will happen to me if Travis leaves with you in a couple of weeks? Do you think the Marx Crew will ever let me walk away? Because they won't, Dee. My association with you and your brother has given me a life fucking sentence. If they don't kill me, then I'll spend the rest of my fucking life being their puppet." I shake my head, swiping at my embarrassing tears. "I've seen too much. Know too much for them to just let me go. It won't matter for you and Trav though, will it? You will be gone. Disappearing to live the life you've been dreaming of giving your brother, while me and your foster family pay the fucking price."

I start pacing, my anger not waning in the least.

"Fuck. I've gone from delivering pizzas to delivering an assassin. Because that's all I'm good for, isn't it? And, yeah, maybe the people you are killing deserve it. I know you know I look in the envelopes when you get out of the car to do the deed. But it's still killing people."

When she still remains silent, I spin from her, needing to get her beauty from my line of sight. None of what has happened is right. Just because I have a thing for her doesn't make any of this right.

"Fuck, Tim!" I look back up to the sky, wishing like fuck that I could see my brother's face, just one more fucking time. "Why me? Why was I the one that survived the car accident?" I shake my head, letting my chin drop to my chest. "Why was I the one Mike West chose to beat to an inch of my life when he could have chosen any of my other mates?" Fuck. I'm an arsehole for thinking that. I'd never want my mates to go through that. "Shit." I drop to my haunches. "Why did I go with Travis into that fucking shed?" I stand and spin to face Dee again. "And why the fuck was it *you*, of all the girls in the world, to walk into my life and ignite the spark that I thought I lost? Why did my dick choose to only get hard for you and not a fucking boring innocent girl that saves ladybugs from drowning in pools?"

I take a step closer to my dark angel, her big brown eyes looking a little glassy.

"Tell me, Dee. Why the fuck me?"

She doesn't speak.

And just like that, I know that I've fallen for a girl who will never fall for me back.

"You know what? Fuck you." I point a stabby finger at her. "And fuck this life." I turn my back on her and storm off. "Have fun walking back."

33

DEE

Jared's retreating back undoes me. His words were so harsh, and I know they come from anger, but it still slices my chest open. The further away he gets, the more I start trembling, a tear slipping from one eye as I fight against the onslaught that is raging to escape.

As soon as Jared takes off in a sprint down the track that leads to the car park, my instincts kick in and I run.

He's hurting. Self-destructive. And who can blame him?

He's been dealt the shit hand, over and over, and all I've done is add to it.

His life wasn't the best when I arrived, but since I came into it, I've turned it upside down. He's taunted me, got angry at me, been playful with me, tried to make me communicate with him, all because he's drawn to me.

It's not his fault, and now he's paid the ultimate price.

The last bit of innocence he had.

He's now a killer.

As my feet pound the leafy floor of the path below me, I

hear a car door slam, so I push harder, moving faster, needing to get to Jared.

When the car engine starts up, I fly from the mouth of the path to the side of the car before reefing the door open and leaping in.

"No!" He screams in the small space. "Get the fuck out!"

I shake my head, letting him see the determination on my face.

"Get out, Dee." He lowers his voice this time, his lip curling in a sneer. "I don't want you here."

I ignore him and put my seatbelt on.

He growls. "Fuck it. It's your death wish."

Shit. His words tell me my instincts were right. He's not in the right frame of mind right now. There's no way I'm leaving him when he's like this.

Jared shoves the car in reverse, and I jut forward as he slams his foot on the accelerator. My heart rate picks up as my eyes dart from his crazed expression to the gravel road as he shifts the car into drive and speeds off, the car snaking out at the back. I hold on to the grab handle above my head with one hand and clutch onto the seatbelt with my other as the dark silhouettes of trees fly by with the hint of light filtering from the rising sun.

"There are two ways this is going to end. Option one." His eyes dart to mine briefly before returning to the road. "You speak to me with your fucking voice."

Shit. He sounds so unhinged.

"Or option two, I wrap us around a tree."

He says that so matter-of-factly that I know he means it, and my heart races as my stubbornness kicks in.

No one forces me to speak. That's my control. But shit. What if he's serious?

The car slides as Jared goes too fast around a corner, a manic laugh falling from his lips.

"What's it going to be?" His blue eyes filled with dark anger dart to mine, and I shake my head, not able to give him what he wants. Not like this, anyway.

If I give him my voice, it will be because I want to, and I trust him. Right now, I don't feel any of that.

"I guess that's your decision, then?" He remarks, shaking his head like he's disappointed in me.

For a moment, his foot lets up on the accelerator, slowing the car a little, and a flicker of relief washes through me.

It's short-lived though, because when we round another corner, he grips the steering wheel tighter before planting his foot. The engine revs as the car kicks back a little before darting forward faster. I feel like he may have damaged the damn gear box, but that's the least of my worries right now, because as the sky starts to lighten above, I can see where the road turns sharply up ahead, and the barrier that runs along the edge of a steep incline into the surrounding bushland.

My eyes dart to him and I catch him watching me instead of the road. He has to see the fear in my eyes. It would be impossible to miss. He doesn't speak as his eyes move back to the road and the barrier moving rapidly towards us.

Fear pushes me and I reach out, my hand gripping his thigh just as I think we are about to go out Thelma and Louise style. His leg jerks under my touch and his eyes dart back to mine as the cloud of anger lifts from them, and he slams his foot on the brake.

The squeal of the brakes struggling combined with the clang of stones from the gravel hitting the underside of the car is loud, and the car starts to turn as Jared loses control of it. We slide sideways, still careening towards the barrier before we slam into it with a loud crunch.

I clench my eyes shut, tears streaming from them as I hold my breath, waiting for us to fall over the edge.

But we stop, and my eyes fly open to see that we are still topside. We haven't gone over the edge.

"Fuck." Jared whispers, his voice drawing my attention. He's looking out his window, and down towards the drop below. Then he turns his wild blue eyes to me, grinning. "That was close."

He starts laughing.

What the actual fuck? He nearly killed us, and he's laughing!

My fear covered face morphs into a scowl, and I punch his shoulder hard, but even as he grips the spot I hit, he laughs playfully.

Is he like bipolar or something? Perhaps a split personality?

His moods are giving me whiplash, and even as I watch him, his smile falls, and a serious expression takes over his face.

"Shit, Dee. I'd never hurt you. I'm sorry. That was totally fucked what I just did." He runs a hand through his hair. "I think I need therapy."

I fucking think so too, but that thought is doused when a metal-on-metal scraping noise snaps us both to attention.

The car shifts sideways, and jerks to a stop, our eyes widening as we realise we aren't safe yet. Jared looks out through his window, and when he turns back to me, he tries to calm his expression. I don't think he realises he failed.

"I need you to open your door and get out nice and slow." He gestures his head to my door, and as if the stupid car hears us, it shifts again.

My eyes fill with tears as I lose control of my fear, because I know that if I move, it might make the car shift. Even if I could get the door open in time to get myself out, there's no way Jared will make it out with all of his weight on the side that's tipping over the ledge.

I shake my head, my lip trembling as Jared studies my face, and he sucks in a shuddering breath.

"It'll be ok. Just open your door nice and slow. I'll lean towards your side."

My eyes dance between his as I contemplate if I should do this, and I know that there's no other way. We can't stay in the car. Even if we called for help, they wouldn't make it here in time.

I grip Jared's wrist and tug on it, silently telling him to move over to my side, but he shakes his head.

"No, Dee. You go first. I'll be right behind you, I promise."

I frantically shake my head, knowing it won't end well. I know we have no other options, but the thought of leaving this car without him is too painful to consider.

"Please, beautiful." He cups my cheek, running his thumb over my tears. "Just open your door. It will be ok."

Sucking in a breath that I wish was more calming, I give him a small nod, and without looking, I reach back and grasp the door handle. I'm so terrified, my whole body shaking with fear I'm not accustomed to, and I slowly and gently pull the handle, hearing the click of the door as it unlatches.

"That's it. Now slowly, push it open." Jared encourages, our eyes remaining locked on each other's.

As the door eases open wide, the car shifts again, this time with more of a jerk, and a whimper escapes me.

"Dee," Jared's other hand comes up to cup the other side of my face. "All that stuff I said before was out of anger and I need you to know that even though things have been hard and scary, and I've been feeling trapped, I'm glad you came into my life. I've never felt more alive than when I'm with you."

He leans forward, so I do the same, closing the distance as our lips touch. Tears stream from my eyes as our tongues dance with a longing that I fear we will never get to explore.

Even as I feel him unclip my seatbelt, I don't break our kiss, desperate to feel him and keep him.

The moment the car shifts again, starting to slide, Jared breaks our kiss and shoves me hard, pushing me out the door.

My head slams into the edge of the door as it shifts, a groaning and scraping noise loud as I leap up in panic, lunging for the open door.

I don't make it, my eyes wide with disbelief as Jared's face watches me without fear as the car slides faster.

I lunge forward, too late as my knees hit the gravel, and a guttural scream rips from my lungs as I watch the black Audi go over the edge.

TO BE CONTINUED

STAY CONNECTED

To stay connected and be in the know about future works
that may include some of the side characters from my books,
join my reader's group:
Sarah JD's Vicious Kittens – a Sarah JD Readers Group
https://www.facebook.com/groups/sarahjaneduncan-
readersgroup

Visit Sarah JD at
https://sarahjaneduncan.com
for updates!

STAY UPDATED

Join my VIP Readers list and receive monthly newsletters jam packed with updates about your favourite Fox Pines characters!

Sign Up Here

https://sarahjaneduncan.com/newsletter/

ARE YOU FOLLOWING HUSH ON INSTAGRAM YET?

Check it out:
@hush_tiny_dancer

https://www.instagram.com/hush_tiny_dancer/

THE HEAVY HEARTS SERIES

https://books2read.com/HeavyHeartsBook1/
https://books2read.com/HeavyHeartsBook2/
https://books2read.com/HeavyHeartsBook3/
or
https://sarahjaneduncan.com/my-books/heavy-hearts-series/

https://books2read.com/KittenBookOne
https://books2read.com/Kitten2
https://books2read.com/KittenBookThree
or
https://sarahjaneduncan.com/my-books/the-insatiable-series/

UPCOMING BOOKS

SUBBING FOR SANTA – A Dark Christmas Romance

https://books2read.com/SubbingForSanta

LILY'S ASH

https://books2read.com/LilysAshSSbook2

ABOUT THE AUTHOR

Sarah JD

Sarah JD, also known as Sarah Jane Duncan is a dark romance author, living in the beautiful Gippsland region in Victoria, Australia, with her high-school-sweetheart-turned-hubby and three grown children.

When she's not busy writing, Sarah can be found sewing dance costumes for her daughter or helping her hubby in their family business.

Sarah writes about females who have to fight against the odds to find their power, find their voice, and find their truth. The heroines in Sarah's stories possess the strength that only comes when you have to fight for your life!